Detroit Debris

Naomi Young-Rodas

TSL Publications

First published in Great Britain in 2022
By TSL Publications, Rickmansworth

Copyright © 2022 Naomi Young-Rodas
previously published 2008

Images: Naomi Young-Rodas

ISBN: 978-1-914245-93-0

The right of Naomi Young-Rodas to be identified as the author of this work has been asserted by the author in accordance with the UK Copyright, Designs and Patents Act 1988.

All characters and events in this publication, other than those clearly in the public domain, are fictitious and any resemblance to actual persons, living or dead, is purely coincidental.

All rights reserved. No part of this publication may be reproduced, stored in a retrieval system or transmitted, in any form or by any means without the prior written permission of the publisher, nor be otherwise circulated in any form of binding or cover other than that in which it is published and without a similar condition being imposed on the subsequent buyer.

www.magicbullet.com
11.22.03

Welcome to Magic Bullet! If you think the government is out to get us in ways the average Joe couldn't imagine, then this is the site for you! If you're the kind of person who gets the significance of today's date, then you're in the right place. Forty years later, the American people are still getting screwed, and here in the 3-1-3 more than ever. Share your thoughts in our interactive forum. Send me your theories. Spread the word.

To get you going here's a snippet from today's news: "...as Iraq has proven a difficult and costly undertaking and as questions linger about the still-unfound weapons of mass destruction, Bush and Blair have been under political fire..." Still not found those pesky WMDs huh? Taking our boys to war for nothing? Wouldn't be the first time, would it? "...influential Pentagon hawk Richard Perle conceded that the invasion of Iraq had been illegal..." no, you don't say!

You get the idea. Send me your thoughts.

FREEP.COM APRIL 12, 2010

EX-DETROIT COPS: PROBE OF DANCER SHANTA BROWN'S DEATH HIT HURDLES

Two former Detroit police officers – a dispatcher and a homicide detective – said in sworn affidavits that police officials tried to cover up investigations into a long-rumoured wild party at the mayoral Mannogian Mansion and the slaying of dancer Shanta Brown.

Arthur 'Danny' Daniels, ex-cop

It was the dancer who started everything. The press was right, police officials did try to cover up investigations into the party at the mayor's mansion, but the mayor didn't have the dancer taken out. I'm not saying he's clean. He's a million miles from clean, but on that point they got it wrong. Someone wanted to take Mr. Mayor down. And who could blame them.

I had history with the *Free Press* you might say, so when the time was right, I called up Alison and said, 'let's meet.'

There's this bar I like up in Ferndale. Actually it's a gay bar. I don't play that way, but I like to mess with people's perceptions. Turns out the girl, I'm sorry, woman. I'd better say right now I treat everyone equal but I'm not into all that PC nonsense, I call a spade a spade and if a female is nearly thirty years younger than me, well she's a girl, but anyways, seems Alison felt kind of at home at that bar. Shame 'cause I thought she was a fine looking woman, but I'm too old for all that run around. Give me a pack of Marlboro's, a good book or an old film and I'm a happy man. I like those Raymond Chandler's. *Lady in the Lake, The Blue Dahlia* and all that. Kind of ironic that dancer called herself Jessica Rabbit. Maybe she'd have called herself Veronica Lake if she hadn't been born after Veronica bought it. Old Philip Marlowe sure would be in his element here with all the corruption we got going on. Anyway, we had some good talks in our time, me and Alison. It makes a pleasant change to meet a journo who really wants to know the truth, 'cause everyone's pretty much scheming one way or another, just trying to get by in this broken town and no one cares about the truth.

That's how it started, but this story goes way back. Back to when I was a homicide cop. I saw my fair share of wackos, as well as all the day-to-day drug stuff. Over 300 murders a year we had when I was at my prime and most of those went unsolved. Not enough money. Not enough police. Not enough police bothered to do a proper job. But I liked catching them. That's what got me going – the chase. The intellectual challenge. I relished a full-on serial killer with a fetish, something to get your teeth stuck into. Something to where they'd say old Daniels is smart. He cracked that one just like a walnut.

That guy who stole ladies' panties, now that was an interesting case. 2358 pairs we found him with when we eventually went to his house. He was truly obsessive. That was his downfall. We might never have caught him if he hadn't taken to going back to particular women's apartments. One woman, a very attractive red head as it happens, he went back to her place four times. I mean, that's not smart. I don't think the killing was the main thing for that guy. The underwear was. I still maintain his first kill was just a robbery gone wrong. After that maybe he got a taste for it, but I wouldn't classify him as a true serial killer. Serial sniffer more like. I should write a book! Anyways, that kind of case gets the grey cells going. You've got to try and get into the mind of the perpetrator. Now 90% of the murders in this town are just shootings, wham bam, no thought, no finesse, and most of them are drug related, so there's not a huge amount of detecting involved.

I'm a bit of a romantic at the core. I want to be a hard-boiled detective like Marlowe, or a Rick Blaine character. I was born too late. The 40s, 50s, that would have been a great time to be an inspector, though I'm not about suit wearing. Can you see me in a double-breasted with this overhang?

Guess I'd still be on the force if I hadn't caught a bullet. But why put up with the grind? With the mindless stuff, and the paperwork? I had way more than my twenty years. Now I follow cases at my own pace. Comfort of my own home. Though you've still got to get out there and talk to people to do real police work. And that stripper, sorry 'exotic dancer' who got killed in 2005? That one kept me going for a long time. I knew there had to be some sicko on the end of that, I'm telling you. No one saw it but me. No one saw any connection. Then they all got caught up with that political BS and the mayor caught with his pants down and too much money in his pocket and they pulled the plug on the murder. Oh yeah, it all got hushed up and shoved in a corner. Paperwork got 'lost'. I'm not denying any of that. But the mayor as trigger man? No, I don't buy it. Don't reckon he bought it either.

I've got this poster above my desk – The Truth is Out There. It's kind of cheesy I know, and it's not like I'm into any of that conspiracy stuff, or alien abductions, or even that I'm a huge fan of the *X Files*, though you've got to admit that Scully is well worth watching. No, it's just that the truth usually is out there and it's a reminder to me to keep looking for it. Take this Brown case – the dancer who got killed. First, I thought it was drug related, because her boyfriend was a known drug dealer and plenty of people came forward to say that she 'danced' for some rather unpleasant characters. But there was something about that which didn't sit right. My light bulb moment was realising she was at the party that was rumoured to have taken place at the mayor's place. Well, I never should have mentioned that. Thirty seconds later I was off the case and almost begging to hang on to my job. Shit, if that didn't make me suspicious of the mayor or one of his cronies...

But I'm getting ahead of myself. The thing that interested me first was the rabbit's foot underneath the seat. People in the department were happy to believe that was just her key fob, because of her professional name, but DeAndre Little, the boyfriend, swore blind he'd never seen her with it and he didn't have a reason to lie about a thing like that.

I'd seen enough to know that was the kind of thing a sicko would do, put that rabbit foot there to let us know how clever he was, that he'd thought things through and planned it all. But it didn't *look* planned. Looked like the guy just got lucky. He saw Shanta in that idling vehicle, he happened to have a gun, he had some beef with her, and he shot her. If it looked like any other shoot-up, all the better for him, but then he messes it up by throwing that rabbit foot in there – it didn't make sense.

Now the question is, was this guy smart enough to fabricate a link to the mayor to cover up what he was doing and throw the scent off? Or did he just get incredibly lucky? And was Jessica Rabbit the first, or in the middle? I don't believe she was his only kill and I don't believe she was the last. I don't know why; call it intuition. I never believed it at the time either, but I got pulled off the case and it got put in cold storage.

So, like I said, I met Alison Krall up in Ferndale. Alison is young and keen. Dark curly hair, tight curls. And blue eyes. Nice combo. Well proportioned. Slight masculine swagger. I couldn't see her in a cocktail dress and heels, but other than that I'd have never guessed. Not that it's relevant. We'd worked together before, but we hadn't seen each other for a while. I liked Alison and we were going to blow all the current press stories about the mayor out of the water.

Alison slides into the booth and orders a beer and says, 'how you doing Danny? How's the shoulder these days?'

'Much better thanks.' I moved my arm around to show her I had the mobility back. Actually, it's only about ninety percent and the physio says that's probably as good as it's going to get. It aches when it rains too, but I guess that's life.

'Cute dog,' said Alison.

'Yeah, meet Jasmin, sometimes I call her JFK, just for laughs. You could say she's the new woman in my life.'

'You're a funny guy officer Daniels.'

'No more officer, I'm a civilian, remember?'

'You look good on it.'

'Yeah, I lost a few pounds. She gives me plenty of exercise,' I said, looking down at Jasmin, who smiled back at me with her big black eyes. Falling in love at my age, it's ridiculous, and with a dog! I should be ashamed of myself. 'But it's tough not to snack since I quit smoking.'

'You really stayed off the cigarettes?'

'Sure did, not had one since that night.'

'I'm impressed.'

'And how about you? How you doin?' I said it in my Joey from *Friends* voice. It made her laugh. I always had liked her laugh. If I'd been a younger man…or maybe not.'

'Good. I got my own column.'

'Yeah, I saw that.'

'And I moved in with Carol. We're in that house she bought in NW Goldberg, you know the foreclosure place?'

'Sure. So, you're all domesticated now?' I said.

'Hardly! I bet Jasmin is better house trained!'

It was good to see Alison hadn't changed. It was just great to see her again. She looked good. 'We should hang out more. We were quite a team.'

'Yeah, you should come over to the house sometime. It's got a nice yard. Jasmin can check it out.'

'What do you think, Jasmin?' I said stroking her ears the way she likes. 'You wanna go to Alison's house?' Jasmin put a paw on my knee and dropped her head to one side. She does that when she's listening to me. 'I think she likes the idea. Let's call it a date.'

'Cool. Now, how are we going to work this thing?'

'Always down to business. You did pretty well with the small talk there, though.'

'Yeah, I'm getting better at the foreplay, aren't I?' She winked at me.

www.magicbullet.com
01.15.05

Got called to the Mayor's Mansion tonight. What a disgrace. It was late. There was a party. A big party. Lots of girls wearing not many clothes. It was freezing too. Mayor's wife came home early, found the Mayor with his pants round his ankles. Metaphorically at least. They were up round his fat arse when I got there. Starts laying into the 'dancers' with her high heels. Steel heels. It wasn't pretty. Two of them ended up in the bus, straight to Detroit Receiving. That one they call Jessica Rabbit looked fine though. She didn't get hurt.

Can you believe it – I'm freezing my privates off and that fat ass Hendricks is partying at my expense! The people of Detroit need to know that the Mayor is spending their hard-earned cash on prostitutes and partying, while his entourage of so-called security look the other way. I've seen his wife riding around in that brand new Lincoln Navigator with the leather seats. I know you have too. Come on people, how long are we going to put up with this? When the scandals start breaking, remember you heard it here first.

Forum

- lovin' the posts man. Keep 'em coming. Glad someone cares about what's going down at city hall.   Frohike

- Thanks. Good to know someone appreciates my efforts. It's hard to get love in this city. It isn't just city hall either, it's all rotten. Junkies, dealers, whores, unemployment... don't get me going. Lone Gunman

- I hear ya. Keep up the good work. I'm recruiting some colleagues to the cause. F

May 18, 2005, www.fileitunder.com

KEMI HENDRICKS = CORRUPT POLITICIAN

Kemi Hendricks, the mayor of Detroit, is essentially THE stereotypical corrupt politician. Kemi fired Deputy Police Chief Nigel Greene, who was investigating charges of corruption and cover-ups committed by Kemi's security detail. Kemi Hendricks is a walking, talking joke. Were he a mayor in any other city – these scandals would have forced him to resign by now.

Back to the Beginning

I was working nights. Seemed like I was always working the night shift. Well, I had no life so why not. We got the call about 3.30 a.m., Monday April 25, 2005. My partner Mick was pissed off about working nights, but to be honest he was pissed off most of the time so who could tell the difference. But his wife didn't like it. I'd already figured the wife wore the pants in that household even if he made out like a macho guy. We hadn't been working together that long and it wasn't working out real well. My long-term partner, Reuben had retired last year and then promptly got cancer and was gone in three months. Crying shame, but don't get me started on that. I make it a policy not to well up while on duty.

So, we turn up. There's already the usual circus of uniforms and EMS. The male occupant of the car who had called in the incident is on the way to the hospital and we're left with a young black female in a none too pristine crime scene. Between you and me, I couldn't be one hundred percent sure the scene hadn't been messed up either accidentally or intentionally. Anyways, the woman was one hundred percent dead. The killer hadn't gone to any effort to hide gun casings. No apparent witnesses, though a nice little crowd had gathered to watch the action.

'Ah shit,' said Mick.

'What's up with you?'

'Another shooting in D Town, just what I need.'

'In case you hadn't noticed, you're a police officer. This is what you signed up for.'

'I didn't expect a shooting we couldn't solve every day of the week.'

'Then you're stupider than you look Mick. Let's just get on with it.'

Mick went through the motions of asking if anyone had seen anything. I eyeballed the vehicle to see what I could work out. The woman's purse was still on the seat (not a robbery then). Inside was her billfold with a bunch of credit cards and a driver's licence – Shanta Brown, d.o.b. 07.05.80; photos of three kids in the plastic pocket. I figured the killer drove by. Shot several times into the Explorer on the passenger side, then took off p.d.q. Once the body was removed, was when I found the rabbit's foot in the foot-well of the passenger side.

Mick didn't get a thing. No witnesses. No make or model of car. No one would even admit they'd heard gunshots, which seemed odd given that there must have been quite a few. I don't want to disrespect a fellow officer, but I had to wonder how much effort Mick had put into the thing. I just hoped that the male occupant wouldn't be too badly hurt and would give a description.

We left the uniforms and the tech guys to finish the scene and went to the address on the driver's licence. It took a while for lights to come on and the door to be opened. The kid looked about seventeen, sleepy, in a bath robe.

'Yeah?'

'Police. Is this the residence of Miss Shanta Brown?'

'Yes.'

'And who are you?'

'The sitter. What's going on?'

'There's been an accident. Do any relatives of Miss Brown reside here?'

'Well yeah, her kids.'

'No adult relations?'

'No.'

'Do you know how to contact any of her relatives?'

'Uh, no. I think her folks are dead. She talks about her grandmother sometimes.'

We took her contact details and made sure that she could stay with the kids – three of them under ten – what a way to end a shift.

Back at the station we wrote up the initial report, left messages with social services to take care of the children and clocked off. It was 8 a.m. All the traffic was coming into downtown, so I had a clear drive home as usual. I was tired, but buzzing. I hit the pillows anyway. I didn't sleep much, but I guess I dropped off at some point. I've seen plenty of shootings in my time and plenty of dead bodies. It doesn't unsettle me anymore like it used to, but my mind immediately goes to work on possibilities.

I thought about the kids and why their mother wasn't at home with them at 3 a.m. Was the man in the car with her the father? I was going to have to track down a next of kin to inform. Why had she been shot? Random violence? Drug related? The latter was always a good starting point.

I woke around 12 p.m., made myself a stack of pancakes with plenty of syrup and started working the case in my head. I decided to go to the hospital and check on the boyfriend or whoever he was. I know, I wasn't on duty again until midnight, but what else was I gonna do all afternoon?

The nurses gave me the usual run around, but it turns out the guy wasn't that badly hurt and I didn't have to sweet talk or pull rank too much to get to see him.

He was watching TV. I introduced myself. Mr DeAndre Little was decidedly unimpressed.

'What was your relationship to Shanta Brown?'

'We're going together,' he said.

'And how long has that been?'

'A few months, I dunno.'

'Are you the father of any of her children?'

'Hell no! I know how to use a condom.'

'Why do you think someone wanted to kill Shanta?'

'You tell me. Youse the police.'

'Well yes, but we're not all psychic.'

'Huh? Oh, that's almost funny.'

His hard man act began to slip a little. 'So do you think you were the target and they just messed up and got Shanta by mistake?'

'Na.' DeAndre flipped TV channels. 'Why would anyone want to kill me?'

'You tell me. Youse the drug dealer, aren't you?'

DeAndre gave me a look. Then an almost smile lifted one side of his mouth. 'A'right, I'll level with you. You gonna find out anyway. I got some business connections. But if that was the deal, they could take me any time. And I ducked. If a brother wanted me, he'd have made sure before he left.'

'OK. Did you get a look at the guy?'

'He had a hat pulled down over his face.'

'What kind of hat?'

'Baseball cap. I didn't see nothing else.'

'What kind of vehicle?'

'Some kind of SUV, I guess.'

'You guess?'

'It happened quick, you know. I saw this arm sticking out with a gun, I ducked, 'cause it's instinctive. But I didn't think to grab Shanta. I feel bad about that. Then I was covered in blood and glass and shit.'

'No idea what colour or make?'

'A dark colour.'

'OK. So, you don't have any idea why someone might have wanted to kill Shanta?'

'Well, we were at this party a couple of weeks back and this guy wanted sex and Shanta refused. He hit her so I beat him up pretty good. Maybe he wanted to show his manhood or something.'

'Does that happen a lot, people wanting to sleep with your girlfriend?'

'Well, she's a dancer, you know. Some guys think that gives them an entitlement.'

'And you don't mind?'

'I don't mind guys looking, 'cause she's a mighty fine sight, who wouldn't, but if they touch, that's a different story.'

'So, she only danced, no extras?'

'Uh huh.'

'At a club or only at parties?'

'She had a regular gig at that place downtown, you know, it's a real popular place. The Bazooka.'

I bit back a smile. 'OK and the name of this guy from the party?'

'Colton Hill. There were plenty of witnesses to my whippin' his ass. You can check it out.'

'I will. I'll check it out.' I made a note of the host's name and address. 'One last thing. Did Shanta have a rabbit's foot key chain?'

'Huh?'

'You know, a rabbit's foot charm on her key chain.'

'No man, that's sick. What you asking that for?'

By the time I was done with Little I felt in need of a burger and some re-grouping so I headed over to Miller's on Michigan Avenue. I ordered the works with cheese, fries and onion rings. What? I needed brain food. A man can't think on an empty stomach. If Little hadn't been sitting in the car next to her, I'd have pegged him for the killing. Uncontrolled jealously. I don't want to stereotype, but I haven't met a 'dancer' yet who wouldn't do a few extras, even if she wouldn't go all the way. And I haven't met a boyfriend yet who was happy about it even if they said they were. And DeAndre didn't seem too upset, but maybe her death hadn't sunk in yet.

DeAndre Little was obviously in the game. I was confident I'd find a rap sheet later, but you didn't need to be Einstein to work it out. There was a good chance this whole thing was somehow drug related. I kind of liked DeAndre even so. I didn't think he was as tough as he wanted everyone to think he was. I smiled again at the 'Bazooka'. Everyone was familiar with Bouzouki. It was a clean, quality strip joint. A place you could take pals to for a bachelor party or out of town visitors if they had that inclination, nothing too sleazy.

Top on my list of things to check out back at the office – the party DeAndre had mentioned, talk to this Colton character, and find out more about Shanta. I figured Shanta probably picked up extra cash dancing at private parties and maybe some other things. But she was only twenty-five with three kids already. She probably had the first when she was only fifteen or sixteen, so maybe dancing was all she could do, and she was just a clean-cut, single mom without many choices.

I got to the station at 8 p.m. I knew Mick wouldn't arrive until the dot of midnight but there wasn't any point me going home and back again. Ballistics were already in. The casings were .40 calibre – standard police issue. Nothing on the type of gun. No weapon was found at the scene. Some people might have jumped to the conclusion that the killer was a cop, but not me. Plenty of guns take that kind of ammo. It's a favourite of drug dealers too. Prelim from the coroner's office said she'd been shot four times. No prizes for guessing the cause of death.

I checked up on DeAndre Little. Plenty of juvenile stuff. A couple of arrests for possession with intent to deal, but nothing major. Nothing violent. Colton on the other hand was a nasty piece of work. Recently out of jail after a stretch for aggravated assault. At first glance he seemed like a good contender. The party host, Mitchell Jones, also had a sheet for various drug offences but no jail time. I ran the checks and got addresses and car details on both men.

'You're keen.' Mick strolled in with coffee and a dog. I noticed he hadn't brought me anything.

'Do you want the good or the bad?'

'Hit me with the bad. My life is shit anyway, let's get it over with.'

'You get to find a next of kin 'cause I already bagged the good angles by getting here early.'

Mick groaned and mumbled, 'workaholic. What's the good news?'

'We get to go to a strip club later.'

'Nifty.' I don't know why, but it really got on my nerves the way Mick said 'nifty' like he couldn't think of anything else to say. It got on my nerves so much I didn't bother to tell him mustard from his hot dog had dripped onto his tie. He was a detective, he'd work it out sooner or later.

'How come?'

'The deceased was a dancer, worked at Bouzouki according to the boyfriend.'

'When did you see the boyfriend?'

'This afternoon.'

'The captain ain't going to approve all that over-time, you know.'

'So sue me, I like my job.'

Mick shook his head. 'You should get out more.'

'And what would you know about it?' I threw him the address book from Shanta's purse. 'Here. See if you can find grandma.'

General Motors to cut 30,000 manufacturing jobs in US and Canada.

General Motors Corp. said on Monday it will cut about 30,000 manufacturing jobs, close or reduce operations at 12 plants in North America and slash the number of vehicles it produces as the automaker struggles for survival.

Steve and Leroy,
soon to be ex-motor industry employees

'Shit, so what am I gonna do now?'

'What are any of us going to do now?' said Steve.

'You'll be al'right.'

'How d'you figure that?'

'Well, you white. You boys are always all right,' Leroy said.

'You're such a racist Leroy. How long we been working together and you still giving me that shit?'

'How long has the black man been a slave in this country?'

'Yeah whatever.' Steve was not going to get into a race discussion with Leroy. Actually, he agreed with the man, being a black man in America sucked, but being a poor white man wasn't much better.

'So seriously man,' said Leroy, 'what are you going do when the plant closes?'

'Maybe I'll go back to school or something.'

'Yeah, with what money?' Steve shrugged. 'At least you don't have no wife and kids to support. Like I said, you'll be all right. What am I gonna tell Rhonda?'

'Oh man, you have got a problem!'

'It ain't funny. She already thinks I'm a useless motherf... that I'm useless. Building cars ain't good enough for her, like it ain't been the backbone of America since they invented the damn thing! It ain't like I'm selling drugs or something. I've got a decent job, or I did have. Drugs, on the other hand, now that's a growth industry.'

'You wouldn't,' said Steve.

'Why not?'

'You've got kids.'

'You telling me drug dealers don't have kids?'

'But, but...'

'But what? How else am I gonna feed them? I could say I've gone into retail. It's just selling a product.' Leroy laughed his deep throaty laugh.

'You're such a stereotype.'

'Oh, and you ain't with your going back to school shit? Just get on with your little white man mid-life crisis and we'll see who's doing better a year from now.'

Steve and Leroy had worked for GM since the 80s. Leroy had gone to the plant straight from high school. It had been a pretty good job back then. He hadn't been interested in going to college even if his folks could have afforded it, which they couldn't. Leroy liked working on cars. He did it all the time anyway so he might as well get paid for it, that's what he figured. He wanted to get himself a righteous car to attract the ladies. And he did. A red 1968 AMC Javelin. It was the '68 model but it was actually introduced in September 1967. Leroy liked the fact that it came out the year he'd been born. It looked like it had been through the riots too when he bought it for $250 from his first month's salary, but he'd worked it up into a thing of beauty. Ran like a dream by the time he'd finished with it.

Steve wasn't really into cars. He bought whatever the cheapest runaround going was, ran it into the ground and bought another. His thing was cameras. He traced the fascination back to when his dad had bought his Polaroid instant camera. At only seven, Steve was enthralled by the way the picture appeared before his eyes and he soon worked out you could manipulate those photos and make them look weird. In his teens Steve had gone through quite a phase of rolling around with his car heater on full blast, taking 'interesting' shots and then heating the photo to make the most of its pliability to create 'art' out of those crappy Polaroids. He could tell his father didn't approve, preferring instead to teach his son to take real photos with cameras with lenses, carefully gauging the exposure and aperture.

Steve had never asked his father why he loved photography. Why, apart from house expenses and holidays, it was the only thing he spent money on. Why he seemed strangely obsessed with cataloguing his children's every moment. But Steve caught the bug. Steve had thought about going to art school, but his father drew the line there. Taking photos was a hobby, not a career, he needed to get out and make money. William B. Novak was not about to let any son of his go to art school, not that he had the motor industry in mind either. Steve also had dreams for a time of being an architect. He loved the clean harsh lines of buildings. When he doodled, he drew great American skylines. But there was no money for that much education, and when William B. dropped dead from a heart attack while Steve was still in his first job from high school his fate as a working man was sealed.

www.magicbullet.com
04.26.05

Sometimes I feel like a garbage man, just cleaning up the dirt in this city. That's what we do really if you want to know the truth. Sometimes we save a life, but mostly it's just picking up the pieces.

But hey, somebody has to do the clean-up right? All I'm asking for is a little respect for the work I do. It's not like I get paid much, not like those city hall miscreants.

Really, someone needs to excoriate this city big time. Clean up all the scum. The whores. The drug dealers. The corrupt politicians. You know what I'm saying? I'm tired of it. Aren't you tired of it, Detroit? Someone could make a real mission out of that. Make a real difference. Actually, I did a little clean up job last night that should go some way to improving things.

Forum

- I feel you man. No one cares about us hard working folk who can barely make a living out here.   Ringo

May 21, 2005, www.fileitunder.com
Kemi Hendricks says, "Quit Buying Prostitutes, Fat Ass!"
WXYZ News reporter Steve Wilson – an ambush journalist, and Michael Moore look-a-like is my favorite local reporter. His gruff demeanor is really abrasive, and it's hard to like his style, but he is able to expose the sham of Kemi Hendricks' rule in Detroit like no other reporter in the area...Wilson's schtick is that he likes to ride politicians, and there are PLENTY of corrupt pols around here for the picking...

We got to Bouzouki just before 2 a.m. I wanted to be able to talk to the girls, not see the floor show. Mick wanted to get there earlier needless to say. I flashed the badge and got us in. As strip clubs go Bouzouki is more of a 'family' kind of place. Sure, there's toplessness, pole dancing and stripping, but it's mainly for bachelor parties. You even see some couples in there. The girls are pretty well taken care of and disreputable types are discouraged. Of course, with a profession like that, if dancers get killed you can never rule out a customer, but I was favouring a drug connection or something related to DeAndre's associates.

We got shown into a dressing room. Five girls were there. The main dancers. One was off sick.

'Evening ladies.'

'Are you here about Jessica?'

'Jessica?'

'Yeah, she didn't come into work tonight and Dave couldn't get her on the phone or on her cell.'

I pulled out a photo of Shanta. 'Is this the woman you mean?'

'Yeah, that's Jessica.'

'We have her as Shanta Brown.'

'Could be. We all have professional names. She's Jessica Rabbit.'

'And you don't know her real name?'

'Linda might, she's the one off sick, they're friends. I just know her here at work. What happened to Jessica?'

'I'm afraid Sh... Jessica was shot last night.'

All the women expressed surprise and genuine distress. 'Is she OK? What hospital did they take her to?'

'She didn't survive the incident.'

After that the women were keen to help us, except one who said she had to get to a second job, but she left her details. Me and Mick separated and questioned two girls each to speed things up a little. We didn't get too far to be honest. It was just background information. First up for me was Chantelle.

'Do you remember any customers acting weird lately?' I asked her.

'No. We don't tend to get that kind of thing. Dave runs a tight show. Guys aren't allowed to touch the dancers except to give a tip.'

'No guys hanging around outside the club?'

'No, not that I've noticed.'

'What about after-hours activities?'

'Well, I guess Jessica could have been into that, but I don't think so. She's got kids. I don't think she'd even be dancing if she could get something else that paid this good. And it works out well, 'cause she can be with the kids more during the day.'

'But you didn't hang out with Jessica outside the club?'

'No, we're just work colleagues. I like her, but we're not close, you know?'

'Did Shanta talk about her boyfriend?'

'No, not really. I'd see him pick her up from work sometimes. He looked a little young to me and a little rough, but that's her business.'

'How do you mean rough?'

'Oh I don't know... he has that kind of gangsta look.'

'Like he might be a drug dealer?'

'Well yeah, but I don't know what he does. All the boys dress that way.'

Back in the car we exchanged notes – Shanta was nice, but none of them really knew her outside of work. She had kids. She liked dancing and was good at it, but they didn't think she did any extras or was ever into prostitution. No weird clients or men coming around. No one knew her friends or her boyfriend.

Working homicide at night doesn't work that well. Most of the people you need to speak to are sleeping. It was now past 4 a.m. and I figured even party gangstas like Colton Hill and Mitchell Jones would be in bed. I did background checks and paperwork. Mick was still trying to track down grandma or any other relative. The captain switched us to days, which meant the rest of the day after 8 a.m. we'd be off, and would start fresh at 8 a.m. on Thursday.

I slept better, knowing I had the drug guys to talk to next. I was feeling confident that Colton Hill would be in the frame and we'd have this murder sewn up by the weekend. Just goes to show it doesn't pay to try and predict these things. Anyways, I slept late, did laundry, re-read

Playback by Chandler. Not one of his best, but still enjoyable. I barely thought about the case until early evening. Then it slapped me in the face like a ton of bricks – Jessica Rabbit. Shanta's professional name was Rabbit. So, the rabbit's foot in the car did mean something and it meant the killer definitely wanted Shanta not DeAndre Little. I cranked up Google. Jessica Rabbit, the gorgeous wife of Roger Rabbit in the 1988 cartoon film *Who Framed Roger Rabbit*. She certainly was attractive so I could see why an exotic dancer might adopt the name. Shanta had been eight when the film came out so she could have seen it as a kid. Kathleen Turner did the voice of the animated character I noted. I didn't discover too much else of interest, except that there also seemed to be a vibrator with that name. I wondered if Shanta was aware of that and intended some kind of double entendre by it.

The link to her stage name made me think the killer had known her in her professional capacity, which hinted more at a frustrated customer than one of Little's drug buddies. Still, it didn't rule them out. They could know her professional name, especially if she'd been paid to dance at any of their private parties. But that rabbit's foot in the car, didn't fit with a drive-by shooting of an emasculated drug dealer. Bang went my relaxing evening. Now the case was wide open and I couldn't concentrate on anything else. I popped open a Vernors and got some Better Made pretzels with cheese dip, while I surfed the net for more clues on Jessica Rabbit.

> Another thing that's bugging me
> Is this commercial on tv
> Says that Detroit can't make good cars any more.
> Motor city.
> **Neil Young, Motor City**

"Don't forget the Motor City…" Steve sang as he worked. It was their last day on the production line and he was happy about it.

'Stop singing that Motown shit.'

'But we're in Motor City, you've got to love Motown.'

Leroy shook his head. 'That's black music for white folks.'

'I am white, in case you hadn't noticed. Anyway, you like Eminem and last time I looked he was white.'

'Tsch. That's just one of my varied and eclectic musical tastes, whereas you just love that raggedy old 60's soul. Why don't you get into some

Marvin Gaye or Curtis?'

'I like Marvin.'

'I mean the hardcore stuff, like "Trouble Man", not those lovey dovey duets with Tammi. Or even better some Howlin' Wolf.'

'Oh no, that stuff is too depressing,' said Steve.

'Life is depressing.'

'Exactly. Music is supposed to lift you, not push you further down.'

'The blues don't push you down, they express how you're feeling.'

'Well, I'm feeling for a double cheese and large fries, you coming?'

'You know that ain't fair, you know I gotta go to that church supper with Rhonda and the kids.'

'Well then you'll be closer to God, and I'll just be in heaven!'

Leroy shook his head. Fifteen years he'd been with Rhonda and it wasn't that he didn't love her. He couldn't imagine life without her, but it wasn't like it used to be. Though she always had been a little stuck up and above herself, he'd kind of liked that about her when they first met. She was a challenge. Rhonda wasn't wowed by his shiny red wheels like the other girls. She expected more than a movie and a drive-thru burger. God knows how her folks ever allowed her to marry him. They sure had been trying to get rid of him ever since. Sometimes he thought he was just Rhonda's big rebellion and now she regretted not having done something less permanent like smoking a little pot or burning her bra. Sure, he earned pretty decent money, he didn't drink or do drugs, and he was a good father. Surely those things should count in his favour. He wasn't an educated man, but he wasn't stupid. He read. He knew what was going on in the world. If Rhonda had wanted some college professor or businessman she should have gone and got one. But they'd had fun, back in the day. Back before they'd had the girls. He remembered staying up all night dancing. And she was hot in bed. No denying that. She may look and sound like a good church woman, but Rhonda loved to love. Or she used to. Leroy didn't like to dwell on how long it had been since they'd been intimate, as Rhonda now liked to call it, it was depressing, but on the upside, she hadn't kicked him into the spare room yet.

But now he had no job. His one redeeming feature was gone and it didn't look like he was going to pick up anything else any time soon. For richer, for poorer. Leroy didn't think Rhonda was going to be too keen on the poorer part.

He picked up a bunch of cheap flowers on the way home. While he still had money he might as well treat her, maybe get in her good books. It didn't quite work out like that.

'Hi, I brought you something.' Leroy leaned in to kiss Rhonda, but she laid a hand on his chest pushing him away.

'We're going to be late.'

'We got plenty of time. Why don't you put these in water while I take a shower?'

'Like you have money to be buying flowers!'

'I have for now, make the most of it.'

'Yeah, I better had,' she said, marching to the kitchen.

Leroy threw his work clothes in the laundry basket, showered and put on clean jeans and a shirt.

'Aren't you gonna wear suit pants?' Rhonda asked.

'It's just a potluck supper, Rhonda.'

She gave him a disapproving look, but let it go. They drove the short distance in silence and Leroy was glad to get there so he could leave Rhonda with the women and join Tony and Smitty. He filled his plate with mash potatoes, ham and corn. At least the food was always good at these gatherings and they didn't have to listen to Rev. Williams drone on. Leroy had been raised in the church. He thought it was good for his kids, but how much of it all he really believed was another question. Left to his own devices he figured he probably wouldn't go to church too often.

www.magicbullet.com
04.29.05

***Detroit News*, April 26, 2005   Dancer killed in drive-by shooting**
Exotic dancer Shanta Brown was killed at approximately 3 a.m. last night when her Explorer was shot at repeatedly. Her boyfriend, DeAndre Little, is in a critical condition at Detroit Receiving.

Not much news you might say – another stripper gets shot in this town. It must be drug-related, or just another unfortunate result of the downtown crime-wave. Except – I heard Miss Brown is alleged to have danced at that *alleged* party at the Mayor's Mansion earlier this year. More trouble for Mr Hendricks, or just coincidence?

Come on folks, there's no such thing as coincidence. The Mayor must be up to his neck in it. When is the media going to catch on and catch up? Nothing I like better than a conspiracy theory. But I'm here to tell the truth. The Mayor is guilty. There was a party. Miss Rabbit was there. The wife didn't like it. The Mayor hushed it up. 'Alleged?' Take it from me – that party happened. Can't sweep it under the carpet this time, Mr Hendricks. The taxpayer wants value for his dollar and you're not giving it.

Forum

- Tell it how it is. Ringo

- Keep dishing the dirt. F

May 25, 2005, www.fileitunder.com
Kemi Produces Hatchet Piece on Journalist
Pissed off politicians have collaborated on the creation of a hatchet piece on investigative journalist Steve Wilson – known for exposing corruption in local politics.

First thing Thursday, I called Linda Gonzales, the dancer who was supposed to be closest to Shanta. She didn't sound sick to me, but maybe she'd recovered since Tuesday night. I agreed to go to her house. I prefer to talk to people face to face, get their body language and reactions. I was on my own. Mick had finally tracked down Shanta's grandmother. She lived in Dayton, Ohio. Any excuse for a day out of Detroit, he was headed down there rather than letting the local PD deal with it. I didn't see that he was going to get a whole lot of useful information, but I was happy to not have him around.

Linda's place was nice, real nice, much better than the house Shanta was living in. She was a little older than the other dancers, but still looked good – light-skinned Hispanic, well-proportioned even in her bath robe. She made coffee. I looked around. Quality furniture, not too much clutter, but plenty of Mexican art and crafts. Tasteful, I guess you'd say. No photos of children or a husband. The coffee had cinnamon in it. Made me want a paczki with it, or maybe a breakfast taco. Linda didn't look like the kind of woman who snacked.

I ran through why I was there. Linda was more upset than the others to hear of Shanta's demise and the nature of it.

'So were the two of you close, Miss Gonzales?'

'Call me Linda. I guess so. We'd have lunch sometimes or go shopping.'

'Can you think of any reason why someone might have wanted to kill her?'

'No. No. Wasn't it something to do with DeAndre? I told her he wasn't good for her.'

'Why did you think that?'

'He's obviously into drugs. Shanta was better than that. She was trying to raise her kids properly. She didn't need to be around that kind of man.'

'So, you think her death is something to do with him?'

'Oh, not intentionally, but these things happen in that kind of life.' She paused to sip her coffee. She left lipstick on the mug. Why a woman would put make-up on before her clothes intrigued me, but I didn't have enough experience to make anything of it, maybe that's what women do.

'Don't you think so?'

'Well, I'm not at liberty to say, but we do have reason to believe that Shanta was the intended target, not DeAndre.'

'Oh.'

'Did Shanta dance at private parties? Are there any frustrated customers out there, maybe wanted more than was on offer?'

'Men always want more than what's on offer, detective.' She smiled. 'She did some private parties, yes. There's good money to be made that way. We were at the party at the mayor's mansion you know.' The alleged party in January was already slipping into urban myth, the mayor and his goons fiercely denying it, most ordinary people confident that it had taken place at taxpayer's expense.

'You were? It really happened?'

'Oh yes, it happened. It wasn't that exciting, except the mayor's wife came home early.'

'And did she lash out at the strippers?'

'We prefer to be called dancers, detective. I think she did catch one. Not anyone I knew. Shanta and I were away from the action. But it degenerated after that. A bit chaotic. We all got ushered out very swiftly.'

'But nothing happened that night that could have led to Shanta's death? Did Shanta talk about the party a lot?'

She paused, as if thinking. 'I suppose she did brag about it. Probably it was the first celebrity party she'd done.'

'Were any of the other dancers at Bozouki jealous?'

'Maybe, but not that I could tell. We're usually happy for each other if someone manages to make some extra money. And I don't think any of them are huge Hendricks' fans.'

'OK, well thank you for your help, Miss... Linda. If you think of anything else, please give me a call.' I handed her one of my business cards.

She rose elegantly to see me out.

I pushed my *Best of Dusty* into the CD player. Linda Gonzales intrigued me. High end hooker was what I figured. She had money and poise. Breeding you'd almost say. I thought dancing at Bozouki was kind of slumming it for her, but maybe she picked up clients that way. If Shanta and her were friends, maybe Shanta was into prostitution too? Maybe I'd need to revisit Miss Gonzales.

So, the party at Manoogian Mansion really had taken place. I wasn't surprised. Kemi Hendricks was brazen if nothing else, he didn't go out of his way to cover up his 'expenses' or creative use of the city's money. So why was he going to so much trouble to cover up this particular party? Had there been more than dancing going on? Was it to save his marriage? Rumour going round the department was that the mayor definitely wanted this *faux pas* hushed up. But what did that have to do with Shanta? Not much, as far as I could tell.

Next up was Colton Hill. He lived south of Seven Mile on the west side, where pockets of drugs and crime sit right in amongst good working people trying to keep their neighbourhood nice. I drove past plenty of empty lots and a new garden project. Sometimes it feels like the city is turning back to nature, it's so green. The address given for Hill was a decent, one-storey, but just down the street were the kind of houses perfect for shooting galleries, the kind with needles not guns. It wasn't hard to see how Hill could make a living right on his doorstep.

Mr Hill took a long time coming to the door. I badged him. 'Homicide. Can I have a word?'

'I'm kind of busy right now.'

'Me too, trying to find the scumbag who killed a mother of three. The question was rhetorical.' I pushed my way in. I don't like to play the tough guy unless I have to, but with some people that's all they understand. I had that feeling about Hill right away. He was a short guy, stocky, built like one of those English bull dogs. Big as I am, I wouldn't have wanted to go head-to-head with him. 'I'm not interested in your drug business.'

'I'm on paper. I don't need any trouble or I'll be right back in the joint.'

'Then answer my questions and there'll be no trouble.' He backed down the hallway and into the living room. The place was a mess, though there were plenty of signs of wealth, a huge flat screen TV, a quality leather jacket slung on the sofa, a high-end Lay-Z-Boy that probably massaged his ass while he cut and bagged. There was white dust on the coffee table where he'd put a newspaper over his work.

'A couple of weeks back you were at a party with DeAndre Little and Shanta Brown?'

He shrugged.

'I'm going to need a bit more cooperation if you want to stay out of jail.'

'I go to a lot of parties. Maybe.'

'I think you know the one I mean, at Mitchell Jones' house, where Shanta was stripping as the entertainment.'

'I don't know no Shanta.'
'What about Jessica Rabbit?'
'That bitch. What she saying now?'
'Not much. She's dead.'
'And I suppose you think I did it.'
'I didn't say that, but you did hit her at the party, didn't you?'
'Says who?'
'I thought we were going to do this the easy way.' I picked the newspaper off the table and dropped it on the floor revealing several baggies. 'You know where possession of a controlled substance is going to get you. Now answer the question and quit pulling my chain.'
'OK. I slapped her at the party and Little tried to beat on me for it, but he's so puny he couldn't do much, and I ain't seen them since.'
'Where were you Monday night?'
'At an NA meeting.'
'Where and what time?'
'The drop-in on Springwells. Nine 'til eleven.'
'Kind of ironic, isn't it?' I said nodding at the table.
'Hey don't judge me man. I'm trying, but I can't go straight. Who do you think is gonna give me a job? I ain't working at Mickey D's for two dollars an hour.'
'All right. Where did you go after that?'
'To my momma's house. I stayed the night.'

I made a note of the address of his mother and finished up with Hill. I decided to check out his alibi before I tracked down Mitchell Jones. Mrs Hill lived in a well-kept house near the Baptist Church in Russell Woods. It was on the way from Springwells to Colton's part of town so he wouldn't have been going out of his way if he had stopped off there. She was polite, but not thrilled to be visited by the police. She was short like Colton, but not stocky. Well dressed and tidy. Her house smelt of baking.

'What's he done now?' she said.
'Who?'
'I guess you're here about Colton?'
'Yes, but how do you know?'
'That boy's always in trouble. I hoped he was finally doing better.'
'Well. He may not be in trouble. But I need to check where he was on Monday night.'
'He was here. Came from one of those meetings. We had a late supper.'

'Did he stay the night?'

'Yes. Left after breakfast.'

'Did anyone else see him here?'

'Probably Mrs Baker across the street. She likes to watch who's coming and going.'

'Could Colton have gone out later and come back?'

'I don't see how. I don't let him have a key and the door was locked when I went to bed and locked when I got up. What's he supposed to have done? I wouldn't cover for him, if that's what you think. Those days are long gone. I don't mess with no drugs. I don't let him in when he's high and he knows I don't approve of the people he hangs with.'

I thanked her. It wasn't conclusive. I'm sure an enterprising man like Colton Hill could get in and out of his mother's house if he wanted to, but I knew she wasn't lying. Hill's alibi looked pretty tight. I checked with Mrs Baker. Sure enough she had seen Colton arrive and leave. It took me some time to extract that nugget of information as she was keen to tell me about all the comings and goings on the street for the last few weeks. I decided to hold off on talking to Jones. Hill had been my best candidate, now it looked like he wasn't anywhere near the frame, so there wasn't much point corroborating that he had been at the party and he'd hit Shanta Brown, that was ancient history and it was starting to look like it had nothing to do with her murder.

'There is very little difference in the problems of crime between the suburbs and the city. The nature of crime might be different, but there are some pretty hairy things going on out there in suburban Detroit. Given the choice of a straight B&E and some of the kinky stuff out there, I think I can deal with the B&E better.'
Coleman A. Young

'So, are you the only white person left in the city?' asked Leroy.

'Seems that way,' said Steve.

'How come you don't move?'

'I dunno, guess I like it down here with you coloured boys.' Steve gave Leroy his best smile. His nigger loving smile Leroy called it. Leroy punched his bicep. 'Yo, don't abuse me brother. I'm the only white man in Detroit who loves you.' Leroy just shook his head.

'Well, your street's turned to shit, in case you hadn't noticed.'

'Your street don't look too great either,' Steve said, waving his beer can in the general direction of Leroy's neighbours. 'At least I ain't paying a mortgage. I'm thinking of buying myself a nice old house that's been foreclosed on. I seen one on Preston Street. They only want a $100 for it. I reckon I could beat them down to eighty or less on account of it's been gutted.'

'And what are you gonna do with a shell of a house in a shitty neighbourhood?'

'Enjoy the peace and quiet! Na, seriously man, I'll be sitting pretty, no rent, no mortgage. I'll fix it up. Dig up the yard, grow some vegetables. I'll be almost self-sufficient. You could come and help me, seeing as you don't have anything else to do.'

'Work for you?'

'No, collaborate. We'd be collaborating man.'

'You can collaborate my ass. I might get into dog fighting. I hear that's a growth area.'

'With your luck Leroy, your dog would get killed in training.'

'Thanks for your support man.'

'Don't mention it.'

'Why don't you get yourself a cheap house?'

'Oh yeah, Rhonda would really go for that. This house right here isn't good enough, you see her moving to some burned out shell?'

They sat on the steps and drank another beer.

'So, aren't there any jobs in construction?'

'You'd think, with all the building they got going on. The mayor's always bragging about how many jobs there are, but I don't see no one hiring.'

'Leroy.' They heard a woman's voice calling.

'Uh oh.'

Rhonda stuck her head out of the door. 'Oh there... hi Steve.'

She always made 'hi Steve' sound like it was a disease or something.

Steve didn't know what she had against him, but he knew when it was time to get going.

'I thought you were going to take the kids to the park?' Rhonda said.

'I am.'

'Well, you can't go now you've been drinking.'

'I've had one beer Rhonda, relax,' Leroy said as he slid the other empty towards Steve who pocketed it. Steve stood up and slapped dust off his work pants. Then he held out his hand to Leroy.

'I'll leave you to it then.'

Leroy rolled his eyes. 'Yeah, see you around.'

Steve walked down the street, listening to the birds sing. Leroy's neighbourhood wasn't so bad. Sure, there were a few empty houses with boarded up windows, but the kids could still play outside. In his pocket he felt the Canon Sure Shot that he took everywhere with him. Maybe he'd take some photos on the walk home.

Steve had inherited an Olympus from his dad along with a boxful of faded slides but no projector and the dream they'd always had of building their own dark room. Maybe he'd build one now, in the new house he was going to buy. He was serious, why not? Why pay rent when he could get a whole house and do it up? He had time on his hands now and he had a little money saved up. Apart from the Nikon D50 he'd blown nearly a grand on a year back, Steve had lived a low-key life. Never married, no kids. No vacations – he liked to stay home when he had time off and watch sports and read the papers on the internet. Oh yeah, he'd spent money on his laptop too, but that was two or three years back and he hadn't gone top of the line, not like the Nikon.

Steve wasn't some bum who stayed at home watching TV all the time. He went to the bar. He'd watch the game with the guys, but mostly he'd rather shoot the breeze with Leroy or do his own thing. Leroy got him. Twenty-five years they'd been working side by side. It was longer than most marriages. And Leroy didn't make fun of his creative side. Some of the other guys, tell them you'd spent Sunday taking photos of peregrines or close-ups of tree blossom and they'd think you were queer.

Steve wasn't queer. He had a thing going with Arlene from upstairs. But they were both free to see other people and Steve had a feeling it was time to branch out. End of an era at the plant – time for a new woman. A new life. Of course, he didn't really need a dark room with the digital SLR, but he liked to think of doing it, just to make his dad happy. Maybe shoot a few rolls on the Olympus for old time's sake.

www.magicbullet.com
05.02.05

I hate addicts. Don't you? My old man used to hit the sauce... I'm not gonna go into any ancient history, but it makes me mad the way he used to mess up and then say 'I can't help it, I've got an addiction' like we were supposed to feel sorry for him. Well I didn't feel sympathy being hungry because he drank our food money. How come one man can be upstanding, say no, never touch drink or drugs while the next man can't? You've just got to be strong. And the women... the things they'll do to score their fix, it turns my stomach to think about it.

But I guess judgement day is coming – something is killing addicts. They're dropping like flies, faster than I've ever seen. There's some powerful poison out there and they can't get enough of it. All the puke and shit we have to clean up, it ain't right.

I'm sorry I'm spouting hate here, but I just had to get it off my chest. It gets me down sometimes the way this city is going to the dogs.

May 27, 2005, www.fileitunder.com
Detroit = F**d!**
Hendricks and modern Detroiters are feeling the sting of a generation of deferred payment for sustaining the infrastructure of a city of 2 million, with the tax base of a city of 1 million.

Mick didn't get anything from grandma except that Shanta was a good, clean-living girl. She didn't do drugs, she didn't hang around with drug dealers and she wasn't a prostitute. But what did grandma know, she only saw her at Christmas and in the summer when she dropped her kids off to stay with her for two weeks. Jessica Rabbit may not have been all bad, but she couldn't be a total saint if her boyfriend was a known drug-dealer, albeit small time, and she danced at parties for men in the life and got roughed up by them. Not to mention having danced at the mayor's secret party. Maybe that was at the bottom of it all.

 I have to say I wasn't too upset at the thought of having to re-visit Linda Gonzales and talk a little more about the party over some of that fine coffee of hers. There are worse ways to spend an afternoon you know. I sent Mick back to Bozouki to see if he could get any more from Dave or the girls. I told him a disgruntled customer was looking more likely. For a change he wasn't unhappy with his detail. Though to be honest, I had a feeling we weren't going to get anywhere with that. Always trust a feeling, that's what I say, even if you can't grab hold of it and make it into something concrete. There's cops that will say intuition is bullshit, leg work is what gets results. But you need both. Intuition can crack a case wide open. Of course, someone like Mick wouldn't know a hunch if it hit him into next week. I didn't have a feeling where this case was going, but I had one about where it wasn't going, and I didn't want to waste my time chasing a load of guys just because they liked to watch girls dance without their tops on. This was personal somehow; otherwise the killer wouldn't have left that rabbit's foot in the vehicle. That was the key to this one. That's what I thought about on the drive over to Linda's.

 Maybe it was a guy who had been spurned by Jessica, but it seemed to me like it would be a man she knew, or someone who'd tried to get intimate with her, not just some john who got told not to touch at the club. Unless the guy was a real sicko, felt so inadequate that a thing like that could push him over the edge. Either way it was a man who would be hard to track down, simply because we had no leads. The rabbit's foot left a message, but it was anonymous, there was no forensics on it. So that meant the guy knew enough to wear gloves, but anyone watching cop shows on TV would know that. Probably had planned it to a certain degree, though the drive-by called for an element of luck and flexibility. I made a mental note to check out where a person could buy a rabbit's foot key chain like that, though my guess was you could buy them at pretty much any convenience store in town, the kind of store where no one would remember you buying it.

Linda was just as gracious as she'd been at the first interview, though this time she was dressed in tight jeans and a lacy sweater. She offered coffee. I didn't refuse.

'So how can I help you officer?' Did I imagine flirtation in her voice? I think I did, imagine it, I mean.

'I'd like to know more about the party at the mayor's. It's another avenue we're looking at.'

'You didn't get anywhere with DeAndre's associates?'

'Not really. We're still looking into that angle, but it's not looking promising.'

'Well, what can I say? The mayor held a party. I'd say there were at least ten dancers there. I knew most of them. We did some individual lap dances, but nothing more. Maybe someone got a hand-job in a darkened room, but it was mainly a regular party, drinking, dancing.'

'Any drugs?'

'I didn't see any, but I expect there was some cocaine.'

'Anyone acting weird around Shanta?'

'Not that I remember. She was a little in awe, like a big kid at her first grown-up party. I tried to keep an eye on her.'

'Ah huh. And what happened when Mrs Hendricks got home?'

'She did kind of go off on one; lots of shouting at the mayor. She hit the girl who was dancing for him with her stiletto. Got her right in the side of the head.'

'And then what? Did the party break up?'

'Yeah, people were in a hurry to get out of there. We left too. There seemed to be a lot of police around outside and a couple of EMS vehicles. I did wonder why when that one dancer was the only person injured as far as I know. Wait, now that was weird, as we went past the ambulance there was this white guy leaning against the side of it. He asked Shanta if she'd dance for him. She told him to get lost and I think he called her a bitch, but I'm not certain because we were walking away.'

'Did he use her name?'

'He called her Jessica.'
'And did it seem like he knew her?'
'I couldn't say. If he'd been to Bozouki he'd know her by Jessica.'
'Can you describe him?'
'He was in an EMS uniform, a pretty average looking white guy, shaved head.'
'Do you think you'd recognise him again?'
'Maybe.'
'And that's the only strange thing you can remember about that night?'
'Yeah.'
'Do you have any thoughts on why the mayor tried to keep the party quiet?'
'Don't you?' She smiled. 'Plenty of reasons. If he used taxpayer's money…which I'm guessing he did, he doesn't need another financial scandal. He's probably embarrassed his wife came home and caught him. Maybe she made him keep quiet about it. It's fairly obvious he'd want to downplay it.'

I agreed, but the mayor wasn't known for downplaying anything. The way this had been hushed up had already created a huge myth around it, which made you wonder what the real story was. Anyways, this EMS guy was something to go with. It was kind of tenuous, but maybe Jessica's refusal had been the final straw. Maybe his girlfriend had dumped him that night. Maybe he was a loser with a history of never getting women and when even an exotic dancer turned him down…maybe he really wanted to be a doctor or a cop and he was sick of being the guy who put people on a gurney. Who knows what makes men flip and go over to the dark side?

Mick was already back at his desk, tidying up before making an on-the-dot departure for home.

'Hey. Did you get anything at Bozouki?'
'Na. Same as before, none of the girls could think of any customers who had been misbehaving and Dave confirmed what a tight ship he ran and that anyone caught messing around with the dancers was barred.'
'Anyone been barred lately?'
'Nope, last one was before Christmas. Before you ask, I already checked him out. He said he went with a bunch of guys for a Christmas party, he drank too much, got a bit too touchy feely with one of the dancers – not Shanta. He's happily married with children and he moved out of state for work back in February.'

I was impressed Mick had actually done the legwork to check the guy out.

'You get anything?'

'Maybe. You know this party at Manoogian Mansion everyone's been talking about?'

'Alleged party.'

'Well Shanta's friend Linda says it happened and they were both there. Said some EMS guy got a bit upset when Shanta declined to dance for him.'

'Not much to go on.'

'No, but he's worth checking out, if I can find him.'

'Good luck. How many EMTs do you think there are in Detroit?'

'He's white.'

'Well, that narrows it down some. Anyway, I'm out of here. Don't work too hard.'

When you've been in the force as long as I have, you get to know people. I made a couple of calls. My friend over at dispatch said, 'party, what party, that never happened man,' and Jim, when I called him, said sure, he could find out which EMS teams were sent to the mansion that night, he'd get back to me. I figured there wasn't much else I could do for now. Seeing Linda had made me crave Mexican food. I picked up some Evie's tamales to go and went home. I opened a can of chilli and smothered the tamales and rooted around until I found my Mercedes Sosa album. You can't say I don't know how to kick back and enjoy myself.

...

Progress on the Jessica Rabbit case, if you can call it progress, was short lived. Friday morning the captain called me in his office. 'You're off the case Danny.'

'Why? I'm just starting to get some leads on it.'

'That's the problem; you've been asking questions you shouldn't be asking.'

I've got to say, at the time I didn't know what he was talking about.

'The word is from on high. Don't ask me about it. Take what I give you and think yourself lucky it's not worse.'

'But...'

The captain held up his hand to stop me. 'This case is bigger than me, bigger than you, bigger than both of us. Just drop it or you're liable to get kicked back to uniform.'

'OK, OK.'

Ten minutes later, as I sat pondering this bombshell and wondering what I was going to do, Jim called me back.

'There's no record of any ambulance being called to the mayor's mansion on January 14.'

'What? But I've got an eyewitness.'

'I'm just telling you there's no record.'

'But....' then I got it. 'OK Jim, thanks for looking.'

So, the cover up was for real. I'd been pulled from the case for asking about the party and either the records from that night had gone missing, or Jim couldn't tell me what he'd found. Finding the EMS guy without inside information would be impossible. Probably it would have come to nothing anyway. So, he called Shanta a bitch, some guys are like that with women, it didn't mean he'd killed her. Maybe it was just as well the captain had closed the case, if it was going to end up unsolved, but I hate loose ends, it doesn't feel right. I like to say I've explored every possibility before I give up on something.

In the small pockets of Detroit targeted for gentrification, poor and homeless residents have been forced out to make way for luxury loft and condominium construction. Meanwhile, most of the city rots away. *Free Press*

For the third time that week Leroy had been turned away from a construction company he'd heard was hiring. The papers were full of the projects for downtown, but with unemployment at over 30% he figured there were just too many people chasing the same jobs. At this rate he'd be lucky if he got a job selling hot dogs at the Super Bowl. He was sitting having a beer with the TV on when Rhonda came home from one of her volunteer projects. He didn't know why she didn't get a job now both the girls were in school. She was the one with the college degree. She'd worked in a bank before she got pregnant. When their first child was born, he'd worked all the overtime he could because they both agreed it was best for her to stay home with the baby, but eight years on that picture didn't look quite right anymore. But his pride wouldn't let him ask her. Surely, she'd make the suggestion herself, wouldn't she? To keep their lifestyle? Keep their house? Just 'til he found something else.

'Busy looking for a job then,' was Rhonda's opening remark.

'I've been looking, all day, all week. I just came back from another sure-fire opening that's closed all of a sudden.'

'I don't think I can take much more of this,' Rhonda whined.

'You can't take it? What about me? You think I like going begging for labouring jobs?'

'I'm going to take the girls to my parents for awhile,' she said.

'What? But it's only been a few weeks, Rhonda. I'm going to find something soon. You can't take them out of school.'

'There's only a week left of school, they won't miss that much.'

'Is this really about what's best for the girls?'

She said, 'of course,' but he could see by her face that the kids were just an excuse. She didn't want to be around him now he wasn't the great provider.

'Talk about kicking a man when he's down. You know I'm trying to get work.'

'I know you are, but I don't think it's good for the kids to see you like this.'

'See me like what? Seems to me the kids are kind of enjoying having me at home more.'

'It's just temporary,' she said. 'It'll be good for them to get out of here for a while.'

'Do you even love me?'

'Of course I do Leroy. I'm thinking of the children. I haven't seen my parents for a while, and it will be great for the girls. There's so much to do in Washington. I know you don't like visiting my folks, and you'll have space to find a job.'

More like they don't like me visiting them, thought Leroy, but from many years of experience he knew there was no point arguing with Rhonda. 'Well, I don't see how you being gone is gonna help me, but seeing as you've already made up your mind.'

Rhonda was packed and gone to Washington the next day, leaving Leroy wondering just how long she'd been planning this trip to see her parents. The house was quiet. Real quiet. He called Steve.

'Yo, what's up man?'

'Not much. How about you?'

'Rhonda left me.'

'What?'

'She took the kids to see her folks.'

'But that's just for a week or two, right?' Steve asked.

'I don't know. Sounded more like it would be for the whole summer.'

'Cool. So, you can play out again?'

'I was hoping for a little more support.'

'Sorry. You wanna go for a beer or something? Hey, let's go to Buddy's. We haven't been there for months. I'll buy.'

'OK. See you there in fifteen.'

'So, you're buying?' Leroy said, looking at the menu.

'Yep.'

'Then I'll have the Meat Deluxe.'

They placed their orders. Steve wiped the condensation off his Bud and took a swallow. 'What did Rhonda say?'

'Said she thought it would be better for the kids if they went away for a while and I could concentrate on getting a job.'

'How's that going?'

'What?'

'Getting a job.'

'Like shit. I can't find a thing.'

The waitress brought their squares. 'How come you always get the Greek, man?'

'I don't know, I just like it,' said Steve.

'Well salad dressing on a pizza ain't right. You wanna get yourself a real pizza.'

'You got pepperoni juice on your chin. Looks real manly,' Steve said.

'Think that's why Rhonda left me? 'Cause of my poor eating habits?!'

'After fifteen years? Na, I think she's used to that by now.'

www.magicbullet.com
08.24.05

More clean up duties last night. It felt good to finally be doing something to cleanse the big D. Some might say I'm putting her out of her misery. Maybe I am. Decontamination and sanitation is what we're talking about if you want to get technical. There's various tools of the trade. One I prefer more than others. I haven't totally perfected my technique yet, but I'm getting there. I've had a certain amount of professional experience. This wasn't the way I figured things would work out. I had another profession in mind, but I'm still providing a service. You could say I'm a civic servant. More than those bums down at City Hall anyway. What a farce! Have you seen the latest on Hendricks? I can barely bring myself to read the papers some days, it makes me sick.

Forum

- Don't get me started on Hendricks, man, I wouldn't know where to stop! Frohike

- Where are the details? I hear what you're saying, but we all know Detroit needs cleaning up. Give us the juicy inside track. JFB

FREEP.COM JUNE 24, 2007 PROLOGUE

It's the tale of a killer no bigger than a few grains of salt, the swath it cut through the heart of America and the reality that it could happen again.

Back to the grind

Anyways, I went back to the regular shit work – drug dealers getting shot. A year or so ago, Flanagan and Burnett put the Shanta Brown case to bed within two weeks – drug related, some dealer got upset 'cause she wouldn't dance at his party. I didn't figure it, but whatever. At the time I had other burgers to flip.

I'd just caught an interesting case for a change. The victim was a drug dealer, but there was something a bit different. There wasn't any question about June-Bey Jordan being in the game, and it sure looked like a drug killing – messy, in broad daylight like no one cared; no one willing to be a witness, but the killer had placed a newspaper on top of the body. Not just accidentally tossed there, but neatly folded to a story on page 5B and doodled in the margin was this name – Yves Dale Harlowe. Nothing else, just that name; and you've got to admit Yves isn't exactly a common name around here.

Of course, the brass wanted it cleared up quick. Not much hope of a conviction or significant jail time. One dealer shooting another dealer over a corner in D Town isn't news and it isn't worth anyone's time to do too much about it. The whole scene is a tragedy, but don't get me started on the war on drugs we're not waging and we certainly aren't winning.

I sent the paper to the forensics boys. It was from a Sunday print edition of the *Free Press* from two weeks prior to the murder. I remembered the issue; it was a special report on fentanyl. The page the killer had chosen to draw attention to was Chapter 8, The Morgue. Its closing line was "many more people would die first." A prophetic message from the killer? Someone who hated the drug scene? Someone who'd lost a loved one to drugs? Maybe to this new thing fentanyl that was dropping addicts all over town? No prints, needless to say. Nothing unusual about the paper, you could pick it up in a hundred locations. The techs said it looked like the name doodle had been copied from a cartoon. In other words, it wasn't the killer's actual writing so they couldn't deduce anything from that. It was all small caps in a funny font like you'd see in comic books.

Obviously, the killer was sending some kind of message with it and that's where it got interesting, for me anyways, not for anyone else as far as I could tell. My partner Mick wasn't interested. He just wanted the case closed, and if someone went down for it even better. I could tell I'd be working overtime on this one, but it wouldn't be paid by the police department. Puzzles captivate me, always have. Not crosswords and that stupid Sudoku thing, nothing autistic, I mean working out the clues that lead you to the man.

I read and re-read that article, all fifteen chapters of it, prologue and epilogue too, but I couldn't work out what the killer's beef was. There was so much material just in that one chapter. There could have been any number of angles that might flip someone over the edge to violence. Goes without saying the killer wanted to make a comment on the drug situation in the Big D, but it had to be more specific than that.

Then the department gets this anonymous call. Says the shooter was white. Says the shooter was an off-duty cop. I didn't like the idea of it maybe being a cop. Even if he could say he was doing a service, getting some lowlife dealer off the street. It isn't good for anyone if a cop goes rogue and I had a hard time picturing it. I put out a few subtle feelers among the narcotics boys, but no one came back with a guy wanting to do that kind of unpaid overtime. But it pushed a button in my brain, what if this was someone who used to be a cop? Maybe they'd had to leave the force for some reason? Or maybe it was just a fight over drug turf and the call was a red herring? Still, I wasn't getting anywhere rattling the cages of known drug associates, so I figured there was nothing to lose by some side research.

I called Glenda down at records; asked if she could get me the files on unsolved shootings with anything odd about them, like newspapers left at the scene, or cops as suspects. She wasn't enthusiastic about it. I said there was a pastrami on rye in it for her and she perked up a little. That woman loves to eat. I'd like to give her a little more than a sandwich, if you know what I mean, but she's married so that avenue is closed. Mick said I was wasting my time. He'd keep after the drug guys and check out the anonymous phone call. 'Real police work,' he said. Fuck you I thought. I don't hate the guy, don't get me wrong, but we have totally different ways of working, and frankly I'd rather be on my own since Reuben punched out.

So anyways, couple of days later Glenda calls me and I go over there.

'How you doing, Danny?' she said.

'Not so bad. How about yourself?'

'Just fine. I hope your back ain't playing up.' And she hefts a big stack of files on the counter. 'That's just the "odd" unsolveds. I didn't get to the cop suspects yet.'

'Jeez. That's a lot of paperwork.'

'You bet. Looks like you boys don't have much of a cleanup rate.'

'Hmm. You got a box?'

As if she already knew I'd ask for it, she lifted a cardboard file box from under her desk. 'You wanna get into the twenty-first century Danny. You could look this stuff up for yourself online, then just request them by file number.'

'Uh huh, where would be the fun in that, and what would you do all day then?'

'Oh you know, read the *Enquirer*, file my nails, take long lunches.'

'Sorry to have put you to trouble, but you know I like to come and see you in person, Glenda.' I put the warm pastrami on the counter in what I hoped was a seductive manner.

'Is there mustard on that?'

'Oh yeah, and pickles, just the way you like it.' I was starting to sound dirty to myself. I needed to get out of there and get distracted with proper police work.

'OK,' she said, taking and unwrapping it. 'Let me know if you still want the other stuff when you're done with that. I might take a little New York cheesecake as payment for that instalment.'

'Careful you don't spoil that fine figure,' I said as I left. I couldn't help myself. The woman is built like storage container, but I like my women big.

I go home, crack open a beer, unwrap the cellophane on a new pack of Marlboros and settle in for some reading. I know what you're going to say – you could stand to lose a little weight Danny, you need to quit the smokes Danny, but I don't have that many pleasures left me, and I'm not looking to live out my years in some retirement home with Jell-O rolling down my chin, so I'll take my chances.

First, I scanned the files looking for any cases mentioning a newspaper left at the scene. I was surprised. I turned up three. None of them mentioned a name doodled on the paper, but that didn't mean it hadn't been there. I was going to have to go to evidence and pull the boxes. None of them mentioned the headline either. I thought it unlikely that they were unconnected. I mean, killers don't generally leave a newspaper at the scene. All three were gunshot victims. Glock .40. It's a service weapon, but there are plenty of Glocks in Detroit, so it doesn't narrow things down as much as you'd hope. The three murders were a dancer –

black, a hooker – white, and a young black man. He'd had some drug related arrests, but he didn't look like he was a major player. So an equal opps killer on the racial front. Possibly a drug connection on all three? Hookers were often addicts, dancers often hung with dealers. But why kill the victims of drugs and the dealers? Or maybe this guy had something against women? Thought all 'dancers' and hookers were whores? But then why kill two black men, drug dealers presumably, assuming my current case was the latest victim of the newspaper killer.

I checked the investigating officers on all three cases. Different officers, different parts of town. No reason why anyone would have connected them. I knew one of the guys slightly. Figured I'd call him for a beer and chat about it.

I turned out the light and smoked in the dark. I like to do that, looking out at the glow of the streetlights, feeling the Big D humming all around me. All the murder and mayhem just out of reach.

>
> Armed with a paintbrush, a broom, and neighborhood children, Guyton, Karen, and Grandpa began by cleaning up vacant lots on Heidelberg and Elba Streets. From the refuse they collected, Guyton began to transform the street into a massive art environment. Vacant lots literally became 'lots of art' and abandoned houses became 'gigantic art sculptures.' *History of The Heidelberg Project*,
> www.heidelberg.org

Steve drove down to Heidelberg and parked. It was Saturday. It was sunny, not yet hot. He walked along towards Mt Elliott taking photos of the art. He'd been coming down here to check out the house decoration and sculpture for years. Now it was starting to get trendy. You saw more white people, more tourists, but the neighbourhood was still quiet.

The house he'd seen listed for a hundred dollars was on Preston Street, just one block north of Heidelberg. It was so quiet. He could hear birds singing, in the city, on a Saturday. Everything was green. Many houses had been torn down and there were swathes of emerald returning to nature. Here and there trash poked through the overgrown grass. It was like a ghost town except for the few people Steve came across tending vegetable plots or sitting on their porches. He had the sun on his back and he felt warm. Detroit wasn't so bad.

The realtor was standing on the sidewalk at the end of a short drive; a youngish black guy looking uncomfortable in his suit. To one side was a vacant lot. To the other a house that looked reasonably well kept. Across the street was a burned-out husk. Steve held his hand out. 'I'm here about the house.'

'Right.' The guy looked surprised. 'Well let's take a look.' They walked up the path. 'There is some fire damage,' he said, 'so watch your step.'

The small front porch looked perfect to Steve. He could already see himself sitting there with a beer. The upstairs had a balcony too; just perfect for sitting out reading on a summer evening. The view across the street wasn't great, but maybe he could just knock that down himself. It looked like a puff of wind would blow it over. They stepped into the living room. The oak floors could be stripped. Not bad, not bad at all. The realtor looked embarrassed and moved them to the kitchen. Well, what was left of the kitchen – a pipe sticking out of the floor was all that remained of the plumbing. Even that didn't deter Steve. He had a cousin who did plumbing. The back wall was completely black from a fire. Steve figured he'd have to rebuild that, or re-plaster at least. The rest of the house didn't get any better and it didn't get any worse.

'What's going on with the lot next door?' Steve asked.

'It's vacant.'

'So, I could use it?'

'I don't... well I guess. I don't see anyone snapping it up to make condos.' The young man smiled a nervous smile. He had big teeth, lots of them. Steve nodded.

'I'll take it. Where do I sign?'

'Don't you want to look at anything else?'

'Not right now. I know, it's kind of expensive, maybe I should check out some others, but I like the neighbourhood.'

'OK, well I'll get the paperwork sorted out and I'll be in touch.' They shook hands.

And that was that. Steve had a house. He watched the real estate guy walk back to his car. After all these years of renting he finally had a house, with a porch. He imagined himself sitting in a swing seat watching his neighbours go by. He started to think about all the things he could do with the place, once he'd made it weatherproof of course. Then he walked around taking pictures of the house from every angle, every room and the views from upstairs. He'd have to work on the back wall fairly soon, check the roof and replace all the downstairs windows which were either broken or completely gone, frame and all. He thought the upstairs ones were OK. He went back up to take a look. Steve walked slowly from room to room, checking the windows, running his fingers along the windowsills. They all seemed sound. He opened the door out to the tiny balcony. The wood of the handrail was starting to rot, but mostly that was in good shape too. He couldn't believe he had a house for just a hundred dollars. There was so much to do. He needed to get himself to a builder's merchants soon and get some basic tools and supplies and contact his cousin Ray to do the plumping on the place.

Steve had never worked in construction, he'd never worked anywhere but at the GM plant, but he was fit and healthy and pretty good with his hands. He'd done plenty of minor repairs for women friends over the years. He figured with a little help from some library books or magazines, he could do a decent enough job of fixing the place up.

www.magicbullet.com
09.11.05

'Juicy inside track'? I'll give you an inside track – fentanyl. Yep, that's the killer of choice right now. All the junkies are just itching to get hold of it. Most people, if something is likely to kill you, they stay clear, right? But no, not your average dope head, they just want the biggest high they can get even if it's their last one. It used to be we could pull them back from the brink, not anymore.

But I'm sensing that's not the juice you want JFB, am I right? You're gunning for more dirt on the mayor? Well, here's a little titbit that hasn't made the papers yet – Hendricks' campaign workers – they're at all the nursing homes helping the Alzheimer cases fill-out their ballots. You wait and see if that f***er doesn't get re-elected. But you can be damn sure I won't be voting for him.

Forum

- Ooh, that's tasty and despicable all at the same time. JFB

FREEP.COM JUNE 24, 2007 PROLOGUE

How are a teenager and rogue chemist in Mexico linked? By a mega drug suspected of killing her and hundreds of others in metro Detroit.

I called Johnson and we met at this place in Greektown. He loves the Pekilia. Whatever. I'll eat just about anything and I like those salads with the feta cheese and olives. I feel a salad every once in a while kind of balances things out.

I didn't know Johnson that well. Our paths had crossed a few times. We'd been in the same bars on occasion. We'd pass the time of day, but I didn't know what kind of movies he liked or his taste in women.

We shoot the breeze for a while to be polite then I get to the point, because you know, I don't have all day.

'You remember that case you had a couple of years back, newspaper found near the body.'

'Can't say I do. You got more details?'

'Michelle Dobbs, prostitute, age forty, going on sixty by the look of the SOC photos. Shot over on Keating. Known drug user. Says here a copy of the *Free Press* was found near the body.'

'Yeah, I vaguely remember it, but a junkie prostitute doesn't exactly stand out from the crowd.'

'Show a little heart Bob, she's still somebody's daughter.'

'I guess. Show me the photo.' He looked at the crime scene photo. 'Oh yeah. We never got anyone for that,' he said.

'I know.'

'They're not re-opening it, are they? What's your interest?'

'Kind of links to an ongoing homicide. Well, the newspaper thing does.'

'I don't even remember the newspaper angle.'

'It's listed, in this report signed by you, as being tagged as evidence.'

'I don't remember nothing weird about it.'

Apart from the feta, I didn't feel like I was getting a whole lot out of this lunch. Johnson pushed himself back in his chair, took a used toothpick from his coat pocket and started picking at his teeth. I figured it was only a matter of time before he belched loudly. I was wasting my time. Then he taps the photo with the toothpick.

'Wait a minute. There was something odd about that one... Yeah, that was the one. The techs found some vomit near the body. They analysed it, got a DNA profile. We spent hours trying to follow that up. Eventually the profile matches someone on the database, some low-level drug dealer. We figure she couldn't pay, he got mad, he glocked her. Eventually we track him down. Well, we track down his mother. The guy had died two weeks previous, liver failure. So, it could have been him or maybe it wasn't. In the end we figured she just got caught in the crossfire. That kind of life, that neighbourhood… only a matter of time, and we closed the file.'

'But he would have been alive when she was actually killed.'

'Seems like it, but I guess he was sick. A liver don't fail over night.'

'Yeah. Sounds like he was sampling his own product. OK. Thanks. I'll see you around.'

'Yeah, good to see you. You're looking good for an old timer.' He belched. Old timer? He's got as many miles on the clock as me and I'm looking a damn sight trimmer than he is, I can tell you.

'Every junkie,' he said, 'wants a breath-taking high.' *Free Press*

Leroy and his nephew Wendell were sitting on a bench overlooking Belle Isle. Wendell was Leroy's brother's youngest son. Coming up on twenty-five, he'd already been in the drugs game since he was fifteen and had been promoted several times.

'I heard you weren't doing so good man,' Wendell said. 'I've got some openings and I always like to use family, 'cause you can trust family.'

'You know I ain't into that, Wendell.'

'You wouldn't have to do anything on the street. I need a pickup man. All you gotta do is drive up over to Canada once a week and collect some stuff.'

'You get it from Canada?'

'Via Canada let's say.'

'And what if I get checked?'

'We got that covered. There's lots of ways around that. And we have a special vehicle. You won't be taking the red devil,' Wendell laughed in a throaty way, 'we got something way less conspicuous. Plus you look like a regular guy.'

'I am a regular guy.'

'You know what I mean. You don't look like a player.'

'I'm gonna have to think about it.' Leroy was already thinking there was no way he could say yes, but on the other hand he sure could use the money and it would just be driving, he could give it up as soon as he got a real job.

'That's cool,' said Wendell. 'Think of yourself as a Youngblood Priest character, getting one over the Man. I know you and dad dig that 70's shit.'

'I could get out whenever I want?'

'Sure, but you're gonna get used to that regular money. No taxes, no deductions.'

'I don't think so.'

'I know you hate it, but it don't have to be as bad as you think. Look at me. Look at my house, my fine wife, my baby boy. You can keep the street at bay if you're smart.'

'Yeah, but if you're in that business that means people you associate with are killing people,' said Leroy.

'It's just capitalism, man. People want a product. I sell them a product. If I didn't do it someone else would and they'd do it worse than me. I got the best product going. I don't cut it with no dangerous shit. My clients know they can trust my stuff. It's the American Dream.'

More like a nightmare, thought Leroy. What am I doing talking to a drug dealer, even if he is my nephew? 'All right, well I'll think about it.'

'OK, but don't think too long. That vacancy needs filling.'

Leroy continued to sit on the bench and listen to the silence. How had his life turned to shit so fast? Twenty-five years he'd worked for GM and just like that it was gone. It looked like his wife was leaving him. He couldn't get any work and now he was contemplating selling drugs. But Wendell had a point. None of this was Leroy's fault. There would always be junkies and there would always be drugs. If someone was going to make money off it, why shouldn't he have a little piece of it? But making money off other people's misery was not Leroy's style. Surely, he could get some kind of honest work, couldn't he?

www.magicbullet.com
11.22.05

Now you know how today is a special day for some people. I don't suppose anyone here subscribes to the Lone Gunman Theory, but I thought we might discuss the different options, just for nostalgia. I mean do you really think the Cubans were involved? You can bet Hoover was manoeuvring things somehow.

How many Lee Harvey Oswalds were there?

Is there a magic bullet?

Forum

- We all know Oswald was just the fall guy. JFB

- I don't think we'll ever know the truth, but 77% of Americans can't be wrong. It isn't the first or last time the government has pulled the wool over our eyes. Frohike

- Ain't that the truth! Lone Gunman

18 other comments, click here to read them

Freep.com June 24, 2007 Chapter 4: The hooker
For two decades, heroin has been her only dependable lover.

I went and picked up the evidence boxes for the three cases with newspapers mentioned. My captain was not happy. Mick was now off sick. He couldn't assign anyone else to me and I was taking too damn long on what was a simple drug-related killing. Could I please get my finger out and arrest somebody or give up and close it unsolved. Sometimes you had to just say they were unsolved, but I hated to do that. It messed with my Zen-like approach to life. I had a pretty good percentage over my time and I wasn't about to let it slip now. Anyways, what else did I have planned for the evening? So I loaded the boxes in the trunk, picked up a pizza with extra jalapeños and went home for a quiet night in.

I put a Dolly Parton CD on low, put on the standing lamp over my Lay-Z-Boy, took a big bite and opened the box from Johnson's case. I'm glad to say the bag of vomit wasn't in there, that must have stayed with the lab boys. There wasn't much stuff. A plastic bag with some cheap jewellery in it, which meant no one had claimed it, because family would have had a right to take her personal effects. A bag with her clothes in. A bag with a crumpled newspaper in. That didn't match with my guy. He was a neat freak. The paper on June-Bey's body had been carefully folded to show the headline. Even the doodled name was neat. I didn't think it was just a doodle. I believe that name was there deliberately. I looked at the paper through the plastic. It was a squashed amalgamation of sports and classifieds. I knew there was no point, but I put down the pizza slice, pulled on some gloves (I always have a box handy) and took the paper out of the bag. An odd, unpleasant odour emanated the minute I pulled the bag open, but I couldn't place what it was. I flicked through it glancing at each page. No doodled names anywhere. I re-sealed the bag. God knows why Johnson even bothered to bag it. I reckon it was just coincidence the paper happened to be near the body.

I finished my beer and ate a couple more slices, then I wiped off my hands and moved to the next box. This was Delaware Loomis. Delaware? What kind of parent names a child Delaware? Anyways, found about a year ago in an alley just south of Eight Mile. Neat gunshot to the head. I didn't worry too much about what else was in the box. I went straight for the bag with the paper in. *Detroit Free Press*, August 4, 2006, folded to a corruption probe into ex City Councilman Alonzo Bates with the headline: "2 Admit Guilt in Corruption Case" and in the bottom right-hand corner, very small and almost illegible was a doodle. I got to tell you I got a little buzz then, like when you take a hit on a cigarette on a really cold night. I pulled out the magnifying glass I keep in the pocket of my Lay-Z-Boy. Bingo, it's another name: Ada Rose Hewl Levy.

I flipped open my notebook. The name on the June-Bey murder paper was Yves Dale Harlowe. I wrote the other name under it. I figured they could be real names but they both sounded odd to me. I open the third evidence box. Go straight to the bag with the newspaper in. It's another neatly folded *Free Press*. My pulse is up a little now. I pull it out. Vertically on the left-hand side. Another doodled name. Only it's not. It says: A Lawyer Shoveled. A lawyer shoveled? What the hell does that mean? I looked to the headline for a clue. July 29, 2006 "Lawsuit Against Hendricks Can Go to Trial, Appeal Court Rules".

July 29 and August 4, only six days apart. If the same killer had done them both he was on a real killing spree and if he was killing that regularly even Detroit's police would have noticed a link by now. I went back to the files. Loomis was indeed killed in August 2006, but on the 22nd, which meant the killer had saved the paper for nearly three weeks. The third case was Rochelle Miller a dancer fatally shot in January 2007. Her newspaper had been kept for six months. That meant the story in the paper was relevant, or at least the headline, otherwise the killer wouldn't hang onto them for so long. A murder every six months or so? How many more had he done? The doodled names had to be important too. No way could it be a coincidence that all three murders had a pristine copy of the *Free Press* with an unusual name or phrase doodled on the same page in a cartoon-like font.

Like I said, I'm not much for word puzzles or crosswords or anything, but I could see immediately that the two names and the phrase had some letters in common. It's got to be an anagram, right? That could take me a while. I ran a hot tub. What? Something wrong with a man liking to bathe? It's a good place to think. I set my cigarettes and ashtray on the toilet seat, just in reach. I write the three names large on a piece of paper so I can see them and stick it behind the taps and I slide into that baby. Some water sloshes onto the floor. I'm always doing that. The way I see it, if you're going to the trouble of taking a bath, it might as well be deep and it better be hot. I let the steam rise until I'm sweating, light a Marlboro and look at the names:

Yves Dale Harlowe
Ada Rose Hewl Levy.
A Lawyer Shoveled

I could immediately see that some of the same letters were in each of the names – Y, W, D, but beyond that I didn't get anywhere for a long time. I went back to thinking about the newspapers instead. The killer clearly wanted to make a statement with it, but what was it? What was most important, the headline? The date? The fact that it was the *Free Press*? Was it just saying, 'look I'm the same person doing these killings and I want you to know it'? If I worked out what the anagram was, maybe that would help me.

I must have dozed for a little, because next thing I know the water is tepid. I get out, towel off and put on my robe, then I go over to my desk and start working those letters. Two hours and five bags of pretzels later, I've cracked it. Lee Harvey Oswald. Fucking Lee Harvey Oswald! So now what? Our guy identifies with Oswald? He's trying to say he's been wrongfully accused? He's into conspiracy theories, so he takes his name from the original and the best? Or it's more subtle than that?

I fire up my computer and I'm on a roll. First, Wikipedia on Lee Harvey Oswald, not much I didn't already know, except that one of his nicknames in the Marines was Ozzie Rabbit from the 1920's cartoon character Oswald The Lucky Rabbit. I file that in my brain for later. From Oswald it's just a few obvious clicks to sites on the Lone Gunman Theory, The Single Bullet Theory, AKA The Magic Bullet Theory, and of course a digression to the *X Files*' Lone Gunmen.

What is my killer trying to say? He's the Lone Gunman? All his murders have been with guns, not a typical choice for a serial killer. Does he think of himself as some kind of hero? The *Lone Ranger* righting injustice?

It's already getting light by the time I go to bed. I get maybe a couple of hours, but my head is too buzzing to sleep. Down at the station, my captain kills all my excitement – he really doesn't care if I have a highly literate killer who likes to leave immaculate copies of the *Free Press* at the scene. Mick is going to be off for the rest of the week, and he needs me on another homicide, so if I'm not going to bring someone in for the Jordan killing, could I please shelve it and get onto the next case. I've left out some phrases like, 'get off your fat ass' and 'shove the Jordan case…' because I don't want you to get the wrong impression about the man. He's just trying to do a job like everyone else and it isn't his fault he's got clear-up rates to meet.

Forgotten but not gone. In ghost of a neighborhood, the few who stay say city neglects them

Gone from this northeast Detroit neighborhood are most of the two-bit drug slingers and gangsters who took over houses for their trade, shot off their guns in broad daylight and terrorized anyone who dared to speak up... Amid the eerie quiet are the forgotten ones -- Detroiters certain that no mayor, no City Council member, could possibly know their world exists... *Free Press*

While Steve was walking around taking photos of his new neighbourhood, he had a thought. A while back the *Free Press* had done a series of articles, 'driving Detroit' or something, with photos and stories from different parts of the city. Maybe Steve could interest them in a before and after kind of story. He'd send them the photos of his house when he'd bought it and then at different stages until he'd finished working on it. He figured it could be a real inspiration to other people to do similar things. Maybe he could even start a whole regeneration of the metro area! Steve chuckled to himself, well maybe not, there were probably people doing that already, but it wouldn't hurt to contact the Freep and maybe he could earn a few bucks on the side too.

First thing Monday morning he called the *Free Press* and after some long delays and several call transfers he was finally talking to Bill who'd done the Driving Detroit series. He briefly explained his idea.

'Well that sounds pretty good, but I'm not going to be around here much longer, I'm retiring. I'll leave a note for my colleague Alison. She'll give you a call.'

She didn't. Well not for a few days anyway and then they arranged to meet to chat about Steve's idea and look at some of his photos.

'Hi. Are you Steve?' The guy was sitting flicking through photos on a Canon Sure Shot. He looked up. 'Please tell me you're not going to offer me pictures you took on that?' she said.

'Um, no. Alison?'

'Yep.' She sat down opposite him.

'You want a cup of coffee?'

'No thanks, I already had enough caffeine today. So, Bill tells me you have this great idea for a photo story, and I'm starting out doing a column, so we're a match made in heaven.'

'Right,' said Steve. Alison was younger and spunkier than he'd been expecting and he suddenly felt really old and a bit out of his depth. 'So, Bill explained the idea?'

'More or less. Let me see some of your photos, 'cause if you can't take a picture we're wasting our time here.'

'Sure, sure,' said Steve, putting the Canon in his jacket pocket and pulling a folder out of his backpack. He'd spent most evenings for the past couple of weeks sorting through his recent photo collection and printing off what he thought was his best work, including some of his own new house. He slid the folder across to Alison who opened it. 'So, first there's just some general shots, you know abandoned houses and buildings, that kind of stuff.'

'Uh ah.' Alison didn't want to give too much away, but the photos were amazing, at least as good as the kind of work they usually used. But Bill had taught her well. She was not to gush and enthuse, but play it cool, make sure the paper got exactly what it wanted and at the right price.

'And these are some of my house. And those are the most recent, where I've done a little work on it. Like I told Bill, I was thinking we could do a kind of before and after story.'

'Hmm, but that's going to take a long time, isn't it? How long do you think it is going to take you to fix the place up?'

Shit, thought Steve, she's right. What paper is going to want to cover something that is going to take months to finish. 'Um, well, yeah quite a while I guess.'

'Don't get me wrong, Steve. I think it's a good idea, but what you need to do is put it all together and then get in touch with me with more of a finished product and I'll write it up. There isn't really anything for me here.'

'Right.' Steve was crestfallen. He'd built his idea up into a huge project, maybe even an exhibition at some downtown gallery to go with it. Steve Novak, the great new thing in photography, and this girl barely out of college had cut him down at the first step.

'That said, I'm sure we could use some of your other photos. You have lots, right?'

'Oh yeah, tons. All sorts of stuff.'

'So, if I emailed you and asked you for something specific, you could do it?' asked Alison.

'Yeah, I should think so. And you'd pay for them?'

'Of course, standard freelance rates.'

'OK. And the house thing?'

'Like I said, get back to me when it's closer to completion. I definitely think we could do something with it. Could be a very good angle, you know more positive, local Detroiter makes good – turns derelict house into attractive family home. You're not planning to sell it and make a load of money, are you?'

'No, I'm going to live in it.'

'Cool. Any family? Photos of kids playing in the yard or anything?'

'Um, no, no family, but I could get some neighbourhood kids round or something if that'll clinch it.'

'We'll cross that bridge when we come to it, Steve.' Alison made to stand up. 'Good talking to you. You got a card?'

Damn, he'd fucked up again, what an amateur. 'I'm waiting on some from the print shop,' he lied. He tore a sheet out of his notebook, wrote his email address and phone number on it and handed it to her. 'Do you?'

'Sure.' She fished in the side pocket of her Dockers cargo pants and gave him a card with her details, then took his piece of paper without looking at it, folded it and put it in the same pocket.

'OK, well I'll be in touch.' What a schmuck thought Alison as she went outside to her bike. He takes a good photo though. She was already thinking of a couple of things she could probably use him on.

Steve sat back down, having half risen to acknowledge Alison's leaving. He watched her ass as she left, it looked pretty good, but cargo pants? And the thumb ring? He bet she'd have a tattoo somewhere too. Gee, he felt old, but overall a promising meeting. His house project was possibly on for the future and she had said she'd get in touch about using some of his other photos. But maybe that's just what she always said. Probably she wouldn't call. Had he just been fobbed off without even realising? He thought about her asking if he was going to live in the house. It hadn't even crossed his mind not to, but maybe there was money to be made in doing up houses and selling them. Certainly worth some thought once he'd seen how much work it was and how much it cost him.

He felt a bit stupid, not even having got some cards printed up, but he'd been concentrating on the photos thinking they would speak for themselves. What was the going freelance rate anyway? He needed to find that out straight away in case Alison did call him. He didn't want to look like an idiot again and he didn't want to get ripped off.

Steve sat there sipping coffee for a while thinking about his new life – his new house, maybe a new career in photojournalism, or at least a few extra bucks for photos he'd be taking anyway. Then he thought about Leroy. He wasn't doing so well. He couldn't seem to get a job and Rhonda had gone off for the summer with the kids. He should call him. Go out, have a beer, shoot the breeze. And he could use an extra pair of hands at the house. In fact, he'd better get back over there and put in a few more hours.

www.magicbullet.com
02.11.06

I think a cleanup professional should have a proper uniform, don't you? An insignia you might say. A logo. A business card. "You mess up, we clean up." Something like that. Yeah, logos are good. I'm just brainstorming here fellas, bear with me. I'll dish some more dirt soon, I promise. A little suspense won't kill you, but waiting for an ambulance might!

Forum

- *What about Ghost Busters? Those addicts are ghosts, aren't they? Lol Ringo*

- *What line of business are you in man? Do you have a cleaning operation, 'cause I could put some business your way. JFB*

- *I was speaking more metaphorically, John. It is John, isn't it? Lone Gunman*

- *Right. That's deep. That's cool. JFB*

- *How about an anagram like nightly acme (mighty clean). F*

- *Oh Frohike, you're such an anagram nerd, give me a break! Ringo*

- *I kind of like it. You might be onto something. Lone Gunman*

Freep.com June 24, 2007 Chapter 8: The morgue

Meanwhile, in the drug houses and on the street corners of Detroit, rumours were circulating that a new brand of heroin was killing people.

Just as I'm finally getting somewhere on the June-Bey Jordan thing, and it's maybe shaping up into a juicy serial aspect, with a moderately interesting perpetrator, I'm back out on the street, schlepping over to Mack Avenue to see about a stabbing victim. And isn't it just too ironic to bear, that after twenty-five years on the force without ever getting shot, and I might add without having killed anyone either, and a near perfect track record serious-injury-wise, I get hit by a ricochet checking out some domestic between junkies who don't even know what day of the week it is. Sometimes you almost want to sympathise with anyone trying to clean up this town, even if they go about it all wrong.

If I hadn't been in pain I might have seen the funny side of it. The EMS guys certainly did. Weird sense of humour those fellas have. I never have liked them much. I almost could have walked over to Receiving and saved myself the wisecracks. Anyways I jumped the line a little by getting taken in by ambulance. I figured they'd patch me up and I'd be back out in time to catch the evening news. Guess that was optimistic since my left arm was dead from the shoulder down. Still, I was surprised when they said I'd need surgery.

When I woke up it was daylight still. Six o'clock. I thought that was pretty good going until I realised it was 6 a.m. the next day. Apparently, I had woken up after surgery, but had then slept like a log. A loud log, the older nurse quipped, not impressed with my level of snoring. I thought, you'd snore too if you were on your back full of anaesthetic and goodness knows what, not to mention I hadn't been sleeping much lately. She looked like she'd be a snorer. Her and the young Hepburn look-alike were doing a nice little good nurse bad nurse routine. I could tell it was going to be a long day.

The captain rolled by at around 8 a.m. on his way to the station. After he'd berated me for not closing the Jordan case and not even starting on the stabbing case, whined about how Mick was still sick and now I was off, and how he'd never get his clearance rates up with all this shit going down, he remembered where he was and asked me how I was feeling. I could feel my arm again, which I guess was a good thing, but I didn't like the way the painkillers were wearing off. He told me to take it easy and not rush back. I wish I'd had a tape recording of that, the guys will never believe he actually said 'don't rush back.' On his way out he finally parted with the coffee and donuts he'd come in with. The guy has no imagination. I must have been feeling bad 'cause I couldn't even look at the donuts. I let Katherine Hepburn have one while her superior was out of the room giving someone else a hard time.

By 10 a.m. I was feeling a bit perkier. I drank the captain's coffee cold and put away a couple of chocolate-coated rings and then I felt even better in a nauseous kind of way. I'll spare you the details, but the doc said the bullet had been a real bitch to get out and I was lucky I didn't have permanent nerve damage. At least ten days in the hospital and then months of rest and physio. If I was back to work in six months, he said I'd be doing real well, but looking at my medical history, which I took him to mean my smoking and slight obesity, he figured longer and maybe I should consider calling it a day. I'd only been there four hours and I wanted to start digging my way out. I didn't see how I was going to last the full prison term. I ain't got nothing personal against doctors, I just don't like them. And I like hospitals even less. Maybe it was visiting Reuben and seeing him go downhill so quick, because I haven't ever had a bad experience myself I could pin my aversion on. Well anyways, you get the picture, I wanted out of there, but it wasn't happening.

I bribed Katherine with the last of the donuts to go down to the store and get me some reading material. I should have been more specific. She brought me back *The Da Vinci Code* and a John Grisham for Pete's sake. But I guess it could have been worse, at least they were both pretty thick.

The Grisham had a nice soporific effect. I woke up in a sweat after dreaming about Jessica and Ozzie making out like rabbits and spawning hundreds of cartoon bunnies. That reminded me of the big breakthrough I'd made before life intervened. Was it that big though? The killer was into Oswald in some way. Him and thousands of others. It didn't exactly narrow things down. Him and Jessica both had rabbit nicknames – weird coincidence or what. Yes, I still thought about the Jessica Rabbit/Shanta Brown case. I still wanted to crack it. It was a matter of personal pride and integrity even if no one else gave a f**k. I needed a cigarette and I needed my laptop.

Fortunately, it was my left arm that was useless so I'd still be able to work a mouse and type one-handed, but I had a feeling Florence Nightingale was the kind to ban electronic devices, including phones. I also needed real food. I'd only experienced breakfast and lunch so far and if that was anything to go by I'd be dropping a suit size by the end of the week. I needed an associate. Mick was no help on account of him being 'sick'. I had my suspicions that his ailment was mainly in his head, but maybe I'm misjudging the guy. Anyways, we're not what you'd call close friends so he's not going to go out of his way to come and visit. Sad thing was, I could think of plenty of guys I could go for a beer with, but I couldn't think of anyone I'd trust to go to my place and pick up some stuff for me. Now if Reuben was still around, that would be a different story. We were even closer than family, but there's no point dwelling on that. I was pondering this dilemma when Katherine comes in to check on me.

'Hey, could you make a call for me? I need some pyjamas and stuff,' I said.

'You can make a call yourself Mr Daniels. There's a phone right there.'

I followed her eyes. There was a phone on the wall by the bed. Come on, give me a break, I've just had major surgery, right? So, I'm not as attentive to detail as usual.

'Oh yeah, sure. Could you maybe pass me the phone? And the notebook out of my jacket pocket.'

She opened the bedside cabinet and took out a plastic bag that contained the contents of my jacket.

'Hey, where's my jacket?'

'They had to cut it off you. Not to mention the blood. I guess they threw it out.'

'What do you mean cut it off? I walked in here conscious and with that jacket on. I didn't give anyone permission to cut it off.'

She shrugged. 'I don't know. Maybe you passed out when they tried to take it off. But all your belongings are here Mr Daniels.' She passed me the phone.

I flipped through my notebook; not many names jumped out at me as suitable. Then it came to me, my buddy Bill at the *Free Press*. We went back aways. We weren't best friends or anything, but he was a trustworthy guy. I dialled his number.

'Hey Bill, how's it going?'

'Yeah good Danny, but I'm on a deadline here, what do you need? Can I call you back?'

I explained the situation, said I didn't mind waiting 'til he was done with his story. It wasn't that kind of deadline; he was on his way to the airport.

'I'll send a colleague of mine. You'll like her.'

'Bill, I'm not in any position to hit on women right now.'

He just laughed and hung up.

A few minutes later the phone rang.

'Hi. This is Alison Krall. I work with Bill. He said you needed some stuff I could help you with.' She said her last name like 'crawl' and like she wasn't having the best of days.

'Hi Alison. This seems kind of odd when I don't know you.'

'No problem. Shoot.'

'Do you have time to get out of the office for a while?'

'It would be a pleasure. What do you need?'

'Well. I'm laid up at Receiving.'

'Yeah, Bill said. What happened?'

This was the best response I'd had so far to my injury and I didn't even know this woman. Maybe Bill was right when he said I'd like her. 'I got shot in the line of duty.'

'That sounds exciting. Any story in it for me?'

I laughed. 'No, I don't think so. It wasn't that interesting. But I need a few things bringing over.'

'Right, sure. Like pyjamas and stuff?'

'Do I look like someone who wears pyjamas?'

'How do I know, I can't see what you look like,' she said.

I gave her my address and told her where the spare key was hidden. Yeah I know I should have tighter security, but sometimes it's handy to have a key hidden. It's not as if it's under the front door mat or anything. And I know some people who wouldn't want a journo snooping around their place either, but I've got nothing to hide. If she's got nothing better to do than go through my stuff, I pity her. Anyways, Bill wouldn't hook me up with anyone too strange.

'Top drawer of the dresser in the bedroom, there's some T-shirts and boxers that will do for pyjamas and there's a spare toilet bag already kitted out in the bottom drawer.'

'Very organised.'

'I don't like to unpack,' I said. 'And can you bring me anything you can find on Oswald and the Lone Gunman Theory – biographies, stuff off the internet, but skip Wiki I already read that. If that's not asking too much.'

'Interesting sickbed reading. Are you some kind of conspiracy theory nut?'

'No. I'll explain when you get here. And bring me a slice, I'm starving in here.'

'Extra jalapeños on that?'

'How did you guess?'

'I'm an investigative reporter. I can deduce these things.'

'Hmm, should I be worried about you going through my place?'

She laughed and hung up. It was a day for people laughing at me.

I was starting to lose hope that this Alison would show up. They'd already brought round dinner, if you could call it that – I was saving the Jell-O for later, and the pain medication – I was saving that too in the hope of getting a double hit at lights out. I'd put the TV on to check out the news, but it was the same old crap, so I was contemplating a few more pages of Grisham when a young woman poked her head round the door.

'What took you so long?'

'Nice to meet you too. How's it going?' She slumped into the chair as though she'd just run a marathon. She had a nice face, but her dress sense sucked. She was in boy's shorts and a faded T-shirt. Younger than I was expecting.

'Sorry. Thanks for coming. Do you owe Bill favours?'

'No, I'm just the newbie. I get all the shit jobs.' She smiled. 'Is the coast clear?'

'What?'

'Are you expecting any medical staff to drop by?'

'Oh, no, they've just been.'

'Good.' She put her bike courier bag on the bed and extracted a pizza box. Flipping the lid, she took a slice herself before offering me one. After cramming most of it into her mouth, she pulled a bottle of beer out of the bag and screwed off the top. 'I guess alcohol doesn't mix with your meds,' she said, half proffering the bottle.

'No that's fine, I'd better not push my luck.'

She took another slice and sat back in the chair. 'Sorry I didn't get here sooner. I had to file a story, then I got sidetracked dweebing on Oswald, and your place is way out there.'

'It's in the city limits.'

'Only just. I had to go back to my place to pick up the car.'

'You cycle to work?'

'Sure, why not? You should try it. You're a heart attack waiting to happen.'

'Thanks for your concern.'

'So, what's the story?' She asked, nodding towards my arm.

'Nothing exciting, a bullet ricocheted and got me in the shoulder while I was attending a very run of the mill misunderstanding between drug users.'

'Bummer. I was hoping for the inside story on a cop shooting.'

'Sorry to disappoint.'

'Does it hurt?'

'Yes, but I'll live. The chilli burn is taking the edge off it.' She smiled. 'Did you bring me any reading material?'

'Sure did.' She wiped her hands on her shorts and went into the bag again. She handed me a wad of papers. 'Miscellaneous internet stuff.' Then she handed me two books: *Legend: the Secret Life of Lee Harvey Oswald* and *Case Closed*. 'All I could get at short notice. I can probably find you some more. What's the deal with Oswald?'

'Well...'

'Are you going to eat that?' I let her have the last slice and hide the box back in her bag.

'Before I got shot, I'd been looking at some old cases in relation to a new case I'd got. It seemed like a regular drug related shooting except that someone, I'm guessing the killer, had left a neatly folded copy of the *Free Press* on top of the body.'

'Ooh, what was the headline?'

'I'm getting to that. There was a name doodled in the margin of the paper. Anyways, long story short I found three other unsolved shootings where a paper had been found at the scene. I pulled the evidence and two of the others had doodled names too. Turns out all the doodles are anagrams of Lee Harvey Oswald.'

'Wow that could be huge. You're saying there could be a killer out there, who's done at least three, maybe more, and he's leaving a signature?'

'Kind of. I'm inclined to think it is the same perp. And that he could have done quite a few we don't know about, but the fact that he leaves the *Free Press* with an anagram of Oswald on it doesn't really take us anywhere. Needless to say, there were no fingerprints or DNA. This guy is clever enough to not leave evidence.'

'Yet he obviously wants people to know it's him.'

'Well, he wants us to know that one person is killing all these people, but that doesn't mean he wants to get caught.'

'I thought all serial killers wanted to get caught?' she said.

'No, they want people to know how clever they are, that's not the same thing.'

'Anything in the headlines or stories? Were any stories highlighted?'

'Not highlighted, but the papers were folded to particular pages, it wasn't just the front page, and a couple had been kept for a while, so I think the stories are important to the killer, but I haven't found a link yet. I just got started on this thing, when...'

'Give me the stories and I'll see if I can come up with anything. It is my home turf.'

'You're too young to be a work nerd, don't you have anything better to do?'

'Maybe, but I want to get my own by-line. If I help you catch a serial killer, they'll have to take me seriously.'

America's Most Murderous Cities, www.forbes.com
Top on our list? Detroit. The Motor City experienced 418 cases of murder and non-negligent manslaughter in 2006. That's 47.3 murders per every 100,000 residents. Detroit also ranked high for violent crime (No. 2), robbery (No. 4) and forcible rape (No. 12).

Leroy sat at the kitchen table drinking coffee. The prospect of another day looking for jobs that never materialised didn't excite him. He wondered what Steve was up to. He hadn't seen him for a while. It was weird not seeing Steve every day anymore. He'd spent more time with Steve than with his own wife. He thought about Rhonda. They'd spoken once on the phone and that had been cut short by her mother calling her to go somewhere. His daughters had barely had time to chorus, 'we love you daddy' before being whisked away. Leroy pulled out his wallet and looked at the creased photo of his daughters from a year ago. How things changed.

He turned to the back of the paper to look at the job vacancies. The *Free Press* was always full of doom and gloom. He was tired of hearing about the crime wave in Detroit, the number of people abandoning the city. Apparently, Detroit was now America's most 'murderous' city. No wonder Rhonda had taken the first opportunity to get out, but why hadn't she taken him with her? Why hadn't her plan been for all of them to move to Washington and start a new life? Now he was left trying to pay all the house bills with no salary to pay them. It was only a matter of time, before his small GM payoff ran out and he wouldn't be able to pay them at all, but he didn't want to think about that. He'd already pretty much eaten his way through Rhonda's not insignificant store cupboard and he was down to cans that were borderline out of date and stale oatmeal. He couldn't eat oatmeal in the summer, it was too damn hot. He circled a couple of ads for handymen, but he couldn't summon up the energy to call. He probably should fix the back screen door, but there didn't seem much point with his family not around.

He started tearing off pages of the newspaper, screwing them up and throwing them into the sink. Half of them ended up on the floor. He could turn on the TV, but there was never anything on. He opened the fridge. There was only one can of beer left. What the hell, he thought, taking it out, it's nearly noon. He ripped back the tab and took a huge swallow.

As Leroy leaned against the counter drinking his beer, he saw the mail van go past. It reminded him he hadn't collected the mail for a couple of days. He went out to the box, maybe there would be something from his girls, maybe even a letter from Rhonda. As soon as he reached in, he could tell it was mostly junk mail. He flipped through it on the way back to the house – supermarket coupons, bills, catalogues, a letter from the bank. He dumped in all straight in the recycle box by the porch.

It had been Rhonda's idea to recycle even though the city didn't have a designated facility. They collected bottles and cans and paper and once a month or so he took it down to a recycle centre. They put the small change they got for the aluminium into a jar in the living room and every once in a while they had enough to take the girls out for pizza or ice cream. Leroy almost ran into the living room at the memory. He slid on the carpet into a kneel in front of the jar and pulled out its cork stopper, tipping it over to empty its contents. It was at least half full. The coins made a satisfying mound in front of him. Leroy had thought the idea was stupid when she'd come up with it – one more thing for him to do, but he had to agree it was nice to take the girls on little treats, all from sorting out the trash. The girls had loved the idea of saving the planet by doing this one small thing, and of course they loved the treats too. Now, it was really going to pay off.

He counted out the nickels and dimes. There was almost twenty-four dollars, enough to get some groceries. And he remembered there were two bags of cans in the garage he hadn't taken yet. If he went to the recycle place now, he could get some gas and a six-pack of beer too. Leroy felt the most uplifted he had in days. He almost ran into the kitchen, finished the rest of his beer – well, he couldn't afford to waste it, picked up his keys and headed out.

He loaded the cans in the back of the truck and headed out for the scrap metal company. The place took all kinds of scrap metal including cans. Leroy had always felt a bit weird about going to the place. He kind of felt like he was doing some homeless person out of his livelihood. Sometimes he saw some of them, the bums, waiting with their shopping carts of cans to get their cash. He never let the girls go with him, although they wanted to. He didn't want them to see that. And the heat was incredible in summer, the air heavy with the sour smell of beer dregs, wasps fighting over the last drop of sugar in the soda cans. It wasn't a nice place for kids. But on this hot summer day it was Leroy's meal ticket.

www.magicbullet.com
03.20.06

Internal affairs are looking into the mayor's party. That's the story in the cop house. And the murder of Jessica Rabbit has gone cold case. The police gossip always makes it to us sooner or later. They never had any idea. But it would be great if the mayor starts to feel a little heat where it hurts. Maybe someone can make some dirt stick to Mr Henricks this time. Wouldn't that be perfect? Apparently, the papers got an anonymous call and now everyone is starting to sing like proverbial canaries. You can't keep the truth down forever. Suddenly a couple of dancers are saying they saw Jessica get hit by the mayor's wife. Yes, she went to Receiving. Oh yes, she was beat up bad. See how they lie? They are all liars. The guy who said that must need glasses 'cause it wasn't Jessica that got beat up. I told you that before. Whatever! Keep it real and keep it here at magic bullet where you hear all the city's dirty laundry aired first.

Freep.com June 24, 2007 Chapter 8: The morgue

'They were quick deaths, investigators noted, almost instantaneous.'

I'm sitting in bed eating a Caesar salad, and chewing that rabbit food got me to thinking. Personally, I think it's kind of ironic the way hospitals are all into health food when they've got all these superbugs that can kill you. Anyways, I couldn't wait to get out of there. A man can only read so many books especially without the use of one arm. I decided to check myself out the next day having surprised myself by lasting nine days. I only had twenty-four more hours in the hospital, but I knew it would be a long haul in physio before they let me go back to work. But maybe the doc was right, did I really want to go back? I had enough years on the job to retire and get by financially. All this time in the hospital, I'd had plenty of time to think and I figured I could let the department pay my full sick leave, then punch out, why not? I wouldn't need to even go back from sick leave. I could miss the retirement party and just slip away quietly. I certainly didn't owe that slacker Mick anything. If Reuben had still been around that would be a different story, but he wasn't. The department wasn't interested in solving murders anymore; it was all about crowd control and containment. I could solve these murders on my own. And it even looked like I had my own rookie researcher lined up in Alison.

Alison came to see me the following evening. She seemed to be wearing the same outfit as the day before and she had another pizza in her bag. It was a meat-feast. I was really starting to warm to Alison.

'I brought you something,' she said handing me a slice.

'I love you.'

'Easy there, you're not my type.'

I was tempted to ask what her type was, but I hadn't known her long enough. 'In a collegiate kind of way. You're not my type either.'

She smiled a kind of lopsided grin and swept curls back off her forehead. 'So, how's it going?'

'I nearly died of boredom at about 3 p.m., they had to bring the crash cart in here.'

'Hmm.' She popped the top on a can of Coke.

'Where's mine?'

'You don't need the caffeine,' she said. 'I looked at those stories.'

'Get anything?'

'Not much. They were by different writers, so we can scratch a personal vendetta.'

'Never rule anything out.'

'What's that, the first rule of policing according to Officer Daniels?'

'Call me Danny. Just something I've picked up in my long career.'

'Whatever. OK put personal vendetta against a particular journalist near the bottom of the motive list.'

'Agreed.'

'We've got corruption. One story related to City Councilman Alonzo Bates, who by the way is now being tried for fraud and theft, then you've got the mayor. But Kemi Hendricks is so synonymous with corruption that may not help us much.'

'Yeah and then the latest story, if it ties in is from this series on drugs.'

'Tell me about the new one,' she said.

'We got called to a shooting. This guy, June-Bey Jordan had been gunned down in broad daylight, but there were no witnesses of course. I figured it was a regular drug-related murder, but there was this paper on top of the body. It was clean, like it had just been bought and was carefully folded to the section entitled "Chapter 8: The morgue". It seemed like the killer had placed it there specifically to make some point. You could go several ways with it, I suppose. Just the title, the morgue, makes a point you could say. Then there's the last line of the article: "many more people would die first" which I thought maybe was some kind of message that more people were going to get killed. Could be someone wanted to say something about the drug situation. I don't know, but I didn't have much else to go on and it was unusual, so that's why I looked into it.'

'And then you found these other two older murders that had copies of the *Free Press* at the scene?'

'Yes, and they were also carefully folded to particular sections, and they all had these names doodled on the page that are anagrams of Lee Harvey Oswald. That can't be coincidence. It has to be the same killer.'

'I agree. The stories must mean something to the killer, but I haven't found any real link,' she said.

'The one thing that crossed my mind was someone who thinks he's cleaning up Detroit. We've got corruption, the mayor, drugs, all major problems and the victims are hookers, dancers and drug dealers. I could see how someone might think he was doing a service, getting rid of that kind of person.'

'But how does that tie in with Oswald?' she asked.

'He was the Lone Gunman. There are loads of offshoots from the basic conspiracy theory. Maybe he thinks he's got the magic bullet that can save us?'

'The magic bullet?'

'Yeah, you know…'

'Yeah, I know what it was, but I've heard that somewhere. I'm sure I've seen something called the magic bullet, a website or something.' She pulled her laptop from her bag and started to open it, looking around for a phone jack.

'There's no internet connection here.'

'Damn.' She slammed the lid shut and shoved the laptop back in her bag. 'I'll go and check this out. I'll catch you later.'

Before I could say anything else, she was gone. Quite a character that Alison. I started reading some of the *Secret Life of Lee Harvey Oswald*, but I dropped off.

> Detroit sits on the verge of bankruptcy, beset by political scandal, a declining population, troubled industry, high crime and unemployment rates and one of the worst school systems in the country. *The Washington Times*

Steve finally got around to calling Leroy to tell him about his house. He'd wanted to call before, but he'd been so busy finalising the purchase and starting to work on the place, plus part of him was reluctant to call Leroy when he knew things were going so badly for him. But they'd been friends for a long time, you don't keep things from friends and you don't ignore them when times are hard, so Steve picked up the phone.

'Leroy?'

'Yeah, who else would it be? Man, I thought you must have moved to Canada or something. You ignoring me too, just like Rhonda?'

'No man. I'm sorry, I should have called before, but I've been real busy. I bought that house I was telling you about. You know the one for eighty bucks?'

'Damn. You really bought it?'

'Yeah. I wondered if you wanted to come over and see it?'

'Sure.' I ain't got nothing better to do, thought Leroy, but didn't say.

'Great. I'll pick you up in about an hour.'

Leroy was already sitting out on his front step waiting when Steve pulled up. He got into the car.

'So, you finally joined the property owners, huh?'

'Yep, but unlike most of them I don't have a mortgage. Of course, it needs a little work.'

'You don't say? For eighty bucks what did you expect, a mansion?' Leroy chuckled. 'It got four walls and a roof?'

'It sure does, and a porch and a vacant lot next door.'

'I can't wait to see this palace!'

As they drove towards the east they fell silent. Steve couldn't help but notice how much of the neighbourhoods they drove through were abandoned. So many boarded up houses and businesses, open areas where houses had been demolished, the quiet of what was once a bustling metropolis. It reminded him of some Wild West frontier and he was on his way to build his homestead. He refrained from sharing the thought with Leroy for fear of cowboy and Indian jokes.

They pulled up outside Steve's new home and got out.

'Well, it's nice and quiet,' said Leroy. 'I hope you'll be able to sleep out here in the country!'

Steve led the way up to the front door which was now secured with new locks. He led them into the living room. 'I figured I could re-finish the wood floors here.'

'Yeah, that'll look good.'

They kept walking towards the back. 'And this is the kitchen.'

'It is? You could have fooled me. Someone had a real culinary crisis back there,' said Leroy pointing to the blackened wall.

'I know, but it's only superficial. I had a surveyor check it out and he said the wall is fine, it just needs re-plastering.'

'Uh huh.'

'You any good at plastering?'

'No, I make cars. At least I did.'

'Still no jobs?'

'No.'

'Well, I sure could use some help fixing this place up. I could pay you in food and beer.'

'I don't know... I'm not sure I want to be labouring for some white man,' said Leroy.

'Oh, I just thought...'

'I'm kidding you man. I don't have anything better to do. Maybe I can put house remodelling on my resume!'

'Oh, that's great. It's going to be so cool. Let me show you upstairs.'

www.magicbullet.com
04.02.06

Thirty minutes it took me to get to a job yesterday and it's not as if there's that much traffic in this ghost town. It's the mismanagement, cuts, lay-offs. How's a man supposed to do his job? It was too late, of course. And we'll take the flack for it.

I've had enough. And now that so called whistleblower trial has started. I've been blowing the whistle for years – nobody listens. How much is that going to cost us? Millions I expect. And I can't even get decent equipment!

Forum

- It's obscene. It won't be the mayor that pays, it'll be the taxpayer. We need a revolution or something. I'm with those tea party folks Ringo

- Yeah, I like a cup of tea too F

- What we need is some white people running this city Ringo

Freep.com June 24, 2007 Chapter 1: The teenager
In the basement, anything goes. That's where everybody buys their dope. They can shoot it, snort it or smoke it down there. They can turn tricks to earn money for more drugs. It's all good.

'Bingo!' Alison burst into my hospital room like the Energiser bunny.

'Nice to see you too Alison. Yeah, I'm doing fine.'

She flopped into the chair. 'Sorry. How are you, Danny?'

'Just dandy! I've finished the tunnel. I should be getting out of here later today.'

'Really? That's great.'

'The doc has to come round and see me first, but yeah, I should be out of here this afternoon. What are you all excited about?'

'I found it, magic bullet dot com. I knew I'd heard of it. I must have stumbled across it dweebing something else sometime. It doesn't get many hits. I had one of the guys at work look into it and it's only had about 150 views since it started, but it has a solid following of a few fans. About four people regularly leave comments on its forum.'

'Hang on, not so fast. There's a website called magic bullet?'

'Yes, well, it's more of a blog really, not a fully-fledged website.'

'And what's it about? Conspiracy theory stuff?' I asked.

'It's a mix. The first entry was November 22 2003.'

'JFK anniversary day.'

'Yes. The first entry alludes to the 40th anniversary and invites people who know the significance of the day to send in their theories on how, quote the American people are still getting screwed unquote. Then he has some stuff about the war in Iraq and how it wasn't legal. There isn't much in 2004, just the occasional entry on various conspiracy theory type things and some local corruption stories and it doesn't seem like anyone much was looking at the site then.'

'And then something changed?'

'Yeah, things start getting more interesting in January 2005. It mentions the party at the mayor's mansion,' she said.

'So, that's been all over the media and blogs and all sorts.'

'Not in January 2005 it wasn't. The entry is for 15 January. That's just a day or two after the party is alleged to have taken place. Whoever put that on there must have been at the party.'

'Oh, good point.'

'Oh indeed. And one of the regular commentators on the forum, who sounds like he's the author of the blog, signs himself the Lone Gunman.'

'You think it's our killer?'

'It could be our man,' she said.

'Or woman.' Alison gave me a bemused look.

'OK, it's not likely, but we shouldn't jump to conclusions, it could be a woman.' I said.

'Right, never rule out anything.'

'Never rule anything out.'

'So, you're impressed, right?'

'I am impressed. I may take you out for a burger and beer to celebrate my release.'

'Wow, you know how to charm the ladies!'

'I certainly do. Now, as impressive as this is, what does it really tell us and how does it help us track down this person?'

'Well. First, we don't know if it is the killer who's writing this blog, or if he is just a follower, or if it's some totally unrelated nut-job. This could all be pure coincidence and speculation and the "lone gunman" on the blog might not have anything to do with the murders. Like you said before plenty of people believe conspiracy theories, especially those related to the Kennedy assassination and there's probably plenty of nerds out there who might use the handle "lone gunman" for their internet surfing.'

'That's possible. But it's certainly worth investigating.'

'Yeah, but we don't have an IP address,' said Alison.

'An IP address?'

'Yeah, you know, each computer connected to the Internet has an IP address. Once we find out the IP address we should be able to get a location for where the computer is. But my guess is this guy would be too smart to do his blog from home, he probably goes to an internet café or several. Even if this is innocent and the blogger isn't the killer, he might use internet cafes.'

'But the police could find this IP address?'

'Oh sure. Don't you know this stuff? You really are old school!'

'We have a special team works with the technical stuff, you know internet porn, fraud, that kind of thing, us old guys just work all the drug killings with good old fashioned police work!'

'Right. Well in theory, your police techs could find the location, or more likely locations where the blog entries were made. Then the uniforms could go to all the internet cafes and make inquiries, like whether a weird looking 40ish, white guy who's into conspiracy theories comes in regularly to use their computers.'

'I sense somehow you're making fun of me.'

'Only a little bit. That is pretty much what you'd do, assuming this guy isn't a total dumbass and does all his blogging in one place. Seems to me he'd still be pretty hard to find.'

'How do you know he's a white guy in his 30s or 40s?'

'Isn't that the standard profile for serial killers? And then you'll find that he "keeps himself to himself" and hates women for some reason,' she said.

I laughed. 'You've been watching too much TV, but yeah, your standard profile is reasonably correct. But this guy hasn't killed only women, in fact based on the newspapers at the scene, which so far is the only link we've got, the victims are two men and one woman.'

'But don't you think he's done more?' asked Alison.

'My gut feeling is he probably has done more, and he's gonna keep doing it. What I don't get is why he's being so subtle. It seems like he wants people to know what he's doing, but no one has picked up the newspaper link, and the doodles of Oswald anagrams, probably most people would think they were just doodles. You'd have to have quite a few before you join up the dots and work out the link.'

'But you worked it out.'

'Yeah, but I also got lucky, and I'm a very inquisitive kind of guy. I'm sorry to disillusion you, but most cops in the city, they get a dead junkie or a dead prostitute, they're not going to go out of their way to try and catch the perp, and if they make an arrest at all, pretty much anyone will do.'

'Maybe that's what he's counting on. He doesn't want to get caught. He wants to go about his business, cleaning up the city or whatever, but he likes to leave his signature. Maybe he's waiting for a really smart cop to come along, to be a proper adversary. Like that film with Samuel L. Jackson.'

'What film?'

'You know the one by the guy who did, "I see dead people", Jackson plays this evil guy who collects comics, and Bruce Willis plays the good guy who thinks he's invincible.'

'So, our guy collects comics now too?' I said.

'No! Oh it's, *Unbreakable*, that's it.'

'I don't think I've seen that. I like *Casablanca* and that kind of movie.' Alison rolled her eyes. 'Actually, I prefer reading.'

'Well, whatever, maybe he's waiting for a really smart cop.'

'If that's supposed to be flattery, I'm not sure it's working.'

'So,' said Alison with a sigh, 'getting back to the magic bullet blog, it seems like it's just random thoughts, almost like he's using it as a diary or a place to vent about things that piss him off. I reckon he thinks not many people are looking at this thing except a few like-minded conspiracy theorists, but he probably likes the thought that anyone could read it and agree with him. We've already found out that he was at the party at the mayor's mansion, that means he had to either be a guest, a cop, or one of the EMS guys.'

The mention of EMS rang some kind of bell, but I couldn't grab hold of it right then. 'Have you read every entry?' I asked her.

'No, not yet, but I think we should, we might pick up something useful.'

Alison seemed very hopeful about this whole thing. I confess, I didn't entirely understand all the ins and outs of setting up websites or blogs, so I wasn't sure whether the technology would lead us to the killer or not, but I liked her enthusiasm and it certainly seemed like she was onto something. I needed to read all the entries myself. Alison was right; if this *was* the killer he may have inadvertently mentioned something helpful in his rants. He was smart, but it also seemed to me like he wanted people to know what he was doing – the newspapers at the scene, a blog – that meant he was catchable. Sooner or later, he'd let slip that little bit of information that would lead us to him, they always did sooner or later, even the clever ones.

Alison was still there when the doctor came round. 'Can you give us a minute, Alison? Don't go away.'

'Your daughter?' asked the doctor.

'No. A friend.' The doctor looked disapproving.

'So, Mr Daniels, I hear you want to go home.'

'That's right.'

'I'd really recommend staying a couple more days.'

'For the sake of my sanity, I think I'll ignore your recommendation.'

'Do you have anyone at home to help you with things?'

'No, but I'll manage.'

'You're not going to be able to use that arm properly for quite some time.'

'I'll manage.'

'OK, if you insist. Here's your referral for the physio. No work for at least three months. Sign here.'

I signed. I slowly put on my pants. I kept on the T-shirt I was already wearing. Then I went outside to the corridor. Alison was still there, nodding to music from her headphones. She pulled one headphone free and moved towards me.

'If you can just put all my stuff in a bag for me, we can get out of here,' I said.

'Like I have nothing else to do,' she muttered.

'Do you?'

She dropped her head slightly to one side and gave me this weird look. 'I guess not. Where are we going?'

'Do you have wheels?'

'Yep.'

'So anywhere that does junk food and beer.'

We ended up at Lafayette Coney Island. I wouldn't really describe that as junk, that's quality, but it sure hit the spot. That's where I discovered Alison likes to eat as much as I do, maybe more. We had hot dogs with everything and chilli cheese fries, then damn me if Alison didn't order a second dog! At least I had the excuse of having been on hospital rations.

'Did you skip breakfast, or something?' I asked.

'No,' she mumbled with her mouth full. 'It's 3.30 p.m.. That's way past lunch time.'

She had a fair point. 'You don't worry about putting on weight?'

'Do I look like I do?'

'No. It's just most women, you know…'

'I'm not most women. I thought you'd have figured that out by now.'

'Yeah, I guess. So, what do you do for fun?'

'Eat,' she said, wiping chilli off her chin. We both laughed. 'Seriously, I could tell you it's none of your business.'

'You could and I suppose you'd be right, but humour me, I don't get out much. And if we're going to be working together on this serial murder thing, I need to know you're not some kind of psycho, or that you support the White Sox or something.'

'What do you take me for?! Though to be honest I'm more of a hockey fan.'

'Who isn't?'

'So, we're really going to catch this guy, together?' Her eyes lit up.

'Yeah, we're going to try.' I looked down at my arm. 'I'm a bit incapacitated right now so I may need some help. And I'm not going to be back at work for months. In fact, I'm not sure I'm going to stay with the police at all. I may as well call it a day.'

'Really?'

'Yeah, I've got enough years. I can retire with a decent pension.'

'But won't it be harder if you don't have all the benefits of being a police officer?'

'My captain isn't interested in this case anyway. That's how come I ended up shot. I don't think it will make much difference. I still look like a cop and think like a cop and I can call in some favours if I need anything.'

'Cool,' she said.

'How come you're so keen to catch a killer anyway? It's not like in the movies. It's mostly boring drudge work.'

'I told you. I'm new at the *Free Press*. I want to do something massive. Get a big story to impress the guys and get my own by-line.'

'So did you go to journalism school or something?'

'Not exactly. I got a job on the student paper. I loved it.'

'So how come you didn't do journalism?'

'The University of Michigan doesn't offer journalism. Anyway, I didn't want to study it, I wanted to do it!'

'What was your major?'

'Psychology,' she said it in an understated way, like it was media studies or general liberal arts.

'Wow. So you wanted to be a head skrinker?'

She laughed. 'No, my brother's a kleptomaniac. I wanted to cure him.'

'You're kidding me, right.'

'No, seriously. He was always stealing from my mom and I'd get the blame.'

'But, there had to be a quicker way to prove he was the thief than four years in college?'

'You're right,' she took a swallow of beer, 'I'm kidding you. I had my reasons, but now I've thrown my good intentions to the wind and become a journalist.'

'There are some good journalists.'

'It's not often you hear a cop say that. Yeah, but they don't do well.'

'Bill's a good guy,' I said.

'I thought he was, until he hooked me up with you.' She smiled. She looked lovely when she smiled. It had been a very long time since I'd had a female friend. I hoped we were going to be friends. And I'm talking platonic here people. Alison didn't do it for me in a romantic way and technically she was young enough to be my daughter.

'So, enough about me,' she said. 'What about you, Mr police?' She pronounced it pohleece, like in *The Wire*.

'What about me?'

'Are you married?'

'No?'

'Girlfriend?'

'At my age?'

'What is your age, just out of interest?'

'Fifty-two.'

'Not SO old then?' She finally pushed away her plate. 'Boyfriend?'

'Do I look gay to you?'

'Who knows these days? Do I?'

'But in Detroit, in the police?' I said.

'You'd be surprised.'

'I certainly would! Anyway, no significant others, as you young people like to say. No pets either.'

'How about hobbies?'

'Not much. I'm kind of a workaholic.'

'What do you do to relax, read case files?!'

'Sometimes. I like to read, watch old movies. Smoke in the dark.'

'Ooh, now a psychology major could probably make something of that.'

'What the old movies, or the smoking?'

'The smoking in the dark, are you scared someone might see you?'

'No. I'm trying to cut down and I like looking out at the city lights.'

'Hmm, so you like the dark and you have a power complex, you like to survey your kingdom.'

I almost choked on my beer. 'No, it just looks nice.'

'I suspect you have a deep hurt that you use your work to hide and you'd probably benefit from years of analysis.'

'Yeah, right.' I didn't tell her maybe she was right. Ever since my wife died three years into the marriage, nothing much seemed to matter except the job and before you knew it, I'd lost years and all I had was the job. Don't get me wrong. I'm not unhappy. I miss Eleanor, but I don't think about her every day. I like my work. I like watching old movies and smoking in the dark. 'Anyways, I think my meds are wearing off. You wanna drop me back home?'

'Sure.'

'You got nothing better to do? No significant other to meet up with?'

'Touché, Officer Daniels. Not currently, but I'm working on it.'

Downtown Detroit, touted as one of the safest areas in an otherwise crime-plagued city, has seen a sharp increase in crime so far this year... Car thefts are up 83%; robberies, 50%; burglaries, 20%, and property destruction, 42% *Free Press*

Leroy woke with the mother of all hangovers. There was an awful ringing in his ears. His focus was blurred, his mouth dry and this noise wouldn't stop. Eventually he realised it was the phone. His hand flailed to the nightstand and he got a grip on the receiver.

'Uh ah,' he mumbled. He couldn't make his mouth work right either.

'Ho, keeping dealer's hours already.'

'Wha... Who is this?'

'It's your favourite nephew, unc.' Oh God, not Wendell, thought Leroy, that's all I need right now. He squinted at the red digits of the clock. 11.41. 'So you had a late one, huh?'

'Yeah, listen, what do you need Wendell?'

'I need an answer man.' An answer, an answer about what?

'What?'

'You know, that thing we talked about.'

Leroy trawled his memory for what Wendell might be talking about. Then he remembered the day down by the water, Wendell's job offer. The ridiculous offer he'd thought no more about. He may be on the slope to rock bottom, but there was no way Leroy could get into selling drugs, or even driving drugs around. 'Right. The answer's no.'

'Well a little gratitude would be appreciated. I'm just trying to help you out.'

Leroy leaned up on one elbow. That was a mistake. The room spun. He swallowed a bit of vomit that swung up hot into his mouth. 'I know you are, and I appreciate the sentiment. I just can't do it. That's not who I am.'

'Yeah, I know it,' said Wendell, resigned. 'But you're making a mistake. It's a onetime offer. I won't ask you again. I got people waiting.'

'OK. I know. I appreciate it really, but I can't. Say hey to your dad from me.'

Leroy dropped the receiver back into place and lay back slowly on the pillow. He couldn't remember the last time he'd slept so late. How much had he drunk? He tried to remember that, but he couldn't. He scooted the pillows back against the wall so he could half sit up, then stayed immobile until everything settled. Something must have set off a binge. OK, so since Rhonda and the girls had left, he'd been putting away a few more beers, and started with them earlier in the day, but Leroy could handle his liquor, he must have drunk a hell of a lot to feel this bad.

When he opened his eyes again it was 1 p.m. exactly and the combined pain of needing to relieve himself and an unbelievable thirst drove him out of the bedroom and into the bathroom where he satisfied both needs, drinking straight from the faucet. He then stood under a tepid shower for a good fifteen minutes. Looking around for a towel he realised what a mess the place was and resolved to tidy up as soon as he'd had some coffee and food.

Downstairs, dressed only in boxers, he filled the washing machine from the overflowing laundry basket, turned it on and went back into the kitchen to see the last few drips of coffee percolate through. He filled a mug, added two sugars and sipped. The contents of the refrigerator did not have the pleasing effect on the eye that they'd had when Rhonda was in charge. He found some bread that looked passable and stuck two slices in the toaster. Then he sniffed his way through the remaining contents and threw most of it in the trash. At least the peanut butter wasn't off.

It was when he was sitting at the kitchen table eating toast that he saw the letter from the bank and it all came back to him. Yesterday had been going pretty well until that point. He'd worked three hours in the morning clearing someone's yard after getting picked up on a corner with some Mexican guys. Then he'd made nine dollars from recycled cans, bought some beer and chips and headed home. Since he was feeling good, he'd opened the mail instead of shoving it in the kitchen drawer as he had been for the last two weeks. The letter from the bank explained in legal detail the process now under way to foreclose on his house. There must have been previous letters. This one said he had only four weeks to sort something out or the 'notice of sale' would go up.

Leroy dropped the letter back on the table after re-reading it. A glance around showed what a mess he'd made looking for previous letters from the bank. He'd found one, but he never found the original letter that must have kicked the whole thing off; the original letter that might have offered him a way out of this mess, a way to pay off the loan in smaller chunks, or sell the house himself, or something. Rhonda had always dealt with the bank. Why had he assumed that the payments were still getting made directly when his salary was no longer going into their joint account? It must be completely overdrawn by now, why hadn't they informed him of that? Come to that why did they have a *joint* account? Rhonda never paid anything into it.

He slammed his fist down on the counter. What an idiot! How had he let things get so bad? Why hadn't he got some help? Got another loan? Because Rhonda had left, that's why. He did the work, he brought home the money and he left everything else to Rhonda, what a stupid… He couldn't go to her now. He couldn't call and tell her their home would be sold if they didn't make the payments. She must have worked out that the mortgage wasn't getting paid. Rhonda wasn't stupid like him. But had she called? Had she asked her parents to lend her money, which he knew for sure they could do? No. She'd left him high and dry blowing in the wind with the rest of the fuckers in Detroit. She was sitting pretty in Washington with her rich parents and his beautiful daughters, while he had to crawl around in the dust trying to scrape a living recycling trash and clearing yards. That is what had set him off on a rampage. That was what had led him to drink the contents of every single bottle left in their drink's cupboard. Not the letter from the bank. The bank was just doing its job. He was the one who hadn't read their letters. But his wife, his so-called wife wasn't doing her job, and because of his own ignorance he'd let all this shit mount up. He didn't know which he hated more, his stupidity or her abandonment. But it sure as hell wasn't going to carry on a minute longer. He would rise up and kick this thing somehow, with or without Rhonda.

With his new determination, Leroy started with the simple things – he cleaned house. He did laundry, he tidied up and wiped and used cleaning products he'd never previously had to think about. His anger dissipated a bit and he felt some kind of empathy with the work Rhonda had done to keep the house clean and make good, tasty meals with not too much housekeeping money. But he was still mad at her. Why hadn't she been in touch? Didn't she want to know if he'd got a new job or not? And if he hadn't, she must know things would be bad for him. Did she care so little about their home of twenty years that she didn't mind if the bank repossessed it or it got sold? He had to assume she didn't. The more he thought about Rhonda the more he convinced himself that she'd planned her leaving for some time and that she wasn't coming back. Him losing his job had been just the excuse she needed. He could maybe, maybe, get his head around a life without Rhonda, but what about his daughters? How was he expected to see them when she'd taken them over five hundred miles away?

Late in the afternoon, Leroy sat again at the kitchen table. He was tempted to crack open a beer, but he resisted. He drank more coffee to ease his still lingering headache and called Steve.

'Yo, how's it hanging?' Steve sounded more than usually cheerful.
'Not so good as it happens.'
'What's up?'
'It's a long one.'
'Hold that thought, I'll be right over.'
'Any chance you could bring a pizza in your best friend toolkit?'
'Sure.'

www.magicbullet.com
04.15.06

So finally, there is speculation about the mayor's involvement in the Jessica Rabbit murder. I can't reveal my sources, but scan the internet and you'll find plenty of people asking the question, did Hendricks kill Brown?

It's not for me to say... Oh what the hell, you know I'm a man who doesn't hide my opinions. I think he's guilty as charged. It makes total sense. I told you first that the party was for real and not a myth. Hendricks is up to his eyes in dirt.

And don't think Miss Brown was all innocence either. 'Erotic dancer', we all know what that means. And her drug dealing boyfriend? They're a prime example of all that's wrong with the big D. Them and the mayor make a pretty little triangle – it ain't sex, drugs, and rockin' roll any more, around here it's drugs, prostitution and corruption. Maybe I should stop paying my taxes.

Freep.com June 24, 2007 Chapter 9: The trail
Death moved east.

So, I'm sitting in my Lay-Z-Boy, watching the sky turn that cobalt blue it turns before it goes completely black, thinking about Alison. She certainly is feisty, young, but you can tell she's got balls. My shoulder is really starting to ache, but I don't want to take my pills until I go to bed. And I'm real tired. I never felt that way before. I'd do night shifts, day shifts, days followed by four to midnight. I'd just drink coffee or soda, smoke a few cigarettes and keep going. It's what most cops do, I guess, even if you're not that interested in the work you want the overtime, 'cause the regular pay won't feed too many kids. I guess you could say I was lucky not having children, or they were. I've seen plenty of cops with families whose children can barely remember what their fathers look like. And what did I have to go home to? Nothing. So, I didn't. The station became my home. I didn't want to go out boozing like a lot of the guys do, driving home drunk and thinking they won't get pulled over 'cause they're police. I couldn't do that, not after what happened to Eleanor. A couple of beers at home maybe, and that would be it. So, what did I have apart from the work?

But now? Now, I'm tired of it all. The paperwork, the office politics, the way no one cares any more. It's mostly picking up young hoods for drug shootings, any beat cop could do it, you don't need to pass the detective's exam or be any psychological genius. Still, twenty-five years and this is the first time I've been shot, it's not bad going. I've been lucky. Not many of the guys I started out with are still on the force. There's easy pickings working as security consultants or at least taking a desk post rather than working homicide. Shit, the way I live, I could make do on just the pension; I wouldn't have to do anything. But surely, I'd go nuts, wouldn't I, without anything to do? I could go private, but the days of that being fun are probably over. I could work my own cases, the few who got away, just for the peace of mind? I sure want to find out who did Shanta Brown. And for right now, I need to catch this newspaper guy. Might as well do it while I'm off sick, 'cause the captain isn't going to like it. I bet he's closed that June-Bey Jordan file already. What are you talking about Daniels? You already decided to quit, you dumbass. Just wait until the sick leave is nearly up to send in your papers. And why waste your time trying to close this case?

Did I make any difference in all these years? I don't know. I guess I took a lot of bad guys off the street, but there's always more to take their place. There haven't been all that many interesting cases though, most murderers are just plain stupid, or high. They shoot someone over a $10 wrap of heroin, or they shove their wife and she falls down the stairs. It isn't like *Silence of the Lambs*, and it certainly hasn't been very Philip Marlowe, but I never expected it to be. Sure, I went into the force with the usual naivety, thinking I'd make a difference, but mine became specific – all I wanted to do was get drunk drivers off the streets, make them pay, stop some other poor sucker experiencing what I'd suffered.

I didn't expect to end up a homicide cop. It's had its moments, but even the real whodunits weren't that exciting. It all boils down to drugs and money in the end. But this guy, the newspaper killer, that's more like it. That has a little more intrigue. OK, so the victims so far have pretty much been down and outs, and in the drugs game some way or another, but the neatly folded newspaper and the anagrams, that's an interesing angle.

I really should look at those printouts Alison gave me from the lone gunman blog thing. Ah what the hell, I'll read them tomorrow. What's the hurry, I'm in no state to go running around after nebulous men of the night. Nebulous – that's pretty good for this late in the evening, maybe I'll take up crosswords in my retirement. I reach for my pack of cigarettes. It's dark now. I'll look out at the lights, blow smoke into the black night. I can make believe it's 1940's LA if I want.

I feel like I've been run over by a truck. I open one eye to see what's pinning me down. It's just my own weight gluing me to the Lay-Z-Boy. I run my tongue over dry lips and try to push myself up. It's then I notice the bandage and sling and remember the gunshot wound. I can't remember the last time I fell asleep in the chair. I may not sleep for long some nights, but I usually have enough going for me to drag my ass to bed. Those pain pills must be good stuff, but they sure have worn off now. I wonder how the hell I'm going to take a shower, but first things first – coffee. Caffeine and pain killers, sounds like an excellent combo. I push myself up with my one good arm, not as easy as you might think and knock the ashtray off the side table. That thing was full of butts too, well it's gonna have to stay there. I should get angry I guess, but I'm just not that kind of guy.

I was angry once, but it didn't do me any good, so I tried to channel it into other stuff. Alison would probably say that just made things worse, but what does she know with four years of college psychology? But, she's a good kid. That reminded me of the papers she'd given me. The bag was still in the hallway by the front door where I'd dropped it. I set the coffee machine going, not as hard as you'd think with one good arm and collected the bag. I dumped it out in the bedroom and left my dirty underwear and toilet bag on the bed and took the books and stuff to the office. Now, I want you to know I'm not usually a slob. I've lived on my own for over twenty years, and some guys who might give them licence to never clear up, but not me. I know how to clean and I don't like looking at a mess. I even cook every once in a while. But with this arm, well I've got to save my energy for the important stuff. Sure, there's some areas of the place that could do with 'updating' as the realtors say, but I've only got to please myself and I like it this way.

Back in the kitchen, I dropped a slice in the toaster and popped a couple of those magic pills then I took my mug of coffee to the office. I decided to tackle the shower later.

I'll spare you the domestic details. I got sidetracked paying bills and looking through the mail I'd gotten while I'd been in the hospital. Then I caught sight of the photo of Eleanor I keep on the top shelf and I got to reminiscing and then the pain pills kicked in and I got dozy and yada yada before you know the day's gone and I never looked at that magic bullet stuff. I know I should feel some urgency, 'cause this guy he's going to do it again, but don't try and lay a guilt trip on me, I ain't Catholic and it won't work. A one armed, about to retire detective and an over eager journalist are not the world's greatest crime fighting team. These things take time. You wouldn't believe how much time this shit takes, I sure as hell didn't.

'This is getting to be just a big wasteland,' said Earl, 41, who makes a modest living as a handyman. 'It's really turning back to that old saying we had in the '80s: Will the last person in Detroit turn out the lights?' *Free Press*

'Here comes the cavalry,' shouted Steve from the front steps.

'Come on in. I hope it ain't white men on horses with guns, I don't need any more shit going on.'

'Wow, this place smells great. I thought you'd be more of a slobby bachelor without Rhonda.'

'Thanks for your confidence in me.' Leroy smiled, 'actually I have been, I just spent the afternoon cleaning and doing laundry.'

Steve dropped a pizza box and six-pack on the kitchen table and opened a beer.

The smell of pepperoni suddenly made Leroy hungry. He flipped open the lid and took a bite that enveloped half a slice. 'Oh man, that's good.'

'You not been eating?' asked Steve.

'Yeah, but not like this. Mostly toast and crackers.'

'What's up other than your appalling diet?'

Leroy nodded towards the letter on the countertop. 'Go ahead, read it.'

'What?' exclaimed Steve. 'You've got less than a month? How the hell did that happen?'

Leroy looked shamefaced. 'I never read their previous letters.'

'Did you call the bank?'

'No, but what am I going to say? I can't make the payments Steve.'

'They must be able to sort something out. Your mortgage must be nearly paid off. How long you lived here?'

'About twenty years.'

'So, you can't owe much. Where are the house papers? Your bank statements?'

'Rhonda takes care of all that.'

Steve gave him a look, but didn't say it. 'Well, you must know where she keeps the stuff. Does she have a particular place she sits to do the bills?'

'I think she does them in the spare room. There's a sort of computer desk in there, maybe in the drawer.' Leroy got up and ran upstairs. He came back with a few folders. 'Thank God she's organised. Everything is labelled.'

'Let's take a look.' Steve flicked through some paperwork and soon found the annual mortgage statement. 'Shit you only owe five grand. You're not going to lose your house over a measly five thousand dollars. Surely you can come up with that?'

'From where? I don't have any savings. All my money went on house bills and stuff for the kids. I already used up the tiny payoff we got, just living.'

'What about Rhonda?'

'Yeah, she could probably get it from her folks, but...'

'But what?'

'I didn't tell her yet.'

'How can you have not...'

Leroy held his hand up. 'I only just read this letter yesterday. I never saw the others. Anyways, I haven't spoken to Rhonda.'

'You haven't spoken at all, but she's been gone weeks now,' said Steve.

'Tell me about it. I keep trying to call. She's never there, or her parents give me the run around, or they're just on their way out and only have time to say hi. She never calls me back. No letters, nothing from the girls.'

Steve opened another beer. 'I'm sorry man. I thought you two were really solid.' He didn't mention that he'd never really liked Rhonda that much. She was the mother of Leroy's children after all.

'Me too. Well, things haven't been so hot for a year or two I guess, but nothing serious. That's just twenty years of marriage, right?'

'Like I'd know!' Steve laughed.

'Yeah, the lucky bachelor boy.'

'It's not all it's cracked up to be, but I guess there are advantages. Anyways, you're going to have to tell her.' Leroy shrugged. 'You're probably gonna have to sell the house. If you can't make the payments, it's better you sell it before the bank does.'

'Can I do that?'

'Sure. You can do a pre-foreclosure sale. You won't get the list price for it, but you owe so little, you should be able to re-pay the bank their five and clear some money for yourself. And you won't have the bad credit-rating or foreclosure stigma.'

'How come you know so much about it?'

'I read a lot of magazine articles. Yours is not the only house getting foreclosed on, in case you hadn't noticed. Plus I used to date a realtor.' Leroy rolled his eyes. He picked up the last piece of pizza. It was almost cold, but he folded it anyway and put it in his mouth. 'Hey, I could give Janine a call,' said Steve, 'see if she can help you out with this.'

'That'd be great.'

'OK. But you need to call the bank, tell them what you plan so they can put the brakes on this thing. Remind them how you always paid on time, you barely owe anything, you just got laid-off. Give them the whole sob story. Don't be too proud man. I can't believe they're even doing this for such a small chunk of money. Banks are just obscene. And you gotta call Rhonda. You can't sell the house from under her. Well you could, but not if you want to see the kids again.'

'It ain't exactly from under her, she's not here, is she? And it's not like she made any mortgage payments.'

'I know, but save that shit for the divorce if it comes to that. For now worry about the house. You tell her, then it's not your problem. If she don't want to hear it...'

'And where am I 'sposed to live after I sell my family home?'

'It's a buyers' market. Buy another. You got two hundred to five hundred dollars spare, you can get plenty of houses in Detroit.'

Leroy swung back on his chair and thought about it. 'So if there's so many cheap houses going, who's going to want mine for five grand plus?'

'Some people still have money. They want a nice house, decorated and fixed up nice like this one and they're still making a killing 'cause this house is probably worth thirty-five to forty and they'll probably get it for fifteen. Then in a few years, when the housing market goes back up, they make a big profit.'

'You think it will ever go back up?'

'Eventually, it always has. People always want houses, right? Look at all those new places in downtown and Palmer Woods. They'll always be rich folks Leroy, always.'

www.magicbullet.com
06.06.06

What a perfect date. I had to write something just to see 060606 at the top. A funny newspaper story too – *Detroit News*, June 6, 2006 'Silent killer returns' One Travis Conner was found dead face down in his breakfast cereal apparently. That's how quick fentanyl is taking them. I thought we'd seen the end of that, but they just keep coming back for more. It would be funny if it wasn't tragic. That stuff is so deadly it's almost as bad as a bullet. I'd rather take a bullet myself. Nice and clean. Perfect. Magic even.

Forum

- Don't get so morbid man. It's such a perfect date and it's a beautiful day outside. I even just shot me a rabbit – that's dinner taken care of! JFB

- Don't worry. I'm not ready to check out yet. I'm just saying when I do go... Lone Gunman

- Cheerful stuff fellas! F

- Trust me, you don't want it long and drawn out. You want a quick death. LG

Freep.com Chapter 10: The dead
Fentanyl is taking out heroin addicts all over metro Detroit.
July, 2007

I pick up the phone on the fourth ring. 'Hello.'

'How's it going officer Daniels, remember me?'

'I don't know, are you that sassy young thing from the *Free Press*?'

'Yep.' Alison laughs.

'I've been better, but all things considered not too bad.'

'Have you looked at the magic bullet stuff yet?'

'I'm looking at it right now,' I lied.

'What? It's been nearly a week!'

'Yeah, well it takes longer to do stuff with just the one arm working.'

'That doesn't affect your reading ability, does it?'

'Thanks for the sympathy.'

'Sorry. It's just I've been going over it some more and I'm keen to swap notes. Do you need anything? I could bring you some groceries or something? Pizza and a beer?'

I looked around the living room. I'd let things slide the last few days. Well, you try managing with just the one arm, I bet you'd let the tidiness slip a little too. The thought of the pleasure of Alison's company vied with the fairly monumental task of making the place presentable and changing out of my sweatpants. 'Yeah, OK, but give me a while, I need to clean up.'

'No need to tidy up on my account.'

'No, but there is on mine. Plus, I want to finish reading through this stuff.' I gave her a short shopping list and a cheeseburger request and hung up. She was going to come by around six, so I had the afternoon to sort things out.

I set the faucet running while I scooted around picking up clothes and shoved them in the laundry basket. Just yesterday, I'd finally got around to picking up the ashtray I knocked over, but the kitchen was a disaster. I opened up the dishwasher and started to load it. It smelt pretty bad. I hardly ever use the thing. I set that to wash and went back to the tub. I'd found that taking a bath was actually easier than the shower. I could rest my bad arm on a chair next to the tub and it didn't get wet. I figured it would be pointless to try and read in there so I had a quick soak and tried to get my brain in gear. I dried myself as best I could and went into the office naked to air dry the rest of me. I apologise for that mental image, but that's the way it is.

I decided to go about the thing more systematically so I could see straight away if anything connected. I took down my framed *Lady in the Lake* film poster. What I really needed was one of those white boards, but at least I had a good expanse of wall to work with. On a piece of paper I wrote down the main points on the murders I thought the newspaper killer had done, with the newspaper found on the body:

Delaware Loomis, black male, drugs, killed 22 August 2006, gun shot,

Free Press, 4 August 2006, "2 Admit Guilt in Corruption Case"

Rochelle Miller, black female, dancer, drugs? killed 15 January 2007, gun shot,

Free Press, 29 July 2006, "Lawsuit Against Hendricks"

June-Bey Jordan, black male, drugs, killed 26 June 2007, gun shot,

Free Press, 24 June 2007, "Chap. 8 The morgue" Anonymous tip off – white, off-duty cop

What we had in common so far was: death by Glock .40, a neat copy of the *Free Press* on the body, probably a drug connection. It didn't look like the dates or locations of the bodies were significant, but I was assuming he'd probably killed more I didn't know about. I pinned the piece of paper to the wall and underlined the key points in red.

I stuck my Detroit city map up on the other wall and marked the locations of the murders with stick pins. I didn't think they were important, the victims had been killed all over the place, but you never know, maybe if I could see where they all were some kind of pattern would jump out at me. You never know with detective work what will be the little trigger that puts the whole thing together.

I looked at the clock on my desk. It was nearly five already, so I figured I'd better put some clothes on before Alison gets here. I went and sat on the bed and set about putting on some chinos and a T-shirt. There were only a few shirts that were big enough to get my bandaged shoulder into and it still hurt like hell. I spent most of my time in my bath robe or sweatpants with no top. I saw it as my Big Lebowski phase. I tell you, putting on pants with the use of only one arm will really make a man sweat, and doing up buttons… but enough of my problems. By five-thirty I was sitting in the Lay-Z-Boy finally looking through the magic bullet stuff. To be honest, I thought it was kind of a long shot, just 'cause this guy called himself the Lone Gunman didn't mean shit, but what the hell, it was something to do.

The first thing that hit me, after the conspiracy theory baloney, was that just like Alison had said in the hospital, the blogger had been at the party at the mayor's mansion, which either made him a cop, a paramedic, or a guest. There was other stuff made me figure he could be a cop. And, not only was he at the party, but he seemed to take a more than passing interest in Shanta's murder. One of the blogs started with the newspaper report of her murder. Why would he care about that?

The doorbell rang pretty much at six. Punctuality, I like that in a woman. Alison came in with two bags of groceries and dumped them on the countertop.

'Shall I put this stuff away for you?' she said.

'Nah, you don't know where anything goes. Just put the milk away and I'll worry about it later. How much do I owe you?' I pulled out what was left in my wallet and paid her. 'You brought burgers, right?'

'Sure did.'

'There's Vernors in the refrigerator.' I left her to follow me into the living room.

We both started on our burgers before we said any more.

'Oh man this is great.'

'What have you been eating?' Alison asked.

'You know, TV dinners, snacks and stuff.'

'You should have called me, I could have got you some stuff before.'

I shrugged. I wasn't in the habit of asking anyone for help, unless it was work related. 'Hey, I didn't tell you. I got a real nice card from my partner Mick.'

'Really?'

'Nah, it was a cheesy get-well card with some kind of fluffy animal on it. Apparently, he solved the Jordan murder. I think he just sent it to gloat.'

'Isn't that one of the newspaper ones?'

'Yeah, the case I was working when I got shot.'

'So, you think he really caught the guy?' Alison asked, putting fries in her mouth.

'I doubt it. Mick couldn't catch a ball that landed right in his lap. He says some guy he picked up for something else confessed to it. Who knows? But if it really is one guy doing these murders and deliberately leaving a *Free Press* on the body, Mick won't have caught him. He's the kind of guy who puts two and two together and gets three.'

'You think highly of him then?'

'Oh sure.' I finished my burger and dropped the wrapper in the bag on the floor. I wanted to wipe my hand on my pants, but that didn't seem appropriate with Alison around, so I did my best with the paper napkin. 'You want coffee?'

'No, thanks.'

'I think I'll grab one.' I had a pot on the go from earlier. Being a cop you get used to drinking old coffee. 'Let's go into the office,' I said, leading the way. I sat in the desk chair.

'That's OK, I'll stand,' she said.

'Here's the story so far,' I said, pointing to my piece of paper on the wall.

'I can see how you made detective,' she smirked.

'I'm a very visual person.'

'Right.'

'So, you start. Did you find anything in this blog that ties in with anything?'

'OK, I'll start with the general stuff.' She had a notebook with her that she must have grabbed while I got my coffee. She flipped it over, real professional like. 'He hates addicts and women.'

'So do plenty of people.'

'Do you want to do this or are you going to be all negative?'

'OK. OK. I'm just being objective here. Go ahead and put that on the board.' I gave her a piece of paper. She tacked it up and wrote hates addicts and women with a date reference.

'And he keeps mentioning cleaning up. Right here on 24 August 2005, he says "More clean up duties last night." What do you think that means?'

'I don't know. Let's assume for a second this blogger is definitely our killer, which by the way we don't know, but let's go with that, it could mean a killing.'

'Uh huh. Does it tie in with any of the dates we have for murders?'

I scanned the wall. 'Well no, but it could be one we don't know about. Or it could mean something else. Do you have any idea what line of work he's in? Is he a cleaner or janitor or something?'

'I can't pin it down to anything specific, but he mentions cleaning a lot and the rest of that August 2005 entry is weird too: "Decontamination and sanitation is what we're talking about if you want to get technical. There's various tools of the trade. One I prefer more than others. I haven't totally perfected my technique yet, but I'm getting there. I've had a certain amount of professional experience. This wasn't the way I figured things would work out. I had another profession in mind, but I'm still providing a service. You could say I'm a civic servant."'

'Hmm. Decontamination and sanitation? I guess he could be talking metaphorically.'

'Yeah, or it could be what he actually does,' Alison said.

'I haven't totally perfected my technique yet. What does that mean?' I was just thinking out loud. 'Again, if for now we assume he's the killer, it could mean he hasn't perfected his MO yet. He hasn't got it how he wants it to be, or he had one that didn't work out right, but we don't have any cases that match that date, so we're stuck.'

'He says he's had professional experience. Experience of killing people? Of cleaning up after death? Maybe he's a mortician or something! Or ex-military, that could be experience of killing people.'

'Yeah, but he also says he had another profession in mind. Put that on the board – he's not doing what he wanted to do, but he's a "civic servant". What else have we got?'

'Oh hold up,' she says, flipping back in her notebook, 'here's something. He says sometimes he feels like a garbage man just cleaning up the dirt. And here, "Sometimes we save a life, but mostly it's just picking up the pieces."'

'Sounds like a cop maybe?'

'Do you think? Or could be a paramedic – sometimes we save a life?'

'Yeah, could be. Listen, I think we should go right back to the beginning and go through the thing chronologically.'

'OK, but I've got more on this 26 April entry, he's talking about cleaning up all the scum – whores and drug dealers, that ties in with our murder victims, and corrupt politicians, that kind of ties in with the newspaper articles he chooses. Then he says, "Actually, I did a little clean up job last night that should go some way to improving things."'

'Wait, is this still 2005 you're talking about?'

'Yeah, why?'

'26 April 2005?'

'Yeah. What is it?'

'Shanta Brown was killed on 25 April 2005.'

'Oh shit! But there was no newspaper, right?'

'No, but he said he hadn't perfected his technique. Maybe he started with the newspaper thing later. And there's other stuff. He mentions Shanta specifically. He quotes the report of her murder. Why would he mention her? Why would he be interested in that one newspaper report if he hadn't been involved?'

'Well, he mentions some other articles in his blog too.'

'Not many. Maybe they relate to murders he's done too. Motherfucker, he wouldn't be that stupid, would he? OK, OK, let's not get ahead of ourselves here. I'm gonna get some more coffee and then let's start at the beginning.'

'I'll take a beer,' said Alison.

I couldn't believe it. The newspaper guy had done Shanta too? But it couldn't be, it didn't fit. Or did it? She'd been shot with a Glock .40 too. And there was that rabbit's foot in the car. That always puzzled me. Why was that there?

Alison was swivelling in my chair when I got back, looking at the wall. I gave her the beer and she vacated the chair, sitting cross-legged on the floor.

'OK.' I took my blog printouts and went through them. 'So apart from all the conspiracy stuff, the first interesting thing we get to is January 14, 2005, when he's clearly at the mayor's party: "Got called to the Mayor's Mansion tonight." He got *called* there, so that means either police or EMS.' Alison got up and added that to the wall under the heading of 'killer' she'd made earlier. 'Then he talks about it being cold, and there's lots of girls, lots of dancers. The mayor's wife lays into them with her heels. Two of them ended up in the bus…'

'In *the* bus… Could mean his ambulance? He's the driver?' Alison said.

'Could be. Let's leave the semantics for a second. Look what he says next: "That one they call Jessica Rabbit looked fine though. She didn't get hurt." He singles her out by name. The only dancer he specifically mentions. So what? He knows her? He wants to know her?'

'Maybe he wants to lay it on the mayor. You know there's all these rumours starting that the mayor had Shanta Brown killed.'

I tried to hold my train of thought. 'There was something about an EMS guy in the original case. I was just about to follow that up when I got pulled off it. Make a note for me will you, to look back into that.'

Alison took another piece of paper, headed it 'actions' and made a note about the EMS guy. 'Can I get another?' she said, shaking her beer bottle.

'You drive here?'

'Yeah, what's that…'

'Then no, you can't have another beer.' She didn't look happy, but in her defence she didn't question me.

'Did you read the comments on this entry?' Alison said.

'The comments?'

'Yeah, you know, at the end when other people comment on the blog.'

'Um, no, not really. Why is there something interesting?'

'No, just that the blogger answers a comment and signs himself Lone Gunman. It confirms that's the name he's using on this.'

'Right. That's good.' She added that to the wall. Personally, I didn't really care what he called himself. I was too excited about the possibility that this guy might, just might be Shanta's murderer. 'Then we've got the clean-up thing on April 26. He says "last night" so we've got a definite reference to the date she was killed.' I got up and highlighted the date. 'Next entry three days later is the newspaper report on Shanta's death, and straight off he mentions the mayor's party. That wasn't common knowledge then, right?'

'No. We didn't get anything definite on the party until last year, although there were rumours before that.'

'This guy is not a fan of the mayor, which really narrows it down.' Alison laughed. 'He says the mayor must be up to his neck in it and the mayor is guilty. But guilty of what?'

'Guilty of corruption? Of having a party? Or does he mean the mayor killed Shanta? Maybe he's trying to put the blame on the mayor? That's what I was saying earlier, but that would be pretty smart if he is, wouldn't it?' asked Alison.

'You're not suggesting this one guy, killed Shanta, put the blame on the mayor and set off that whole media scrum, and is single-handedly taking out prostitutes, addicts and dealers on a crusade to clean up Detroit?! That's too much for one guy. And you said hardly anyone looked at his blog,' I said.

Alison looked a little dejected, but she didn't let it stop her running with the thing. 'Maybe he just got lucky, he mentions the mayor and Shanta and other people thought the same and it just snowballed. That's how rumours start. Plenty of people have been reporting on Hendricks' corruption and high living for years and there's loads of blogs about his possible involvement in the Shanta Brown case. Could be someone else with a more popular blog saw this and made more of it.'

'OK. So, what are we going to put on our murder board?'

'Hmm, so far we've got police/EMS. Hates addicts, hates women. Father was an alcoholic…'

'Yeah where did that come from?'

'2 May, 2005: "My old man used to hit the sauce…"'

'OK it's a bit of a leap but I'll give you that one.'

'We've got that he was at the party and he tries to put blame on the mayor, but that may not have been his intention, because there's lots of stuff about corruption and politicians getting away with stuff while he's the only one who cares, and he's trying to clean things up.'

I hated to admit it, but I was starting to get tired. My shoulder ached again and I wanted my house back to myself. I didn't know my tolerance for company dropped through the floor with pain. 'Listen, Alison,' I said, 'I hate to break up the party, but it's getting late and I think I need to mull this over some more.'

'But we're just getting started here.'

'We're not all young and bushy-tailed though.'

'Oh.' she said. In fact, she looked a little abashed. It was kind of cute how she so easily forgot my advancing years and my injury. 'Sure, Danny. I'm sorry. But can we just make a to-do list?'

'A to-do list?'

'Yeah, you know…'

'Yeah I know what it is. So, you're a list-maker, huh?

'Wanna make something of it?'

We agreed that she would go through the blog again making a note of any other murder reports he mentioned and anything else that might prove useful, and I would look through the Shanta Brown file and see if there was anything to follow up on the EMS angle.

'And don't forget the IP address?'

'The what? Oh yeah.'

'See if one of your colleagues can get an address on this guy.'

'OK. I'll call you.'

'Take care Danny. Let me know if you need anything.'

> The dried ferns that blow across the vacant lot at Woodward and the Fisher Freeway are like little rolling clichés, bits of tumbleweed emphasizing where life used to happen. *Free Press*

Steve thumbed through his address book, his little black book of women, so he liked to think. Actually, it was just a notebook that he made notes about his photographs in and kept addresses and numbers in the back. It had a pocket in the back cover, and if he ever got them he put business cards in there. He pulled out the one for Century 21 and dialled Janine's number.

'Hi. Is that Janine?'

'Yes.'

'It's Steve Novak. Remember me?'

'Oh yeah. How's it going?'

'Good, good.'

'I heard they closed down GM. What are you up to these days?'

'This and that,' said Steve. 'I just bought a house actually.'

'And you didn't call me? That hurts Steve!'

'Now, don't take it badly. I didn't need a realtor. I bought one of those houses going cheap in McDougall-Hunt. Only paid eighty dollars for it.'

'You call that a house? Was there anything left?' Janine laughed.

'It's not in such bad shape considering.'

'Well good luck with it. Listen I'd love to chat, but time is money, was there something specific you wanted?' Ever the businesswoman. Since they had split up, perfectly amicably, about a year before, Janine hadn't really wanted to keep a friendship going although they had been out for drinks a couple of times, but they both assumed she would be the first person he'd call if he ever needed advice on buying or selling property.

'There is. A buddy of mine from the plant. He's not doing so good, hasn't been able to get a job. And well the bank wants to foreclose on his house. But he doesn't owe that much so I said he should go for a pre-foreclosure sale. I thought you might help him out.'

'Where is it?'

'In North West Goldberg.'

'Hmm, OK, that's better than some places and would this be for old times' sake, or for money?'

'If you could cut him some slack on the percentage that would be great, but I don't expect you to do it for free. He just needs steering through it and you know all the ins and outs.'

'OK. Give me his number. I'll see what I can do.'

Steve gave her the information and hung up; thinking Janine had been even colder than usual and he could probably scratch her from his black book. He just hoped she'd help out Leroy, after that he'd let that contact slide. Next he called Leroy and told him Janine would be in touch and if she wasn't to call her in a couple of days.

'Thanks man,' said Leroy.

'I hope it works out for you. Listen, do you want to come over to the house and help me out with it? I could use a big muscle type lifting these AC units.'

'I'd love to, but I figure if I'm going to be selling this place, I need to do some work on it, spruce it up, maybe some fresh paint and clear out a load of stuff. Plus I still need to talk to Rhonda and tell her what's up.'

'Good luck with that.'

'Thanks, I'm gonna need it.'

'OK, well I'll probably be working on the house all week if you need me. I'll catch you later.'

Steve headed out to Preston Street. He'd agreed to meet his cousin Robert over there to check out the plumbing, or lack of it. When Steve pulled up, Rob's truck was already parked in the vacant lot and he was wandering around at the back of the house.

'Yo, how's it going?' They slapped backs. Steve and Robert were similar ages and had spent a good part of their childhoods riding bikes around, playing baseball and hockey and generally hanging out. They were still close but didn't see each other much since Rob spent most of his time off with his wife and three kids, and being self-employed he didn't have much free time either.

'Pretty good,' said Robert. 'I already had a look out back here. Open her up and let's see what's what.'

They went through the back door into the kitchen. After what seemed to Steve to be a very cursory look around, Rob announced the basic pipe work to be sound. 'You've got all the important stuff, the ground pipes and the connection to the city sewers and everything, you just need the cosmetics – a sink, taps, that kind of thing.'

'Great. But I don't have a whole lot of money.'

'Well, if you're not overly picky about colour, I know a wholesale place with plenty of cheap stuff that is perfectly useable. How's the bathroom?'

'It looks OK to me. You wanna check it out?'

'Sure.' They went upstairs.

'Toilet's OK and the tub. They could probably both do with a flush through, there hasn't been water in this system for quite a while. And I'd get a new shower, but otherwise not bad. I could get you fixed up in a couple of days.'

'That's fantastic.'

'Don't get too excited, there's no such thing as a free lunch.'

'What do you want?'

'You still into photography?'

'Yeah,' said Steve.

'Well, Sarah's confirmation is coming up, so I figured you could do the photos.'

'Sure thing. Little Sarah is sixteen?'

'Yep, unbelievable huh. I want quality, a nice album not just a handful of Polaroid's or some disc with digital shit on it!'

'OK, OK.'

'And you're buying all the materials here. I'm just donating my expertise.'

'You got a deal. Let's go see what your wholesale place has.'

www.magicbullet.com
08.21.06

You know what I trod on today? A spike. Good job I had those standard issue thick rubber soles on. It's getting to be a weekly occurrence. That's all I need to get bad AIDS or something. Maybe I'll go out later with my broom and sweep up, but this city needs more than a good sweeping, it needs to be razed and start again.

It is hot, hot, hot in the city and Motor City is burning. And you know what that means – insurance premiums going up. Why don't we just burn the whole place down?

Forum

- You're so down on Detroit, can't you hear the birds singing? Ringo

- Maybe you need a new location, or a vacation. Kick back! F

- Sorry. I'm just mad right now. The heat is getting to me. Normal service will resume soon. LG

- Yeah, let's get back to some dirt on Hendricks, that always cheers me up! Ringo

Freep.com Chapter 13: The truth
A detective's hunch pays off.
August, 2007

After Alison left, I was real tired. I guess that bullet took it out of me more than I'd thought. I tried to watch TV for a while, but it was no good, I was beat, so I gave up and hit the sack.

I woke up late the next morning. Well, late for me, it was around 9 a.m. and I felt pretty perky. I'd been stuck in the house for days, so I figured rather than sitting around looking at the Brown file, I'd go out, get some cash, maybe do a few errands, and swing by and see my old friend Ron. He's one of those technical guys. He works in sex crimes pulling pervert's computers apart and that kind of thing.

Once I'd managed to get dressed and actually get in the car, driving wasn't as tricky as I thought it would be. Fortunately, I have an automatic and since it was my left arm got shot I was able to put her in gear easily. Driving one handed was a piece of cake. It was nice to be out. The sun was shining and there was a little breeze. It felt real good. After stopping at an ATM, I headed straight downtown.

'Hi Ron, how's it going?'

'Not bad. You look like you've been in the wars.'

'Tell me about it.'

'Should you be at work?'

I didn't like to tell him I wasn't back at work. 'Oh you know, what else am I gonna do?'

'So what brings you to these parts?'

'The usual. You busy?'

'Same as always,' he said.

'So you might have time to do me a favour?'

'I might have known! Yeah, I guess. What do you need?'

'Can you find an IP address from this blog for me?'

'Sure. What's in it for me?'

'A box of doughnuts?'

'That's such a cliché. Not all policemen like doughnuts you know. Make it some breakfast tacos and you've got a deal.'

'OK.'

'So what's the blog address?' I handed him the piece of paper with it written on. 'Give me a couple of hours.'

'Any particular kind of taco?'

'Na, whatever.'

I drove over to Elvie's and since I had time to kill I had a cup of coffee and a couple of tacos myself. It made me think of having coffee with Linda Gonzales and reminded me I needed to call her. Gees, that was a lifetime ago and I still hadn't got anywhere with that. I knew Flanagan hadn't got the right guy for Shanta's murder, but who the hell cared about it apart from me? And why did I care? Someone had gone down for it. Probably no one innocent, most people in this city are guilty of something. So what if it wasn't the right man? Catching the real killer wouldn't bring those kids' mother back. But that case rankled, it always had. I hated not solving cases and this one had been pulled from under me just as I was starting to get somewhere. I promised myself I'd look over the case file again tonight just in case something jumped out at me. Going through all that blog stuff with Alison had got me to thinking about the Brown murder all over again and maybe our newspaper guy was involved. He certainly had some interest in it.

I bought some tamales and put them in the cooler in the trunk and drove back to Ron's office. He didn't even look up when I walked in and dropped the paper sack on his desk.

'Oh man, they smell great,' he said.
'Am I back too early?'
'No, I've got it.'
'That's residential,' I said looking at the address.
'Sure is.'
'Hmm, I was expecting an internet café or something.'

Ron looked at me like he was surprised I'd know what that was. 'Well, this isn't a very popular site, in fact it's getting even less popular, very little activity lately. This guy probably isn't all that technical; either he doesn't know IP addresses can be traced, or he doesn't care. Pretty much any idiot can set up a blog these days. But this is fairly innocuous stuff. What's he supposed to have done any way?'

'If I tell you, I'll have to kill you.'
'Right, sure.'
'Na, seriously, I don't know yet that he's done anything, but I want to check him out. So, you've seen this kind of stuff before?'
'Yeah, there's hundreds of conspiracy theory sites, but this one is more like a diary. Still not unusual though, lots of bloggers use it as an outlet to vent, they don't much care if anyone reads it or not. This guy seems to be a bit hung up on cleanliness, maybe he's OCD!'

Alison had picked up on that too, the guy was always going on about cleaning up, but I'd assumed that meant killing people, maybe it didn't, maybe the guy really did just have a thing about cleaning. 'Thanks a lot, Ron.'

'Any time. Take care of that arm.'

'Sure.'

I looked at the address Ron had given me. It was out in Dearborn. That probably made the guy white, or an Arab. I should have figured the guy wouldn't live downtown. I decided to drive out there, take a look at the house, and see if it gave me a feel for the guy. It was an effort getting into respectable clothes and driving around. I figured I wouldn't do it again for a few days.

First, I called Alison. She wasn't at her desk, but I left a message instead of calling her cell. I gave her the address and asked her to look it up in the public records directory and see if she could get a name on the owner from the tax records, or anything else useful. I could have found out for myself, but I was afraid that if I stopped moving I might not get going again and I didn't want anyone else in the department knowing I was 'working'. I'd already chanced things a bit by talking to Ron, but my crew were unlikely to talk to him. I guess it didn't matter, but I didn't want the captain calling me and chewing me out for working when I was on sick leave. Plus, since Mick had got someone for the Jordan murder, that was officially closed and I had no business messing with it.

The drive out to Dearborn was pleasant enough. I took the Edsel Ford west, past the Arab American Museum on Michigan Avenue and dropped down to Lithgow Street – a pretty typical street in a pretty typical part of Dearborn. I drove slow past the guy's house. A slightly smaller than average place, but it blended right in, nothing out of the ordinary. No car in the driveway. The house didn't have a garage. I didn't want to park outside and draw attention to myself, so I drove around and parked at the top of the street and walked. The house was about half way down. No one was around so I went up the steps to the front door and gently eased up the lid of the mail box. I figured if the door opened or anyone asked I could come up with some story. I've had years of experience. The mail hadn't been taken in yet. There was the usual junk and a letter from the city, looked like a payslip maybe, addressed to Michael Harvey. Nice innocuous name, in a nice innocuous street, it was almost screaming serial killer at me. I bet if I ask the neighbours they'll say he keeps to himself, just like Alison said! Thinking of neighbours I dropped the letter and went back to the street. I decided to not risk looking around the back. I could always come back once I found out more about the guy.

Driving back I pull into the first eating place I see, Noah's Deli on the corner of Roemer and Michigan. I slide into a booth and jot the name Michael Harvey into my notebook, not that I'm likely to forget it, then I order a Double Trouble and thought of Alison, how could I not. That thing was pretty hard to eat with one hand, it was so packed. I can certainly recommend it if you're out that way. Anyways, I'm just about to leave when my cell phone rings.

'Yeah.'

'It's me Alison. I got what you wanted. That address is registered to a Mrs E Harvey, but if she's alive she'd be pretty old. The taxes are paid by an M. Harvey.'

'I've just been there. I got a Michael Harvey.'

'You've been there?'

'Sure, sleeping dogs and all that.'

'What?'

'Never mind,' I said.

'Anything interesting? Was he there? Did you see him?'

'Woa! No, no and no. I'll tell you about it later.' It was getting near my nap time, especially after that monster sandwich. I needed to get home and re-group before I could take Alison's level of enthusiasm.

'Oh, OK,' she said, sounding deflated. 'I can dig a little more, see what else I can find. You want me to come round later?'

'I'm a little beat Alison. Also, I want to go through the Brown case again, I didn't get time yet. I'll call you OK?'

'OK.'

'But call me if you find anything really juicy,' I said.

'It would be a big mistake for anyone to believe that the Great American Dream is apple pie and a happy ending.'
Coleman A. Young

Leroy was tidying his house as a form of procrastination. He knew he had to call Rhonda, but he didn't want to call Rhonda and he was both worried and not worried about what Rhonda would say. However, either way he was going to have to sell the house so he needed to clear out a lot of stuff. At Steve's urging he had eventually called the bank and discussed his situation. Because of his good record of always paying the mortgage on time and never defaulting before, they had agreed to give him a few more weeks to try and sell the property himself before they started foreclosure proceedings. Leroy assumed he was lucky in this, but he didn't feel lucky and so far Steve's ex-girlfriend Janice had not found him a buyer. To be honest he wasn't convinced that they would find a buyer, but being despondent and drinking was not helping the issue so he was trying to keep busy. He didn't need Rhonda saying he was more of a loser than he already thought he was, not that it was his fault he no longer had a job.

He started with the garage. He boxed up his small collection of tools. For now, he'd decided to lend them to Steve who would probably need them for his house renovation and had the room to store them, likewise the lawn mower and gardening tools. There was a collection of used paint. He went through them disposing of any that were too dried out and using up the rest to touch up paintwork inside the house. He didn't know what to do with the girls' bikes. He didn't want to get rid of them in case they came back, he hoped they would at least come back to visit sometime, but where would he store them? He would ask Rhonda. He'd decided to call her in the early evening, hoping to find her at home at the pre-dinner hour.

Leroy found a lot more stuff he knew he'd never use again and made a little money selling it for scrap. He stopped on the way home and bought a few groceries. He didn't need much. Every time he worked with Steve on his house, he ate with him and he was trying to run down the pantry and freezer in anticipation of having to move. He'd given up trying to pay the utilities since the bank had told him they were going to foreclose. It was a relief to not have to think about where he'd find the money for the bills. Sure, he kept getting red bill demands, but he knew he still had a few weeks grace before everything got cut off and he figured he could always stay with Steve if things got too bad. Leroy and Steve had been friends a long time, but he still found it hard to believe that his best friend was a white man while his black friends and relatives had abandoned him just when he needed them most.

He tried not to dwell on that as he sat on the sofa in the living room flicking through his record collection to see what he could bear to part with. He couldn't believe Rhonda would let the bank take their house, their home of twenty years, the place they'd raised their family. The house had good memories, at least it did for Leroy. Surely Rhonda would get her father to help out, wouldn't she? As far as Leroy was aware, her father was easily well off enough to give them the five thousand the bank wanted without it hurting him much.

Leroy put on Curtis Mayfield's *Superfly*. That was one album he wouldn't be selling. He loved it even though it kind of depressed him too. The more he listened and the more he thought, the more Leroy became resigned to the idea that his father-in-law wouldn't bail them out. He'd finally got the perfect way to separate Leroy from his daughter. Oh he'd make sure she was taken care of, and his grandchildren. He wouldn't be surprised if they weren't already looking at houses in Washington for her and the kids, conveniently placed near the grandparents so there were ready-made baby sitters. All these years he'd worked to support his family and now because the plant had closed Rhonda was going to dump him and run back to mummy and daddy. He wondered if he'd ever see his kids again.

Leroy put *Trouble Man* on the turntable. He dropped the needle and went over to the drinks cabinet to see what he could drink for Dutch courage.

Much later Leroy was on the phone to Steve. He would have gone over to see him but between the Dutch courage and the post-Rhonda drinks he was in no state to drive.

'Well, I finally bit the bullet and told her.'

'And?' Said Steve.

'I should go into fortune telling, I knew exactly what she'd say. Her father will not be helping me out. She'll be staying in Washington and so will the girls, they're already enrolled in schools down there. I said both our names were on the title papers and she said I'd made all the payments so really it was my house and she wasn't going to fight me about it, she didn't want anything to do with it. Can you believe that woman?'

'Shit, that's harsh.'

'On the upside she told me to do whatever I had to with the house and she didn't want any money from me.'

'I guess that's something. At least that leaves you clear to sell it without her raising hell and wanting half of any profits.'

'Like there's going to be any profits.'
'You never know. Think positive.'
'That's easy for you to say.'

Freep.com Chapter 15: The requiem

...even as community leaders resolved to do better, fentanyl's killer reputation still beckoned.

August, 2007

Next day I ached, so I was glad to have a day pottering between the Lay-Z-Boy and the office, stretching my grey cells and not my body, though it was a Herculean feat fishing out my copy of the Shanta Brown file from the bottom shelf. I left the box on the floor and piled papers and notebooks out on my desk. I had much of it in my mind, but it had been a while since I'd looked at that baby. Then of course I had to have some coffee and tamales. Hey, I'm on sick leave here. I shouldn't be doing anything but watching the TV and feeling sorry for myself.

Boring as it may appear to the innocent bystander the secret to good police work is a methodical approach, so I started at the beginning and went through the whole file. It was going to take time, but it was the only way to go. I'll spare you civilians all the details and get to the main things that struck me in relation to the newspaper killer possibly having killed Shanta. I made my own little to-do list too just to keep Alison happy.

First off, the Lone Gunman, aka the magic bullet blogger, aka the newspaper killer (maybe), aka Michael Harvey (apparently), was talking about the alleged party at the mayor's mansion on January 14, 2005, before any rumours or news of that party had been made public. That meant he was there, which pretty much meant he was a cop or a paramedic because a guest wouldn't publicise the fact and certainly not in the way the blog did. Shanta and Linda Gonzales had attended the party and Linda had said an EMS person had had an altercation with Shanta and called her a bitch. The blogger also mentioned Shanta by name, that is by her stage name Jessica Rabbit, saying she "looked fine" and hadn't been hurt. This meant he knew her somehow. He called her Jessica so my guess was he knew her professionally. Maybe he was a regular at Bouzouki. I didn't hold out much hope for getting anything new from Dave at the strip joint after all this time, but I made a note to check it out.

On April 26 2005, the blog talks about doing a "clean up job last night" which was the night of Shanta's murder. If clean-up meant killing and not something janitorial that gave us a link, but I'd have to check there had been no other murders that night. On April 29 he quoted the *Free Press* report of Shanta's murder and suggested the mayor was involved somehow. "The Mayor is guilty." But the mayor was guilty of plenty of things. That was the trouble with this magic bullet blog, it was too vague. Was the killer teasing us, giving us just enough to suspect, but not enough details to incriminate himself, or was this just the style of these things? I needed to look at some other blogs, or talk to Alison.

I looked up at the board, not much else seemed to relate to Shanta Brown. Except... I remembered something else from the night with Alison. I flipped through the pages... "Internal affairs are looking into the party." That was the thing that had made me figure the guy could be a cop, but it was possible the rumour mill extends to the Fire Department and EMS or he could have a friend on the force who was feeding him information. "And the murder of Jessica Rabbit has gone cold case. The police gossip always makes it to us sooner or later. They never had any idea." Who never had any idea? The police? Was this a confession? Or was he saying he knew who the killer was? He says police gossip, so he's not a cop himself. Back to the paramedic angle.

I was deep into this stuff when my cell beeped. A text from Alison: "Mrs. E. Harvey deceased. Michael Harvey IS a paramedic! Stuck with work stuff, will report more later." So I broke for lunch and a nicotine aided review of evidence. Yes, that is a euphemism for sitting in my chair thinking about stuff, which I did for some time.

Back in the office, I made a column on the board for Shanta aka Jessica Rabbit and jotted down the notes I'd made from the case file. There was plenty of stuff to follow up on:

DeAndre Little, her boyfriend, had said the shooter drove some kind of SUV, 'a dark colour'. What kind of car did Michael Harvey drive?

Check with Bouzouki — does Michael Harvey go there? Was he a customer in 2005? Did he know Shanta?

Talk to Linda Gonzales again. She'd said the EMS guy was white with a shaved head. We needed to get a photo of this Michael Harvey too.

Shanta Brown's professional name was Jessica Rabbit, Lee Harvey Oswald's nickname was Ozzie the Rabbit, a rabbit's foot had been found in Shanta's car, the magic bullet blogger seemed to be one Michael Harvey who was obsessed with Oswald and shared a name with him and liked to go by Lone Gunman – all coincidence or was there something meaningful in any of it? I'd always felt that it was her killer who put the rabbit's foot in Shanta's car.

I powered up my computer. First, I googled Michael Harvey, well it was worth a try. Never let it be said that I'm not up with current technology. That led me to Michael Harvey the British musical artist amongst other people who I didn't think were our guy. I followed a few links, but nothing that seemed related to any paramedics in Detroit. Then for the hell of it I googled mayor Hendricks. There was plenty on him. The whistleblower trial of Mr Hendricks had just started and looked set to get ugly, but that was a tangent I didn't want to take right now. The lone gunman was clearly not a fan of the mayor, but who was? Him bad-mouthing Kemi Hendricks did not feel like a major clue. I'd let Alison look into that, it's her area of expertise. But some links from the *Detroit News* led me to the Big Tent Circus blog – very interesting stuff. Also, not a fan of the mayor, this blogger was eloquent and educated, a bit of a political pundit, which made it all the more surprising when a recent blog claimed that "Brown was executed because she knew too much about sex, politics and power in Michigan's largest city." I made a note of that to discuss with Alison. The Big Tent blog looked very professional, had a lot of archives and a lot of topics, it also had links to other blogs and websites. So I figured I'd take a look at Magic Bullet for comparison. I never had looked at the live blog yet, only the print-outs Alison had given me. It was worlds apart. The background was dark blue with white text and there were no links or topics, just the automatically generated archive of older blogs. Harvey had just posted something, but unfortunately it wasn't very exciting – predictable pleasure at the mayor's situation and hope that he'd get what was coming to him. I could have spent hours going through more entries and looking at other blogs, but I'm not that kind of guy. Reuben used to call it 'busy work' – it looked like work but it didn't really get you anywhere.

Instead, I logged into the police computer and ran a check. There hadn't been any other murders in metro Detroit on April 25 2005; Shanta Brown was the only one. While I was there I ran a DMV check on Harvey, which came up with him driving a brown 1997 Honda Accord – shit that would give a man an inferiority complex! So not a dark SUV. But that didn't rule him out. Maybe two years ago he was driving an SUV, or he borrowed it, or stole one, or DeAndre Little could have been wrong. He never was the greatest witness.

I logged out and sent Alison a text asking her to check out blogs and the latest on the mayor and saying we'd catch up soon. I was too tired to read, so I heated up the last of the tamales and watched a little of *The Blue Dahlia* 'til my medication kicked in.

> Approaching the derelict shell of downtown Detroit, we see full-grown trees sprouting from the tops of deserted skycrapers. Our excitement is... matched only by the sheer disbelief that what was once the fourth largest city in the US could actually be in the process of disappearing from the face of the earth. *The Guardian*

Steve wiped sweat from his forehead. It was hotter than Hades. I've got to get an AC unit in here soon, he thought. He was just about to go back to work when his phone vibrated in his pocket.

'Hello.'

'Hi, it's Alison.'

'Oh hi, what's up?'

'I've got a story I need some photos for. Are you up for it?'

'Sure. What's the scoop?'

Alison briefly explained the project and Steve agreed to meet her at the *Free Press* offices later in the day. The basic idea was about how nature was re-emerging in Detroit now that much of the metro area had turned to wilderness. Steve knew he had plenty of photos back at his apartment that would suite. He cleaned up, locked up his new back door and drove home. Not that he considered it home anymore. His apartment was just a stop-over, a storage facility until he could move into his new house and start living the 'artist's' life he'd always dreamed of.

Steve fired up his computer and began looking through photos. He'd recently arranged them by topic and he had a whole file on nature in Detroit, trees growing up through houses, wildflowers amongst rusted machinery in abandoned factories, a hawk hovering above a prairie-like wilderness. He saved his favourites to a USB stick. He still had some time before he met Alison, so he packed his camera bag, grabbed a soda and headed out to drive around and maybe get a few new shots, just to show he'd earned his fee. No, it wasn't even about that. Steve just loved driving around Detroit taking photos. He hadn't done it for a while because he'd been working on the house so much.

Steve drove along Buchanan towards Grand River. Mattresses and broken furniture vied with grasses and ground creepers. Steve parked and walked around. It was the hottest part of the day and any wildlife was hiding. He could see the heat haze shimmer above the overgrown field. When did my city get to become a wilderness, he wondered? Steve had always lived in Detroit and so the gradual decay had seemed natural. For years he'd been photographing the factories as they closed, the odd derelict house here and there, but it was only now that he wasn't working, when he had time to pause that he really saw and heard how silent the city had become. He felt a slight breeze dry the sweat on his neck, he smelt the heat and the hayfevery grass seeds. He didn't smell gasoline, or rubber, or factory smoke. The sky was clear and blue. Detroit had changed, but Steve loved it even more, where else could you get nature, art and great food all in one place? Not to mention the endless photo opportunities, though Steve knew others were already jumping on that bandwagon, and soon it wouldn't be enough to take a picture of flowers growing through floorboards next to a junkie's needle, but for now Steve was in the right place at the right time for once in his life and he intended to make the most of it.

Alison was pleased with the photos. He transferred the selected images for her to match to her text and she gave him a pre-prepared cheque for $200. Steve couldn't believe it was so easy. Why had he never gone freelance before? All those years at GM when maybe he could have been playing at taking pictures the whole time.

'So, do you want to go and get a beer or something?' Steve asked.

'I have to finish this off and post it.'

'Sure. How about later? What time do you get off work?'

Alison knew he was trying to hit on her, but she had no plans, and she figured it might be fun to try to string him along for a while, see how long it would take him to figure things out. 'Around seven, I guess.'

'Uh huh. You wanna get something to eat? Greek, Mexican, whatever?'

Well, she did have to eat and she had a free evening. Carol had to work tonight. 'OK, how about Mexican? No, scratch that, why don't we go to Scotty Simpson's?'

It had been a long time since Steve had eaten fish and chips at Scotty's, but since he'd already been halfway down memory lane on his drive around, why not. 'It's kind of a long way out, isn't it?'

'Not really, anyway it's worth the drive. You never go out of downtown or something?'

'Sure, I do.'

'All right then. Meet you there at 7.30.'

And he was dismissed. Alison had a real way of cutting you off when she was finished with you. Steve started to wonder if meeting her later was a mistake. She clearly didn't do small talk. Ah well, what the hell. If nothing else he'd get a good meal out of it, which wouldn't cost him the earth. He didn't need another Janine in his life, always wanting to eat at places that required a tie and jacket and expecting the kind of gift he couldn't afford for birthdays and Christmas. The only question was, did he go and work on the house a little more, but then he'd need a shower and change of clothes. No, he may as well cruise around some more and take more photos and look around for stuff for the house. He'd already found a fantastic front door with leaded glass, a beautiful banister for the stairs and enough doorknobs for all the interior doors. What he really needed now was some marble for his kitchen worktops.

Steve headed to the Brush Park historic district. He loved looking at those historic houses. He could spend hours taking photos of them. There was Gilded Age, French Renaissance Revival, Victorian, even Gothic revival. He couldn't imagine a time when Detroit was prosperous enough that these mansions were inhabited by just one family. Many were abandoned and boarded up, even falling down to the point where they would have to be demolished, some had been made into condos, some were attracting a few new residents. Steve walked down Alfred Street taking photos. In the end he felt too exposed to break into any of the boarded-up houses looking for pieces he could use. He just basked in Detroit's former glory and some of its more bizarre architecture.

Despite the photography detour, Steve was still early for his 'date' with Alison. He sat at the Formica table sipping ginger ale with plenty of ice looking through the photos he'd taken. He glanced at the menu and decided he'd have the straight up fish and fries, maybe with a side of coleslaw. A few people were seated at the other tables. It wasn't a great location for a date, the tables were too close together. Maybe that was why Alison had chosen it. Just then she burst through the door, came over and sat down. She looked tousled. Her dark curls flopping over her eyes. She swept them back and pulled her T-Shirt away from her chest to remove it from her damp skin. Steve pictured the damp skin, a single droplet of sweat rolling down her cleavage, the hint of sourness mixed with some fragrant deodorant. Woa, let's not get carried away here, he thought, she must be fifteen years his junior for a start and why would she be remotely interested in him.

'Did you get the story finished?' He asked by way of introduction.

'Yep, looks good. It will be in tomorrow's Metro section.'

'My first newspaper photo credit.'

'It probably won't be your last.'

'Really?'

'Yeah, your work is really good. You could almost do one of those coffee table books, you know Detroit debris or something.'

'Hasn't that already been done?'

'I don't think so. Anyway, the market could probably stand another one or two. I bet they'd love that shit in Europe, the decline of the great U S of A, post-modernist America, all that.'

'OK, I'll look into that. So, what are you eating?'

'The baked Cajun fish and fries of course.' Of course, thought Steve. He raised an eyebrow. 'What? I like spicy.' Oh dear, thought Steve, spicy I'm not. He went up to the counter and ordered. Alison waved at him and said, 'maybe some onion rings too.'

Steve had to admit the fish was great. Not the healthiest of meals, but he'd been burning plenty of calories working on the house. He was hoping he might have lost a few pounds, but he just seemed to eat more. Still, he did feel a bit more toned.

'So, do you come here often,' he said, regretting it as soon as he'd said it. They had been getting along so well talking about work, now he had to go and do a stupid pickup line.

'Not too much. I have varied and eclectic food tastes.'

'Really?'

'Nah, I'll eat anything.'

'What's your favourite kind of food?'

'Carbs! No seriously, it depends what mood I'm in, but I like my food hot like my women.'

'Do you cook?'

'Do you?' asked Alison, noting that he was completely oblivious to clue number one. Danny would have picked up on that straight away, which reminded her she needed to call him and see how their case was going. Things had gone too quiet.

'Um, no not much. I'm thinking of growing some vegetables though. I might even get some chickens.'

'Chickens?'

'Yeah, why not? Fresh eggs every morning.'

Steve sat and watched Alison put the last fry in her mouth. He didn't know what to say now. He wanted to ask her to go on somewhere, have a drink, but he didn't feel like they'd reached that point yet. Overall it was going well though. They had a rapport. Alison wiped her mouth, screwed up her napkin and threw it on her plate in a very un-lady-like fashion.

'What's with the thumb ring,' Steve blurted out, again wishing he'd think more before he opened his mouth.

'I guess it's a gay thing,' said Alison. She couldn't bear to let things go any further. Steve was a nice enough guy. She loved his photos and seriously thought they could work on other projects, but that was it.

'Oh right,' the penny finally dropped, 'right'. More silence. 'So you won't be wanting to go on anywhere then, maybe have one drink too many and go back to my place?'

She laughed. 'No.'

'OK then. So do you have a girlfriend?'

'Not right now.' She did, at least she hoped, that's how Carol saw it, they'd been dating for a while now, but she didn't want to share that much of her private life with Steve.

'Me neither.'

'No, I couldn't tell,' she said sarcastically. Steve smiled.

'OK, well let me know if you do the book. Maybe we could work on it together. I could write an introduction or something,' she said, pulling $10 from her pocket and dropping it on the table. 'See you around photo boy.'

And with that she was gone. She would have been too much to handle anyway, thought Steve. At least she doesn't find me unattractive, not me specifically anyway. As he drove home, he tried not to imagine her naked and tried to focus on the book they would work on together. He pictured the cover, their names one above the other against a backdrop of the Michigan Theater or Michigan Central Station. Thinking about the book didn't work to take his mind off Alison, still it was something to bear in mind. Fame and fortune as a revered photographer was surely more important than a quick roll-around in the sack. Wasn't it?

www.time.com Can Kemi Hendricks Grow Up?

Detroit's Kemi Hendricks was named one of America's worst mayors by TIME in 2005. Have his fortunes changed since then? Not if you go by court decisions.

August, 2007

'Boy, have I got something good for you.' Alison bounced through the door and almost danced down the hallway.

'Come in Alison, glad you could make it.'

'But Danny, wait 'til you see what I've got.' She rooted around in that cycle courier bag she always has and pulled out a glossy eight by ten of a not old, not young white guy with hair cropped so short he could be bald, in fact he probably was bald. I got a weird feeling in my stomach and knew what she was going to say before she said it. 'Who do you think that is?'

'Michael Harvey?'

'Bang on.'

'And how did you come by this photo,' I asked.

'I took it.' Alison looked so pleased with herself, I almost resisted having the conversation I knew would come next.

'OK, I'll bite. How did you come to take this photo?'

'Well,' she said, finally sitting down.

'We had the address, right, and I had a little spare time yesterday, so I sat outside his place for a while, just in case.'

'You sat outside his place, on your own, are you...'

'Relax. It's Dearborn. I've been in more dangerous places. Anyway,' she said hesitatingly, 'I wasn't on my own.'

I groaned silently. 'OK. Come on spill. Don't make me regret that I asked you to help me with this. I don't need "endangering a civilian" added to my record just as I'm about to retire.'

'So, there's this woman I'm kind of seeing...'

'And God forbid that you could just take her out for dinner or buy her flowers, you thought you'd take her on a stake out!'

'She's really into crime books.'

'So, you've told her about the case?' Alison didn't look at me. 'Rule number two, Alison, don't get involved with women while on a case. No, make that rule number one, and rule number two is never rule anything out.'

'I didn't tell her *everything*. Anyway, she might be helpful, fresh eyes and...' her voice trailed off.

'Wait a minute. You're seeing a woman?'

'Yeah. Hadn't you figured that out?'

'No, as it happens. So do you like guys too, or...'

'Sure, I like guys, but not in that way, pretty much just women.'

'Oh.'

'It doesn't matter, does it?'

'Not to me,' I said.

'Is that why you're still single Danny?'

'Huh?'

'Never get involved while on a case?'

'We're not talking about me. Anyone could have seen you. How long were you there outside a potential murderer's house?'

'Not that long. He came home about twenty minutes after we got there. Came home and stayed home. I thought it would be fun to tail him if he went out somewhere, but we got bored pretty soon when he didn't come out again.'

'Alison,' I said, aiming for something between fatherly and experienced police professional, 'do not follow this guy. Do you hear me?'

'OK, but how else are we going to catch him?'

'I don't know yet, but not by following him around. This isn't the movies, you're not going to catch him shooting someone and make a citizen's arrest.' I could see Alison thinking she could do precisely that and wouldn't it greatly impress her new flame. 'Not to mention the danger, and, *and* he could see you and it could totally mess up our chances. We have to find evidence to nail him. So far, we don't have anything that proves he's the killer. We just have a hunch that he's writing this blog and a hunch that the blogging lone gunman could be the killer.'

'But your tech guy traced the IP address to that house that means…'

'It means some computer at that house was used to write the blog. It doesn't mean Harvey wrote it. There could be someone else living there. And the blog could have nothing to do with it.'

'But there's so much stuff that fits,' said Alison.

'I know. There's way too much that fits and I know you're keen, but we've got to do this slowly and properly if we want a hope of catching him. We wouldn't have enough right now to even get a warrant to check out his house or set up surveillance.' Alison looked disappointed. I had to remember this was all new and exciting for her; she didn't have years of experience of going down dead-ends, or thinking your evidence is going to nail a guy and then finding it's been contaminated, she didn't know that what caught the killer nine times out of ten was mundane checking of minutia and not a small amount of luck. Still I wasn't upset to have a little of the buzz of the chase back. It would be nice to go out on a big one. Maybe Alison could write a piece specifically on me – city cop of longstanding, Arthur Daniels catches serial killer just before retirement. Well, let's not get carried away.

'Did you find out anything more from the blog, or were you too busy playing private eye?' I asked her.

Alison blushed slightly. 'Not much. There was this bit in February 2006 when he's talking about logos and business cards, where is it, oh yeah, "I think a cleanup crew should have a proper uniform, don't you? An insignia you might say. A logo. A business card." And in the comments this guy who calls himself Frohike, suggests anagrams, so I wondered if that's where he got the idea for the anagrams on the newspapers he leaves on the bodies?'

'Could be. It all seems kind of complicated to me. A neatly folded paper on the body would have been enough, especially if it was clear that the headline or date was important.'

'Maybe he just likes showing how clever he is.'

'Hmm.'

'Maybe he's been snubbed in the past or failed a test or something and been made to feel stupid, so now that's part of his thing, he needs to show he's cleverer than everyone else and he's leaving all these clues and still no one can catch him.'

'Could be, but why he does it is not going to help us catch him, we need to know how he gets away with it, if there's any pattern to it, we need evidence.'

Alison doodled on her notepad. 'But maybe getting inside his head will tell us those things.'

'OK. You get in his head, I'm fine in my own thanks!' She smiled. 'Did you ever find any links in the papers he left?'

'No. The only thing that seems to link them is that they are *Free Press*.'

I looked up at the map where I'd marked the locations of the murders we knew about. That didn't help. They were fairly spread out. 'I had a look at Magic Bullet. It's not very professional, is it?'

'No. It's almost like he doesn't want anyone to read it, yet he seems pleased when people leave comments.'

'I came across this other blog, Big Tent Circus?'

'Yeah, I've heard of that. He's a pretty well-respected political analyst.'

'His latest piece claims Shanta was killed because she knew too much about sex, politics and power.'

'Wow.'

'Yes. Are you following all this stuff with the mayor?'

'Not me personally, but the *Freep* is all over it. You know how we love to have a dig at Henricks.'

'I thought it was all about the truth?'

'Oh it is. We wouldn't kick him just for the hell of it, only when he's already tripped and fallen over by himself!' she said.

'You think there could be anything in the idea that he had Shanta killed?'

'It seems a bit extreme even for Henricks, but I guess it could happen. You got taken off the case as soon as you started asking questions about the party, right?'

I nodded. 'Well, keep an eye on it. See if anything comes out of all that stuff.' I looked back at the picture of Michael Harvey, a paramedic with a shaved head. 'Can I keep this?'

'Sure, though I ought to make you pay for the way you scolded me about it.'

Motor City's burning and the flames are running wild, they reflect upon the waters of the river and the lake and everyone is listening and everyone's awake, black day in July...
Gordon Lightfoot, 1968

Leroy and Steve were sitting in the shade of Steve's porch drinking sodas.

'I should have burned the motherfucker down.'

'What you talking about now, Leroy?'

'My house man, my house. I should have made on the insurance like everyone else.'

'Yep, there's the sweet smell of burning houses hanging over D Town. Those fire engines are keeping me up.'

'I'm glad you think it's funny. It ain't your house they foreclosed on,' said Leroy.

'But didn't Janine sort you out? Haven't you got a buyer yet?'

'Bank says I've got to sell it in a week, or they're going to put the sale notice on it and I won't get anything.'

'And Rhonda? Her folks definitely won't help you out?'

'No. I didn't even try asking her. She was very definite last time I spoke to her that she wasn't going to bail me out to save the house and she didn't care what I did with it. I'm on my own.'

'Don't get despondent, we'll find someone to buy it.'

'Well, you'd better hurry and find some rich friends, 'cause Janine's been trying and it ain't shifted.'

'And it's all clean and painted, and smelling of fresh coffee and pie?'

'Ain't no pie, but the rest of it's good. I got rid of a load of stuff and painted and everything. It felt good. When I asked Rhonda what she wanted me to do with her stuff she just said someone would come and collect it, and her lawyer would be in touch about visiting the children. Cold huh? What did I do to her that she's so cold with me? It's like I'm a stranger, not her husband of twenty years and the father of her children.'

'No use asking me about women. There's this woman at the *Free Press*, Alison. We've become kind of friendly with me selling them photos and stuff. So I asked her out on a date, but it was weird, she didn't dress up or nothing, it was just like boy's night out or something. Then it turns out she's gay.'

'She's into women?'

'Yeah.'

'That's the best I've heard yet man. I know you don't exactly have a way with the ladies, but to turn one gay...!'

'I didn't turn her, she was that way already. Anyways, your track record with the ladies isn't so hot either. You ever been with anyone except Rhonda? No, I didn't think so. Did Rhonda mention the D word yet?'

'No, I reckon that'll be in the letter from the lawyer too,' said Leroy, not rising to the bait.

'I really thought that trip to Washington was going be temporary,' said Steve, shaking his head.

'Yeah well, can you blame her really? Can you? Who the hell wants to live here? What's Detroit got going for it? There ain't nothing here no more. I should just leave too.'

"We must not let the doomsayers and the naysayers cause us to lose faith in our city."

Leroy laughed. 'Don't give me any of that Coleman shit!' He kicked the toe of his Timberlands along the edge of the porch. 'What's so great about The D?'

'Well, I don't wanna get all smug or nothing, but I've got me this nice big three-bed, two-storey. I ain't gotta work, I ain't gotta pay no rent.'

'Ah huh. And this mansion of yours, it got power yet?'

'Well not right now, but it's summertime. I'll get the power on before winter.'

'You might wanna get it re-wired first,' said Leroy laughing. 'And water? You got water.'

'Sure do, hooked up a few days ago. You've seen the new plumbing and everything.'

'Hmm, and how are you going to pay for that?'

'I'm not sure I wanna let you in on that.'

'Oh come on, you going to keep secrets from me now, after I've been helping you to fix up this dump and I'm gonna be homeless soon too!'

'Aw right. It's not like it's a secret. There's a lot of empty houses right?'

'Right.'

'So, there's money to be made.' Leroy looked confused. 'There's people that pay good money, you know, for pipes, and copper and shit.'

'You stealin' out of people's houses?' Leroy said, looking shocked.

'Only empty ones. If I don't do it someone else will.'

'Suppose you're gonna strip my house next week too!'

'Of course not, you're gonna sell yours. I'll call some people. But I'm telling you, don't move out until the new folk move in or someone will strip it bare before the ink is even dry on the paperwork.'

'Tsch. You're lowdown man, lowdown.'

'A man's gotta do what a man's gotta do.'

'Tsch.'

'You wanna piece of the action or what?'

'You bet! Just tell me where to be.'

Big Tent Circus, weblog
...Brown was executed because she knew too much about sex, politics and power in Michigan's largest city.
August 2007

I had a nice warm feeling as I drove out to see Linda Gonzales again. I don't know what it is about that woman, but there's something about her I like. I had some Mexican cumbias on the car tape deck to get me in the mood. It was going to be a busy day. I was due to see the physiotherapist in the afternoon.

Linda looked just as elegant as she had two years ago. She waved me in and I followed the heavy scent of her perfume into the living room. The lounge hadn't changed much either. She came in from the kitchen with coffee and cinnamon covered cookies. I was having slightly unprofessional thoughts, especially when she leant over the coffee table and flashed me her cleavage.

'It's nice to see you again, officer, but I heard they caught the man who killed Shanta.'

'They caught *a* man, I don't believe it was *the* man.'

'I didn't think it mattered.'

'Not to a lot of people, no.'

'What happened to your arm?'

'I would say shot in the line of duty, but that makes it sound more glamorous than it was.' I sipped my coffee. 'A ricochet.' I shrugged.

'So let me guess – this is unofficial, you're on sick leave, no one knows you're here and you'd like it to stay that way?'

'You've been reading too much Raymond Chandler, but something like that.'

'I haven't read any Chandler.' She said it like *shandler*. If she hadn't been a prostitute, I might have asked her out on a date, but ever the detective I pressed on with the matter in hand.

'You remember how you told me about the EMS guy who spoke to Shanta at the mayor's party?'

'Yes.'

'Do you think you'd recognise him again?'

'I'm not sure, maybe.'

'I pulled Alison's photo of Harvey out of the envelope I had it in. 'Is this the man?'

She looked at it a long time and I didn't push her. 'Yes, I would say that's him.'

'Would you swear to that?'

'I suppose so, if it would make you happy.'

There were lots of things she could do that would make me very happy, but that wasn't one of them. I think she sensed me struggling with an appropriate answer.

'I'm sorry to be flippant. Yes, I would swear to it if you need me too.'

'Thank you Miss Gonzales.'

'Linda,' she said, with that soft Spanish d.

'Yes. I know it's a long time ago now, but is there anything else you can tell me about that night at the party. Anything you didn't tell me before?'

'No. I told you everything.'

'And this man, was he ever at Bouzouki?'

'I don't think so, but he could have been. You don't remember all the clients, only the ones who do something unusual, or are very regular.'

'Well thanks for your help. I'll call you if we ever need you to identify this man.'

'Do that.'

'Oh, one more thing, do you know a Rochelle Miller?'

'I don't think so. Should I?'

'She was a dancer too.'

'Was?'

'Yes. She died earlier this year.'

'I'm sorry to hear that, but the name doesn't ring any bell.'

'OK. Well, thanks for your time.'

So, I had a witness who placed Harvey at the mayor's illicit party, bad mouthing Shanta Brown. It was a start. It was finally something you could call evidence. Not much, but that first piece of the jigsaw. I bet you know where I'm going next, don't you? Yep, you got it, I went for pizza with extra jalapeños and I tried not to think about Linda Gonzales in an unprofessional way. I thought briefly about Alison and hoped she wasn't doing anything stupid. I hoped she was looking at newspaper articles and blogs and maybe even looking at some of her college textbooks and working out what made our psycho tick, as long as she wasn't actually out on the streets following him.

I thought about what I should do next. I wondered if I could actually place Michael Harvey at the party independently of Linda Gonzales, but when I'd looked into it at the time there'd been no record of any ambulances going to the mayor's residence, so that seemed unlikely. I could talk to DeAndre Little again, see if he remembered anything more about the shooter's vehicle or anything else useful, but I doubted Little could remember much beyond last week. I could go and see Dave at Bouzouki though I really doubted I'd get much there. Me and Mick had done that over pretty good. There were plenty of things I could do, but which one would lead me quickest to the jackpot? On that unsettled note, I headed to the physiotherapist.

I'll spare you the detail on the physio session. Suffice to say that my therapist was about as far from Linda Gonzales on the attractiveness scale as you could get, and the medical centre itself was no great shakes either. I do not want to dwell on the prospect of going there three times a week. Take my advice, if you can avoid getting shot, do that. And here's another piece of free advice – lay off the jalapeños if you're planning to sweat at all.

Considering how little I had actually moved my arm, it sure whacked me out. I didn't even get to dream about Linda before I fell asleep.

> Setting fire to houses to claim the insurance and kill off the mortgage is not uncommon in Detroit...But it is more common for owners to just walk away from their homes and mortgages. *The Guardian*

Steve was stuck as to who he could call about Leroy's house. Janine clearly wasn't having much luck and he couldn't think of any friends or relations who could afford to buy Leroy's house or would want to sell their own to buy it. Then suddenly he thought of Alison. It wasn't that he imagined she had a lot of money, but he thought she might be looking for a house and she might be the kind to have well-off parents she could borrow money off. He couldn't embarrass himself much more than he already had on their 'date' and she was still speaking to him, so it was worth a try.

'Hi Alison, how's it going?'

'Not bad, but I don't have anything I need photos for right now.'

'I'm not calling about that. I wanted to ask a favour actually.'

'Uh oh. No I won't go out with you, not even if it's just for show.'

'Very funny. It's not for me, it's my friend Leroy. Long story short, he needs to sell his house before the bank forecloses and he loses everything. He only owes ten thousand and I just wondered if...'

'If I had a spare ten thousand dollars?!'

'No. If you might be interested to buy it, or if you know anyone who might be looking for a house. It's in great shape, a pretty good neighbourhood. It's a steal for that kind of money.'

'So how come no one has stolen it yet?'

'He doesn't have much time. If he could afford to wait, I'm sure he'd find a buyer, but...'

'OK. Listen, I'm not interested and I don't have that kind of money, but I do know someone who might be, and I stress *might* be interested. Let me talk to her and get back to you.'

'OK, thanks Alison.'

Steve was nervous on Leroy's behalf. It would be awful if he lost everything for the sake of five thousand dollars. He found it hard to believe that Rhonda's family wouldn't help them out. Leroy's life had fallen apart so quickly and so totally. He wondered if there was something else going on between Leroy and Rhonda he didn't know about, but he couldn't believe that Leroy had done anything bad enough to make Rhonda do what she'd done. Even if the spark had gone out of their relationship, Leroy still loved his children. OK, so he couldn't provide for them financially right now, but Leroy wasn't a quitter, he'd get another job sometime. Steve felt bad the way he had done so well out of the plant closing. He was free of the daily grind, he had a house he owed no money on, no debts to speak of and he was making money doing what he loved – taking photos, but he'd never had the pleasure of a wife and children to spend all his money on. Part of him wished he could buy Leroy's house, but he couldn't do it without taking a loan and he didn't think Leroy would be able to live with Steve owning his former home. He didn't want to put a dent in Leroy's pride, it was damaged enough already.

To take his mind off things while he waited for Alison to call back, he worked on the house. It was really starting to take shape now. He'd fixed up the damaged wall and Robert had already done all the plumbing work and had found a friend who was willing to check out the wiring in exchange for Steve doing his daughter's wedding photos. All the major work was done, and Steve was onto more cosmetic work, like refinishing the wood floors. Fortunately, he felt his phone vibrate in his pocket because he wouldn't have heard it above the sound of the sander.

'Hi, it's me, Alison. A friend of mine is interested in at least looking at the house.'

'That's fantastic.'

'Don't get your hopes up, and don't get Leroy's hopes up either in case she doesn't like the place.'

'OK. Shall I give you his number so she can deal directly with him?'

'Sure.'

Steve gave Alison the details.

www.time.com Can Kemi Hendricks Grow Up?
...Much of Detroit remains an urban war zone, having seen its population more than halved from a 1950s peak of nearly 2 million.
August 2007

I finally tracked DeAndre Little down to the Ryan Correctional Facility. It took some time. He was doing three to six on a possession charge and he wasn't happy about it. Wanted to know how I could help him. I said I'd see what I could do if he talked to me about Shanta. Truth was I couldn't do a thing about his jail time, but I figured he had nothing to lose. It got him out of his cell and in my experience, guys usually liked an excuse to talk as long as it wasn't going to get them into trouble.

'How's it going DeAndre?'

'Oh you know. I'm lovin' the food, and the threads are fine.' He pulled at his standard issue blue shirt.

'Uh huh. I brought you some smokes.' I handed him two packs. That at least I could do. He fought down a smile. He liked to play the tough guy, but I didn't think he was all that. He struck me as pretty bright. 'So, I wanted to talk about Shanta, if that's OK with you.' He shrugged. 'Anyone else been to talk to you about it?'

'Nope. Nobody cares. Anyway, they arrested Fat Eric didn't they?'

I nodded. 'Do you think he did it?'

DeAndre laughed. 'Uh huh, he's too fat, he couldn't move fast enough.'

'Do you remember much about that night?'

'Not much. We were sitting outside my place, talking about where to go and then there's all this gun fire. First, I thought it was out in the street. I ducked. Wish I'd pulled Shanta down with me. I still got hit and I don't know what happened after that.'

'The shooter was in a car?'

'I thought so at the time, but you know those Explorers sit up high, so it would have had to be an SUV too.'

'Do you remember anything about the vehicle?'

'Na.'

'At the time you said it was some kind of SUV, a dark colour.'

'That's what I figured.'

'But you didn't actually see the vehicle.'

'No.'

'Could the guy have been on foot or in a building?'

'Could a been, I guess.'

'And he was on the passenger side?'

'Yeah.'

'So that's why you thought the target was Shanta and not you?'

'I dunno. But yeah, makes sense. And if a player wanted to get me, they could get me any time, you know.'

'But why would anyone want to kill Shanta?'

'Cause she was at that party at the mayor's place and he wanted to keep that quiet? I dunno.'

'So she was definitely at that party?' I wondered why DeAndre had never mentioned this at the time, but I decided not to pursue it.

'Oh yeah, I dropped her off. He was paying good money. She took the rest of the week off on the back of that.'

'And did she tell you about the party?'

'Yeah. She said the mayor's wife came home and caused a scene. Beating on some of the girls with her high heels and screaming. Then the police came and an ambulance, but she figured they were the mayor's special police, you know his security detail, 'cause they didn't take no statements or nothing, they just got everyone out of there, real quick.'

'And you really think the mayor would bother to kill a dancer just to keep the party quiet?'

'Well, it weren't his only misdemeanour, was it?' DeAndre smiled.

I smiled back. It certainly wasn't. The mayor had got himself in all sorts of trouble. 'But do you really think he did it?'

'If he did, he paid somebody. He didn't pull no trigger himself. But I don't know. I don't figure it to be honest, but he sure got the homicide case closed down. That he did do, I'm sure. But you'd know about that Officer Daniels.'

'You don't need to call me officer, I'm on my own time here.'

'Then what do you care?'

'I don't know. Let's call it unfinished business.' He shrugged again. 'OK. Let's say it wasn't the mayor or anyone he paid and it wasn't someone coming for you, got Shanta by mistake, what do you think? Did anyone else have anything against Shanta? An unhappy customer? One of the other girls she danced with?'

'Uh huh, she didn't have no unhappy customers.' DeAndre's bravado shone through. He wasn't going to speak ill of his woman. 'And the girls? Na, I don't figure it, they'd just cuss each other out or something. They had like a code or something, them against the clients, they wouldn't never kill each other over nothing.'

'Anyone who wanted to hire her but couldn't?'

'What couldn't afford her? Yeah plenty,' he laughed, 'Shanta was fine. Weren't many in her league. But that ain't no reason to shoot a woman either.'

'What about other players? Anyone want to try and take her from you?'

DeAndre thought a while. 'Na. But I remember now. After the party, Shanta said there was some guy there, an EMS, yeah a paramedic, made a pass at her. Said he kind of gave her the creeps.'

'You didn't mention that before.' DeAndre shrugged again. 'Did she say anything else about him? Did she know him? Had she seen him at the club?'

'She didn't say.'

'Black or white?'

'She didn't say, but I reckon white. A brother wouldn't have played it like that.'

'But she didn't make a big deal about it?'

'Na. She knew how to handle herself. Happened all the time, guys wanting her that couldn't have her.'

'Any other thoughts on the whole thing?'

'No. I know the case got dumped by the police and the mayor, but maybe it was just one of those things. You know, wrong place, wrong time kinda deal? I don't see why anyone would want to kill Shanta.'

'Do you know a woman called Rochelle Miller.'

'I dunno, sounds kind of familiar.'

'She's a dancer too.'

'Hmm. There was a girl used to be with Tyrone, called Rochelle, don't know if that's the one.'

'Tyrone?'

'Yeah, he's in my crew.'

'And where can I find him?'

'He's in here too.' De Andre laughed. 'You won't get much out of him though. Got knifed last night.'

Just my luck, I thought. If DeAndre did know Rochelle Miller, he didn't know she was dead, but then he would have been inside already when she was killed. It probably wasn't even worth following up, but you know me, I like to be thorough.

'OK well I appreciate your time Mr Little. Oh, just one more thing. Why did Shanta call herself Jessica Rabbit?'

DeAndre laughed. 'She just loved that stupid film. Her folks took her to see it when she was a kid, before they got divorced and she said that was the sexiest rabbit she ever saw.' He shook his head. 'If I ever got mad with her, you know, just foolin' telling her off for something, she'd do that line from the movie: "I ain't bad, I'm just drawn that way." She thought it was the funniest thing.'

'But she didn't have a rabbit's foot key ring?'

'No man, you asked me that back then. She wasn't into superstitious stuff like that. She just liked the movie, you know?'

'OK.'

'So, what are you gonna do for me man?'

'I'll talk to some people.'

'Yeah, 'cause I'm up for parole soon, you know. And I've given you some time here.'

'I appreciate that.'

Out in my car I pushed Dusty into the tape deck, so to speak, Dusty always helped me think while I was driving, and lit up a Marlboro. It didn't seem like I was any further forward. The rabbit's foot in the car was still weird, but I didn't know why. DeAndre had confirmed what Linda had said about the EMS guy at the mayor's mansion, but that didn't really help me, he hadn't seen the guy and even if he had, he wasn't a reliable witness. He might know a Rochelle, but he didn't know if it was Rochelle Miller and the guy who would know was fighting for his life. Still, I made a note to look at the Miller case file and see if there was anything that linked her to Shanta other than the newspaper at the scene. That wasn't really any reason why there would be a link, just because one was an exotic dancer and the other a prostitute, but any link, however remote might take me a bit closer to nailing this guy Harvey. I had a feeling. I wasn't doubting anymore. Harvey had killed Shanta and Harvey was the newspaper killer. I just had to find a way to prove it.

'The only one who could ever reach me was the son of a preacher man.'

'Sing it Dusty, sing it.'

...occasionally scrappers boldly dismantled awnings and carried pipes down streets in broad daylight...
Driving Detroit, Free Press

Steve and Leroy were in a deserted house on Suffolk Drive in Palmer Woods. They'd already stripped a load of piping out and were going back for other saleable items like the doorknobs. The rich folks liked new houses that looked old. They were just crazy for antique fittings.

'People really buy this stuff?' Leroy asked.

'They sure do.'

'Don't you feel bad about it?'

'Well yeah in a way. But if I don't do it someone else will, or the house will just rot or get burned.'

'I feel like Bubbles out of the Wire. Remember when they were stealing pipes and shit?'

'Yep. Life imitating art imitating life.'

Leroy laughed. 'Don't get all high brow with me man. How much do you reckon we'll get for this stuff.'

'One-fifty, couple o' hundred maybe.'

'Is that all?'

'Hey how much do you want for an hour's work? And hopefully I won't need to do this much more because I'm selling more photos now. I can get two hundred dollars or more if Alison needs something specific for the paper.'

'That's sweet man. You sure have it made. The closing of GM has been the making of you!'

'Yeah, it has. Best thing that ever happened to me. I don't have much cash these days, but I'm doing what I want and getting by. You gotta make it work for you too Leroy. I know Rhonda left and you couldn't have predicted that. But when you get money from your house sale, you should seriously think about buying one of these cheap houses and doing it up. I really think you could make some money.'

'Well, I haven't sold it yet. But it's looking promising. This young lady came to look at it on Saturday and she's coming back tomorrow. I really appreciate you saying I can stay at your place if I need to move out in a hurry.'

'Shit. You'd do the same for me. It won't be for long. You're gonna be back on your feet in no time. Well, either way it won't be for long 'cause you're kind of a slob Leroy. No wonder Rhonda left you!'

Leroy punched him on the arm. 'Don't worry, I wouldn't be able to stand your humour for too long! I may buy one of those cheap houses just so I don't have to listen to you bitchin' about it anymore.'

They went out back and loaded more stuff onto Leroy's truck.

'You know, I only do this for cash for the things I can't trade,' said Steve. 'I've done this deal with a lady down the street. She keeps chickens. She gives me half a dozen eggs in exchange for the beans I'm growing.'

'Come on, you ain't got beans growing already!'

'Well OK, I have the eggs on account for the beans I'm going to grow,' Steve said.

'What about meat? What do you trade for that?'

'I'm thinking of going vegetarian.'

'Now that I don't believe!'

'OK, maybe not totally, but I could cut down to having meat just a couple of times a week. It wouldn't kill me.' Steve stepped over a hole in the floorboards. 'See that piping over there, near the sink? That's good stuff. Load that up in the truck.'

'Yes boss, right away boss.' Leroy shuffled and touched his hand to an imaginary cap.

Steve laughed. 'I'm going to check upstairs.'

Leroy hauled the pipes out and laid them in truck bed. Back inside he found Steve crouching down taking photos. 'What the hell are you doing? Are we stealing or are you working on your latest art project?'

'We're not stealing, we're recycling. Think of it as a community service.'

'Right, how is completely stripping out this house providing a service?'

Steve stroked his chin. 'Well it's preventing the addicts using it. Even junkies need water.' Leroy rolled his eyes. 'OK, at least it isn't hurting anyone. The owner is long gone. Plus, I can probably sell these photos to the *Free Press*. I sold them a few last week. They're always doing features on the state of the city, the re-birth of nature and all that. Check this out, there's flowers growing through the floorboards.'

'Beautiful. Can we just get out of here? This is making me nervous.'

'OK. But I think you'll come round to my way of thinking when we cash this lot in.'

Leroy and Steve stood outside the recycle centre where Steve had pocketed a sizeable wad of bills.

'We're going to split that money, aren't we?'

'Sure, but let's count it somewhere else. We'll probably get mugged counting money round here.'

'You have no faith in your fellow Detroiters, Steve.' Leroy laughed.

Back at Steve's place he handed over half the money to Leroy. Later as he sat counting the ninety dollars that had been his share of the scrap haul, Leroy didn't think it seemed right somehow, making money this way. He still thought of it as stealing, but maybe Steve had a point. If they didn't do it, then some doped up bum would and shoot the proceeds straight up his arm, and what else was he going to do? He'd turned down the opportunity to be a drug dealer. This may be illegal, but it was morally better than that.

Huffington Post, **Detroit Mayor Sent to Jail**
Mayor Kemi Hendricks was jailed Thursday for a bond violation in his perjury case, his pleas for leniency rejected by a judge who made it clear the mayor would get no special treatment...
September 2007

It was a while before I heard from Alison again. She was busy doing her thing (newspaper stuff) and no doubt busy with her love life, but I didn't ask about that, and I was busy hating my physiotherapist, popping pills, trying unsuccessfully to quit smoking and lose some weight on the advice of some dumbass doctor half my age who doesn't know a butt cheek from a haemorrhoid, but don't get me started.

Anyways, Alison called, chirpy as ever. Sometimes it made me feel old hanging around with the Energiser bunny. I thought being with young people was supposed to make you feel younger?

'Hi Danny. Have you forgiven me?'

'That depends. Have you done anything else stupid?'

'No. I did what you said, boring meticulous police work. I've looked at so many newspaper articles and blogs my eyes have gone funny.'

'That's good. What have you got?'

'Michael Harvey spouting off about cuts to the EMS.'

'What?'

'OK, so it's only a very short mention, but he was interviewed by Tom for his article about ambulance response times.'

'Nice. Anything helpful in it?'

'I'm not sure. How about I buy you lunch and tell you all about it?'

'That's the best offer I've had all month. Where are you taking me?'

'Erm…'

'Wait, I've got physio today, better make it near there. How about Louie's Ham in the Eastern Market? Do you know it?'

'Sure. See you there in thirty?'

Alison was already sitting in a booth looking smug when I got there. I slid in the other side and we ordered. I took the Reuben. I figured sauerkraut counted as healthy. Alison is still too young to care so she ordered the Big Breakfast with hash browns on the side. I must say I admire the way she can put it away and not put on the pounds.

'How's it going with the therapy?' she asked.

'You make it sound like I'm seeing a shrink.'

'Are you?'

'No. I am not. The therapy sucks, but as you can see, I've lost the sling and there's a little more movement.'

'That's good.'

'I don't know how much more of that loud, lardy therapist I can take though.'

'You're not a quitter.'

'You're damn right. I am not. That doctor just out of diapers over there wants me to quit smoking and lose weight.'

'He may have a point.'

'Don't you start.'

'How about you agree to stop smoking if we catch this guy?'

'When we catch him.'

'OK, when we catch him.'

'I'll think about it. What's this big scoop you're all excited about?'

Alison handed me a copy of the *Free Press* from July. The headline read: "Detroit paramedics fear they're losing the battle to save lives." Apparently, the average ambulance response time in Detroit is about thirty minutes, if you're lucky and an ambulance actually comes at all. "Paramedic Michael Harvey, member of the Detroit EMS union, said 'we're taking the flack for substandard equipment and staffing cuts. Since a city audit in 2004, at least two hospitals have closed and we've been decimated by staffing cuts. We have to drive further and further.'"

'Says here the average response time in Dearborn is four minutes. If things are so bad, how come Harvey doesn't get a job with the Dearborn EMS?'

'Who knows?' says Alison, mopping up egg yolk with her toast. 'The point is, Tom talked to this guy. Harvey obviously feels strongly enough to be interviewed and he's clearly not in hiding. If he is the killer, he thinks he can't be caught, he's not afraid to do his job, go about his daily business and be interviewed by the press, and he says stuff that won't win him any friends in the Fire Department.'

'OK, so Harvey exists, he is a paramedic and he's not afraid to speak his mind, but how does that help us?'

Alison tossed back curls while she put bacon in her mouth. I concentrated on my sandwich. 'I thought maybe I could approach him about a follow up article, something in depth about how paramedics on the ground feel about it. See if I can't interview him at his house and snoop around a bit.'

'I believe we spoke about that kind of thing.'

'Oh, come on Danny, don't be such a stick in the mud. It's a great idea, isn't it?'

I had to admit she had a point. Since he'd already spoken to a reporter, he might be up for it and maybe we would learn something. 'There may be something in it. But let's think this through. He probably won't want to do it at his place and I don't like the idea of you alone with him there anyway. Go for somewhere public, then I can be sitting close by and maybe I can get a feel for this guy too.'

'OK.'

'See what you can set up. Thanks for lunch. I gotta run.'

'But you haven't even told me what you've been up to? Have you got any leads?'

'Not much to be honest. We'll catch up soon. Call me if the fish bites.'

...

Meanwhile I'd been reading the notes on our interviews at Bouzouki in preparation for going and having another word with Dave the club manager. All the dancers had said there had been no trouble at the club, no dodgy clients, or disgruntled customers, no one following them or anything and they all seemed happy with the way Dave ran things.

Mick had done the follow-up at Bouzouki while I'd been interviewing Linda Gonzales. One guy had been barred, Mr J. Johnson and according to Mick he'd just had a bit too much to drink. He was happily married and had moved out of state in February, in other words before Shanta even got killed. I didn't think there was any point in asking Mick if he remembered the guy – he wouldn't. Mick couldn't remember the details of any case open longer than a week. And I didn't feel like calling him to check if he remembered anything. Nearly three months I've been off work and not a call or a visit from that jerk, just that lame get well card saying he'd closed the Jordan case. At the time I remembered just taking Mick's word for it that he had properly checked this guy out. Normally not double-checking anything Mick did was a mistake, but there's only so many hours in the day without doing double work, and I didn't think we were looking for a client at Bouzouki. But now, as I looked at that name, Mr Johnson, pretty much the most popular white surname after Smith, I had to wonder if that really was his name or if the guy had been lying. Anyways, something to think about when I spoke to Dave.

I'd agreed to go to Bouzouki in the afternoon since I didn't need to see any of the dancers this time and I haven't gone to bed later than ten o'clock since I got out of the hospital. It's just as well I've decided to turn in my papers, I don't think I could handle the night shift any more, that gunshot has made me into a real lightweight, if I don't get my nine hours a night, I'm useless.

I flashed my badge at the door and asked for Dave. It seems I was expected and I was taken straight through to his office in the back. The club was pretty dead, though three ladies were still dancing to very loud music.

'How you doing officer?' said Dave. He didn't seem annoyed to be talking to me again.

'Thanks for seeing me.'

'No problem, but I thought this thing was all cleared up long ago.'

'Yes and no. I just want to check a couple of things. You said at the time that there weren't any problems with guys bothering Shanta Brown.'

'That's right.'

'Then my partner came back and got information on a guy who'd been barred for touching the dancers.'

'Yeah, there was a guy barred, that's just our policy to avoid trouble. He'd just got a little too amorous you know, too much to drink, it wasn't anything heavy.'

'OK. And the guy's name was Johnson?'

'If you say so. I'd have to look at the list.'

'Could you do that?'

'Sure.'

Dave opened a filing cabinet behind him and started looking through it, so I asked him how long people got barred for.

'Six months,' he said. 'We operate a three strikes and you're out scheme. If you get barred three times, then you get banned for life. Ah, here we go.'

He sat back at his desk with couple of sheets of paper stapled together. 'So, this Johnson character, was this his first offence?' I asked.

'Yep, looks like it. Jack Johnson. He showed a Michigan driver's licence as ID. We make a note of the ID number, that's what I gave your partner.'

'You're saying every Johnson who comes in the place you're going to check to see if he's barred?'

Dave smiled. 'In theory; in practice, the guys on the door usually remember anyone who's caused trouble and that's when they'd check the list, or they'd just not let the guy come in. Entry is at the discretion of the management you know.'

'Could I have that driver's licence number, just to double check?'

'Sure.' He turned the list to face me so I could copy the number down.

'Wait a minute. There's a Michael Harvey on this list.'

'So?'

'Do you remember what he got barred for?'

'I'm no good with names. One of the bouncers might know.'

I pulled out the photo of Harvey I'd taken to keeping in my coat pocket. 'This guy?' I showed it to Dave.

'Uh huh. That guy was a pain in the ass for a while. Used to come in with some other guys, they'd drink a lot and get loud, mostly harmless enough, but he started bad mouthing the girls, calling them whores, that kind of thing. We don't tolerate that. This is a clean establishment, our dancers are professional.'

'Was this before or after Shanta got killed? There are no dates on this list.'

'I don't know, to be honest. I'd have to say it was around the same time.'

'You don't know? How do you know when their six-month ban is up if you don't have the date they were banned?'

'That'll be on the computer,' Dave said apathetically, and started tapping some keys.

I couldn't believe that they had such a disorganised system, but then I figured the door men probably knew the troublemakers, they wouldn't need to come and check on the computer or filing system and most guys if they were banned from a club they'd be embarrassed, they wouldn't want to get shown up in front of their friends by showing up again too soon.

'Here we go, December 2004.'

'And are there any details of the incident?'

'Nope, just his name, ID details and date he got banned.'

'Would Shanta have been working the night he got banned?'

'Probably, but we only keep the shift details for about a year. But she usually worked the last shift and he always came in late. I guess when he got off work.'

'What do you mean, when he got off work? Do you know what he does?'

'No, but those guys they never came in before midnight. I figured they were police or Fire Department, just got off a four to twelve. They just had that vibe about them. You can tell. You know what I mean, officer?'

'You mean you can always spot a cop even when they're off duty?'

'Something like that.'

'So, you don't know if he had something against Shanta in particular or he just bad mouthed the dancers in general.'

'I don't know. I'd say in general. He didn't seem like a nice guy.'

'Are there any door men still here who might remember him?'

'The guy on the door right now, Bobby, he's been here since '89, and I've never known him forget a face.'

I stood up and reached across to shake his hand. 'Thanks a lot man.'

'Always happy to help. We don't want any trouble here.'

I couldn't believe it. Harvey had been right there on this banned list and we'd missed it. But we hadn't known anything about Harvey then. We didn't know to look for him. Maybe if I'd got further with looking into EMS guys at the mayor's party, we would have found him. Still, I kicked myself for letting Mick do the follow-up at the club. Maybe if I'd asked about clients who'd been barred, I'd have looked into Harvey. In fact, Johnson had also been banned in December 2004, before Christmas Mick's notes said, so why hadn't he picked up on Harvey as well? I could kick Mick sometimes.

As I walked back to the door, I hoped my luck held with Bobby.

The doorman was a large black man. I would not have wanted any argument with him. He moved to open the door for me.

'Can I ask you a couple of questions?'

He nodded.

'Are you Bobby?'

'Yep.'

I showed him the photo. 'Do you remember this guy?'

'Yep.'

I prayed that at some point he would say more than one word. 'Do you remember what he got barred for?'

'Talking ugly about the ladies.'

'OK. When was this?'

'A few years ago.'

'Has he been here since?'

'No, not since I had words with him.'

I found it hard to imagine Bobby having words with anyone. 'What do you mean?'

He sighed, like it was completely obvious what he meant. 'After he got thrown out, he came back after about a week and wanted to come in. I told him he was banned. He started causing a scene and I put my hand on his chest,' he put his hand on my chest to demonstrate, 'and I told him not to come back. He called me a filthy nigger and told me to get my hands off him, but I didn't and he left.'

'And he hasn't been back?'

'No.'

'Thank you very much Bobby.' He didn't reply.

Back in my car, I just sat for a while. I lit a cigarette and I smoked it slowly. Would it have made any difference if I'd gone back to the club instead of Mick? Would I have found Michael Harvey and if I'd checked him out would it have led to an arrest? I'd never know the answer to that one. But how could Mick get one guy who was banned in December 2004 and not another? That seemed stupid even for Mick.

And if Harvey had been banned in December and then been ugly to Shanta at the mayor's party in January, why had he waited until April to kill her? It would have been easy enough, wouldn't it, to hang around outside the club at closing time and follow Shanta? Even if she never left alone, if she left with other dancers or was met by DeAndre, there would have to have been easier times to kill her than while she was sitting with him in his car. It wasn't planned. That was the only way I could figure it. He just happened to see her sitting there, and he was mad, mad that he'd been thrown out of the club, mad that Bobby had upbraided him, mad that she refused his advances at the mayor's mansion. But four months was a long time to hold that kind of anger. And that theory also meant he was walking around always carrying a gun, and that he happened to have the rabbit's foot with him to leave in the car.

But if he planned it, why wait so long? And why make it look like a simple drug related drive-by and then spoil it by leaving the rabbit's foot? Was he smart enough to wait that long, because if it was too soon after he got thrown out of Bouzouki he might have been questioned as a suspect? Could a psycho hold his rage that long? I'd have to ask Alison or talk to some psychologist. Maybe he couldn't. Maybe he'd killed some other women while he was waiting for the perfect moment to get Jessica Rabbit.

'We have to reach high. Maybe get knocked on our ass. And then get up and reach again.'
Coleman A. Young

Leroy virtually bounced his way over to Steve's house. He couldn't wait to tell him the good news. Steve was out in the yard planting something.

'How's it going farmer Jones?'

'Pretty good. I've got beans there, potatoes here, and tomatoes on the porch.'

'I never thought I'd see you gardening.'

'Me neither, but it's not gardening, it's food production. Any news on the house yet?'

'Yeah, I'm afraid I've got bad news.' Leroy tried to put on a serious face, but his heart wasn't really in it. 'Your friend Janine is going to be mad at me.'

'Why?'

'You know that lady who was coming to look at the house, Carol?'

'Yeah.'

'Well, we did a deal, I sold to her privately, so Janine won't be getting any commission.'

'That's OK, Janine makes enough money. Anyway, I already erased her from my little black book, she's not as friendly as she used to be.'

'I still appreciate you trying.'

'That's fantastic, I'm so glad you sold it. So, what now?'

'She beat me down to eight thousand, but that still leaves me a bit to play with. As soon as we sort out the paperwork and transfer funds, I'll pay off the bank. She's keen to move in, but she has to give notice on the place she's renting so there's no great rush.'

'That's great. Well, you know you can always stay with me if you want to.'

'That would be great. I'm getting kind of tired of being alone to be honest and now that I'm clearing out the house it doesn't feel like home anymore. It would be good if I could start moving the tools and gardening stuff over here.'

'Fine with me. I could use some gardening stuff.'

'Just as long as you don't expect me to do any digging!'

'OK. Listen, we should go and celebrate.'

'Yeah, I guess.'

'You don't sound too enthusiastic.'

'I know it had to be done and I got out of the bind with the bank, but losing my home of twenty years doesn't seem like much cause for a celebration.'

'That's true, but you've got to think of it as a new start, what's done is done, you've got to move on.'

'I guess.'

'When are you getting a new place. There's some just up the street.'

'Don't rush me man, I've barely moved out of this one yet. I've got to let the dust settle. No house is going to be like that one.'

'Have you heard any more from Rhonda?'

'No, just from her lawyer. She wants to file for divorce.'

'Well, you knew that would happen. What about the kids?'

'There wasn't much detail, but she's proposing they get to spend the holidays with me and the rest of the time with her.'

'That's something.'

'Yeah, but I wish she hadn't moved so far away. I'd rather see them every week. I miss them. They'll forget who I am.'

'They'll never forget who you are. Come on, let's take the truck and collect some of your stuff and then I'm taking you for a beer before you get too maudlin. You should be happy man.'

Huffington Post,
Remember Kemi Hendricks, the Detroit mayor who faces perjury, misconduct, and obstruction of justice charges? The hip-hop politico who just days ago tried to sell our half of the Detroit-Windsor Tunnel to Canada?... Good news comedy lovers: Mayor Hendricks wants to hang out with Barack and Michelle Obama at the Democratic National Convention...

September 2007

'The eagle has landed.'

'Excuse me?'

'I have an interview scheduled for two o'clock tomorrow,' said Alison.

'OK, that's cool. Where and when?'

'The Gateway Deli Café, West Fort Street. Do you know it?'

'No, I've never eaten there, but the Detroit Fire Department is less than a block away.'

'So maybe he's going to work after? It's real close to the *Free Press* building too.'

'Probably. I'll get there before you, so I can just be sitting there looking inconspicuous. Try and sit near me if you can.'

'OK, roger over and out.'

'Wait, Alison. Is this a real assignment? Is this actually going to be in the paper?'

'I don't know. I hadn't really planned for it to be.'

'Our guy might get pissed off if it's not.'

'That might not be a bad thing. He might make some kind of mistake if he starts getting nervous.'

She had a point, but I didn't like the idea of Alison putting herself in any kind of danger. 'OK, well just make it sound real, don't ask too many questions that don't relate to the topic.'

I was going to have to reschedule my physiotherapy to make this date. I wasn't that upset about it. I sat and thought about Michael Harvey. We didn't know much about the man. He was a paramedic. He lived in Dearborn, but worked in Detroit. He lived in his mother's house. He liked to go to strip clubs and had been annoyed that he'd been barred from Bouzouki. He badmouthed exotic dancers when he got drunk *and* when he was sober since according to Linda he was the paramedic who had called Shanta a bitch at the mayor's party. We had only circumstantial evidence linking him to Shanta's murder and nothing so far linking him to the newspaper murders, except that the Magic Bullet blog was written on a computer at his address and the blogger called himself the lone gunman, which was a very tenuous link to the Lee Harvey Oswald anagrams doodled on the newspapers found at the scene. Maybe this whole thing was a waste of time. Maybe Michael Harvey was just a slightly lonely guy who liked to vent via a little-read blog and go to topless bars. Maybe Mick had caught June-Bey Jordan's murderer and the neatly folded *Free Press* left on his chest had nothing to do with it. I laughed. It was farcical to think that Mick could catch a killer on his own.

He couldn't even follow up on men banned from Bouzouki. Anyways, I increasingly liked Harvey for the Shanta Brown murder and that would do for now.

Next day I sat in the Gateway Deli Café nursing a cup of coffee and pretending to read the paper. I didn't like the look of the food, but I couldn't eat anyway. I had a strange nervousness in my stomach about how this would all turn out and if Alison would be OK. I needn't have worried. Alison, it turned out, could hold her own with a variety of slime-balls and weirdos.

They came in a little after two. They must have met outside either by design or coincidence. Harvey held the door open for her in a gentlemanly manner and she steered them to a table close but not too close to where I was sitting. Harvey was facing me, so I had a good eyeball on his expressions. He was wearing his uniform and looked like his photo. He was very neat and tidy, his shoes shiny and not a hair on his closely shaved head out of place. They ordered soft drinks and Alison flipped open her notebook.

'Thanks for agreeing to meet me, Mr Harvey.'

'Call me Michael. No problem. I love talking about the state of the emergency services in Detroit.'

'Don't you worry about your job with all the cuts?' laughed Alison.

'No, people will always need paramedics, I'd just move somewhere else.'

'You don't like it in Detroit?'

'Oh sure, I love Detroit,' said Harvey sarcastically. I willed Alison to move on to something else, and she did.

'So, we're looking for some personal stories about being a paramedic in the city. You know, your side of things, to show it's not the fault of the EMS staff, it's the system and the city, that kind of thing.'

'Sure. Of course, it's the city. There have been so many cuts, we're driving all over the place. It took us forty minutes the other night to get to this old lady. She was dead anyway, but maybe she would have made it if we'd got there sooner.'

Harvey droned on and Alison nodded. He had a monotone, expressionless way of speaking and didn't really seem that passionate about anything, although I could see him clenching and unclenching his fist around the paper napkin that had come with his coffee. I watched him without appearing to watch him. He kept his eyes on Alison. I know I'd told her to make the interview sound credible, but I was starting to think this wasn't going to get us anywhere.

Alison finally started steering the conversation more towards corruption by city officials.

'Yeah, they're all corrupt,' he said, 'I'm glad to see the mayor is finally getting what's coming to him.'

'You mean the whistleblower trial?'

'Yeah, son of a bitch has been screwing us ever since he got elected.' Alison scribbled in her notebook. 'Don't quote me on that,' he added. He sounded just like the Magic Bullet. 'I was at the party, you know.'

'Excuse me?'

'The alleged party at the mayor's place, January 2005. I was there.'

'Really?'

'I can give you whatever you need on that.'

'That's good to know. Some of my colleagues are working on the mayor story but I'll pass that on. I'm sure they'll want to talk to you about that.'

'I'd rather talk to you. And I'd have to be an anonymous source on that.'

'Of course,' said Alison leaning forward. 'So, was it as bad as the rumours?'

'Worse. Alcohol, drugs, half-naked women.'

'And the mayor's wife?'

'She really went off on one. That's why we got called. Some of the dancers got injured.' I looked at Harvey then. You could tell by his eyes that he thought those kind of dancers were little better than hookers. 'It isn't right,' Harvey said, 'spending taxpayer's money like that. My hard-earned money, while my colleagues are getting laid off, and we have to drive around in sub-standard equipment, and the city goes to shit. Some of the streets don't even have signs anymore. How are we supposed to find our way to a call-out? We can't know every street in the city.'

'No, you can't, and I'll be making that point in the article.'

'Good. Can I see it before it goes to press?'

'That's not usual.'

'Can you at least let me know when it's coming out?'

'I can try. Do you have an email address?'

Good girl, Alison, I thought, but I thought he'd fob her off, that he'd say he'd call her or something, but no, he leans in and says, 'lone gunman at hotmail dot com.'

'Lone gunman, that's unusual.'

'Harvey's a common name. I got tired of trying to find a name and number combination that hadn't been taken already.'

'I hear you,' said Alison. 'So, you think it was a lone gunman?'

Too subtle I thought, but Harvey jumped right in.

'Are you kidding me? Oswald was set up, everyone knows that.'

Alison did not disabuse him of his belief. She stayed at the table while he got up and left. I left a couple of minutes later. I wanted to make sure he was going to the firehouse. I followed him on the other side of the street until I saw him enter the Fire Department building, then I called Alison and we agreed to meet at the Lafayette Coney Island two blocks away.

Alison was already there. I straight off ordered a coney island and chilli fries. My appetite had come back.

'So,' said Alison, 'what do you think?'

'Slimey.'

'Yep. He sure has a hard-on for the mayor, doesn't he?'

'I'm not sure that's the phrase I'd use, but I know what you mean. He nicely placed himself at the party too. Were you taping that?'

Alison held out a device not much bigger than a pack of gum. 'Digital recorder. I got it all.'

'Good. Don't lose it.

'Listen, I was thinking...'

'Uh oh.'

'He's going to be at work until midnight now, right.'

'Right. Don't say it, but I'm thinking the same thing.'

'You are?'

'Yeah. But let's wait until after dark. I'll pick you up at the *Free Press* around 9 p.m., OK?'

'OK.'

'And don't bring your girlfriend and don't tell her about it.'

'As if I would!'

Right, I thought. I bet she calls her within ten minutes. I bet the girlfriend really gets off on this crime solving stuff. I tried to steer away from that thought.

I picked Alison up as arranged and we drove out to Dearborn. On the way over, I explained the rules. I could touch, she couldn't. No lights turned on. Flashlights always pointed downwards. It was quiet on Harvey's Street. We parked a few houses away and walked around to the back of his house. It was easy to jimmy the lock and gain entry into the kitchen that was at the back. I moved on down the hall.

'Don't you want to look here?' asked Alison.

'We can check it at the end maybe. Kitchens don't usually have anything very interesting unless you're looking for a drugs lab. Here,' I handed her some gloves, 'you'd better use these.'

'You said I wasn't to touch anything.'

'I know, but just in case. Harvey must not know that anyone has been here.'

First door I came to was closed. I opened it and strobed it with the flashlight. It had obviously been Harvey's mother's room and it looked like she could have died yesterday. A single bed covered with a handmade quilt. The bedside chest was covered with some old-timey crocheted cloth and held a Bible, a lamp and a black and white wedding photo. I assumed it was ma and pa Harvey. Michael took after his father in looks. I opened the wardrobe. It was full of old lady's clothes and shoes. I didn't waste too much time there, but unless Mrs Harvey had died very recently, it was strange that he'd keep the room exactly as it had been. It was spotlessly clean too.

We moved down the hall into the living room. Heavy drapes were fully drawn. I warmed to Harvey – so much easier to snoop undetected if your snoopee had thick curtains that he closed before he went to work. There was the usual, a TV, an old stereo, a very nice and expensive looking leather chair, a slightly dated sofa, mum's choice I figured. There was a bookcase in the corner. Alison went straight to that and started scanning book spines.

'Man, check this out,' said Alison. I walked over. 'They're nearly all about Oswald and JFK, conspiracy stuff. There's not a single novel here. What are those? Comics?'

She made to pull out a magazine. 'Wait. Let me do it.' I pulled it out. *Red Diaries*, four issues from 1997, *The Big Book of Conspiracies*, 1995, *WEIRD*, started in 1997 and he had every issue through 1999. I flicked through it. Issue one was all JFK stuff: 'We Blow the Lid off the JFK Cover-up', 'Lee Harvey Oswald: How Many of Him Were There?'

'Hang on. This looks like the way the doodles are done.'

'What?' said Alison.

'You know, the doodled anagrams. It looks like this font.'

'OK. Do you want me to take a photo?'

'Sure.'

She pulled out a small digital camera from her pocket and took a few close-ups of the typeface. 'There's a comic shop pretty close to here, on Michigan Avenue.'

'Green Brain Comics? Yeah, I noticed that,' I said.

'What do you think the chances are that Michael is a regular customer?'

'Probably pretty good, though he might order stuff over the internet.'

'Yeah, but I bet he likes to browse too,' said Alison. 'Do you want me to go in there and see what I can find out?'

'I'd better do it. I can pull the badge and ask them more specifically about Harvey.'

I slid the comic carefully back onto the shelf. Harvey struck me as the kind of guy who would immediately notice if anything was out of place. Maybe even had a hair glued with spit across his bedroom doorjamb like we did when we were kids. Speaking of bedrooms.

'No computer yet. Let's check for his bedroom.'

Stairs led up from the living room, so we took them. They led up to a big bedroom with a bathroom off it. The walls were very dark navy blue, depressing. There was a large bed – made up and with clean looking bed clothes. Under the window, again with heavy curtains, was a desk with a laptop. It was set up like he never moved it, with a proper keyboard connected. On the wall opposite the bed was a pin board. I swept the light over it. There were newspaper articles. Some were about JFK and conspiracy stuff, but others were about murders in the city or death notices. The article about Shanta Brown that he'd quoted on Magic Bullet was there, along with a tiny piece on the death of Rochelle Miller and death notices for Delaware Loomis and June-Bey Jordan, and at least six other people.

'Check this out,' I said to Alison, 'he's got articles or death notices on all the newspaper victims and some others.'

'Wow.' She snapped several pictures.

By the side of the desk were a stack of *Free Press* papers going back two years. 'He's a fan of the *Freep*!'

'Sure is.'

'The preferred reading matter of all intelligent killers, apparently,' Alison quipped. 'Should we look on the computer?' she asked.

'I don't know. It would be better if we could get it under a warrant. Nothing we find now is admissible because this is an illegal search. I don't want to push our luck. Let's call it a night.'

'Are you sure? It doesn't feel like we have that much.'

'We've got the comics, maybe with a match to the anagram doodles, we've got the death notices of all the people killed, that should be enough to get a warrant and do this properly.'

'OK, if you say so.'

I wondered about breaking the glass in the back door to make it look like a break in, but I was pretty sure I'd put everything I'd touched back the way it was and I didn't want to risk attracting any attention by making noise. I pulled the back door shut, heard the lock click and checked it was locked. The old skills hadn't failed me.

Back at the car, I pulled away and headed back to the city. I didn't want to be in his street any longer than necessary.

'What next?' says Alison.

'Well, I can check out the comic shop, see where that takes us. And I guess I'd better go and see my captain about getting a warrant on Harvey's place.'

Alison nodded.

'Shame we didn't find a gun,' I said, thinking out loud, but then that would have been too easy.

'Yeah. All the murders were by gunshot, weren't they?'

'Yes. A Glock .40, which is what most police use, but it's a really common gun in Detroit too, not hard to get hold of one.'

'It seems a strange choice of weapon,' Alison said.

'How so?'

'Well if this is some kind of personal crusade. I don't know it seems too impersonal. You'd think he'd stab them or something.'

I laughed. 'You've been watching too many movies, Alison. In my experience practicalities have a lot to do with the choice of weapon. A gun is easy. In a lot of places the sound of gun fire is not unusual. You don't need to be too close to your victim so you're less likely to get any incriminating blood or anything on you. Less cleanup, and as long as the gun isn't found it doesn't leave much evidence. All round it's a smart choice.'

'Hmm. I guess you have a point. But it doesn't feel right somehow. Does Harvey have a licence for a gun?'

'No. I already checked, but we both know that doesn't mean he hasn't got one.'

Alison's amateur psychology amused me, but I didn't criticize her for it, many a good thought came out of just such ponderings. 'That reminds me, you know I told you about Bouzouki and how Harvey had been banned?'

'Yeah.'

'That was in late 2004 and then he talked ugly to Shanta at the mayor's party in January 2005, but she wasn't killed until April. So, if it was Harvey who murdered her, why did he wait that long? I can see how he'd be angry about being embarrassed and snubbed, but like you just said, it doesn't feel right that he'd wait four months to get payback.'

'Maybe he didn't have an opportunity before.'

'Yeah, but he could have followed her. He knew where she worked, it would have been easy.'

'Maybe he got sick or something. Or he tried to get over it and then one day he happened to see her and it brought it all back and he got angry and shot her.'

'Could be, but that would mean he had that rabbit's foot already with him just in case he killed her. The rabbit's foot only relates to Jessica Rabbit. It's no good as a message on any other body.'

'Where did you find it?' she said.

'Passenger side, almost under the seat.'

'On the floor?'

'Yeah, on the floor.'

'It could have just been there Danny. Can you be sure the killer put it there?'

'I guess not, but the boyfriend was sure it wasn't Shanta's and it wasn't his.'

'But we can't rule Harvey out just 'cause of this rabbit's foot thing.'

'No, absolutely not.'

'So maybe lay off the rabbit thing for awhile?'

I smiled. 'OK.'

'See,' she said, 'we need to know why he does it. If it's some kind of campaign to clean up Detroit, then Shanta Brown doesn't fit. She was just someone he got angry with.'

'Maybe she was the first and he saw how easy it was and that he got away with it. No one suspected him. We didn't even interview him when we talked to people banned from Bouzouki, my partner somehow missed him. He thought he'd got away with it, so why not do it again if it was so easy?'

'Yeah, and he started leaving papers on the bodies as some kind of calling card because the police are clearly not as smart as him. He wants people to know there is one person killing all these people, but he can't be caught.'

'That's a depressing thought to go to sleep on.'

'But we're going to catch him!'

I wanted to believe her, I really did. I pulled up at the *Free Press* Building. 'Are you going to be all right getting home?'

'Yes officer. I'm a big girl now. Anyway, who says I'm going home?'

'Just be careful. And email me those photos you took tonight.'

She leant towards the car and blew me a kiss. 'I love it when you get all paternal!'

The youth of today, what can I tell you, they're shameless.

Kemi Hendricks, Disgraced Ex-Mayor of Detroit, Living Life of Luxury,

If ever a public figure should be down for the count, it is Kemi Hendricks.

Stripped of his job as Detroit's mayor, locked in jail for 99 days and saddled with a felony record, he is legally prohibited from seeking the only occupation he ever wanted – elected leader.

Huffington Post

'Hey, did you read this thing in the *Washington Times* about Hendricks?' said Steve.

'No. We don't get the *Washington Times*.'

'Oh it's we now is it, we're not married you know Leroy.'

'Thank God. Once was enough!'

'It's online.'

'And how would I have read it, I don't have a computer.'

Steve hadn't thought of that. 'It says, "the latest tawdry scandal involves the city's youthful and charismatic former mayor, Kemi Hendricks," bla bla. Now he's approved a multimillion-dollar settlement for those police officers who claim they were fired because they looked too closely into that party the major had.'

'Alleged party.'

'Oh get real, we all know it happened. On the hush hush and not very QT.'

Leroy groaned. 'You been reading Ellroy again?'

'Maybe.'

'Well don't, it makes you all paranoid and shit.'

'It makes me think about plans man, capers we could pull.'

'Capers? How old are we?'

'You know what I mean. I've got journalistic connections. You've got drug connections. There's a lot of corruption out there just waiting to be tapped into. Seems like you and me, two reasonably intelligent types have got be able to come up with a money-making scheme.'

'I do not have drug connections. Just because I'm black, don't be saying I'm into drugs.'

'Your nephew.'

Leroy was quiet. His nephew was a drug dealer and he knew it. 'I don't have anything to do with him,' said Leroy. 'Anyway, why do we need a money-making scheme? You've got your rent-free house and your *Free Press* photography thing and I've got a bit of cash from my house.'

'That won't last long.'

'Are you saying I'm irresponsible with money?'

'No, I'm just saying if you buy another house and you haven't got any other income, it won't last that long.'

'Hmm. So we're going to blackmail the ex-mayor?' said Leroy.

'I dunno, I haven't thought it through yet.'

'You mean like extortion and bribery and stuff?'

'I had something more subtle in mind.'

'Oh, more subtle. That's OK then, 'cause I can't be getting behind anything illegal, you feel me?'

'Really? This scrap metal removal isn't exactly legal, you know,' said Steve.

'I know. I've been telling you that. You got me into this. I didn't want to do it.'

'And what would you be living on now if I hadn't cut you in?'

Leroy tried to ignore Steve. He'd only been staying with him for two weeks and they were already getting on each other's nerves. He needed to buy a cheap house and move out quick, get Steve to work on his house for a change.

Steve continued, 'There's stuff that's a little bit wrong, but mostly morally right, and then there is proper bad stuff.'

'So stealing is morally right now, is it?'

'You've got to see it in context brother. We're recycling. People want this stuff, it's here for the taking, no one gets hurt.'

'Keep telling yourself that,' said Leroy. 'As soon as I get a real job, I'm out of this game.'

'Yeah well, good luck with that. And no, I don't *feel* you. When did you start talking like a player?'

'What are you saying?'

'You sound like a slinger, you don't need to play that act with me.'

'What do you know about it, you don't even know what a slinger is?'

'Sure I do. I seen the Wire, I read *The Corner.*'

'You read that whole thing?'

'Most def.'

'Man, that's a tome.'

'Sure nuff is.'

'OK, just stop it now.'

'I'm just down with you brother. I feel you, you know, you my main man.'

'I think you're mixing your time frames. "Main man" is kinda retro.'

'Yo whatever. Let me think about this. I'll have you out of the gang and back speaking the Queen's English before you know it,' said Steve.

'Yeah, 'cause that's my main concern, the state of my English! Anyway, we won the war of Independence, remember? It don't belong to the Queen any more. I need to get out of here, living with you could be the end of a beautiful friendship.'

'Not to mention that you need to get laid.'

'You can talk. At least I don't turn them gay.'
'I already told you, she was gay before.'
'Yeah, whatever.'
'At least I've slept with more than one woman.'
Leroy had no answer to that.

Huffington Post,

Hendricks, a one-time rising star in American urban politics who brought youth and vitality to the struggling Motor City, now wears a court-ordered, electronic ankle tether -- an accessory widely viewed as a fashion "don't"-- at least for sitting government leaders.

September 2007

I was sluggish getting going. Our little search of Harvey's place and the relatively late night were taking their toll and my arm hurt like a moth…It was getting much better, but that brought its own problems. I was starting to forget about the injury. I was doing a little too much with the arm. Sometimes I paid at the time with a twinge to end all twinges, other times I paid later. Sometimes my whole body hurt just from getting old. Maybe that doctor with his bum fluff moustache had a point – I probably should lose a few pounds and take more exercise. Maybe I'd get a bike like Alison. Maybe once I'm retired, I'll get a dog. I kind of liked the idea of a dog.

Retired? Gees what would I do all day? A bit more time for movies and reading wouldn't be such a bad thing, but what the hell would I do the rest of the time? Well, I'll think of something I suppose. I could always write my life story – a homicide detective in one of America's most dangerous and criminal cities – there's got to be a market for that. Alison could proofread for me.

I checked my email. Alison had sent over the crime scene photos, sorry I mean the photos of comics taken at Harvey's place. If this case was going to hang on comparing comics to doodles on newspapers my captain would laugh himself sick, not to mention putting my balls in a vice and squeezing gently, but you don't get to pick the way a case goes.

I blew the photo up as much as I could without it going fuzzy and held up one of the doodles next to it. Before you ask, yes, I do still have the evidence boxes from the Loomis and Miller murders; it's not as if anyone else is interested. I'd have to get some artistically technical person to verify it if I was going to court, but to me they looked like a perfect match. I wondered if Harvey traced the letters or copied them. No doubt an expert could tell you. The things some people are expert in, you wouldn't believe.

So that loose end tied up, I spent a miserable morning looking through the paperwork on my pension and composing an 'I retire' letter. I consoled myself by ordering pizza and watching *Casablanca*. What, you want to make something of it? So, I like old movies, sue me. I couldn't face the captain. I'll tackle him tomorrow.

I had decided to deal with the comic book shop tomorrow too, when I remembered they didn't open that early. It wouldn't take long and I could pick up a sandwich to go at Noah's. The diet starts tomorrow as they say.

Not being a comic book kind of guy, personally I couldn't really see the attraction. Why not just read a proper book? But there's clearly a huge market for this kind of thing and not just for kids. Green Brain Comics was packed. Not with people, but with comics of every kind. I browsed a little, trying to look like a customer. I'm not usually prejudiced but I'll confess I have a slightly stereotypical view of what your average comic reader looks like. A glance around disabused me of that view. There was a mix of people there.

After a while I decided to cut to the chase and approached the counter.

'Hi.' I took my badge from my pocket and showed it discreetly. 'I'm just making a few general inquiries.'

'Sure. What do you need?'

I showed the young man at the desk, who did fit my stereotype (long hair in a ponytail, slightly greasy, nerdy look), the photo of Harvey. 'Does this guy ever come in here?'

'Michael? Sure, every couple of weeks or once a month at least.'

'Is he interested in anything in particular?'

'Yeah, he's a conspiracy theory nut, anything to do with conspiracy theories, especially JFK.'

'And there's a market for that kind of thing?'

'Oh absolutely. There's lots of titles. Some exclusively deal with conspiracy stuff, some mention it occasionally or tangentially. Like *100 Bullets* for example, in issue 4 it has a JFK storyline.'

'Right.'

'Can I ask why you're interested?'

'I'm afraid I can't really say. It's part of an ongoing investigation, but Michael hasn't done anything wrong. It's just some background checking.'

I didn't want him telling Harvey some cop had been asking questions about him, but the young man didn't look too convinced with my explanation.

'Do you know Michael well?' I asked.

'I wouldn't say that. We might chat a bit about any new stuff that's come in that might interest him, but that's about it.'

'Does he come to any of your events?'

'I'm not sure. I don't think I've seen him at them. He's kind of a quiet guy.'

'OK, well thanks a lot for your time. Oh, do you have a copy of the *100 Bullets* issue you were talking about? Maybe I'll take a look at it.'

He went and came back with a book from near the back of the store. 'I think you're going to like that, but you really should start from the beginning.'

Looking at the cover I was dubious about how much enjoyment I'd extract from the contents, but I'll try most things once. 'I'll start with this. See how I get on,' I said paying him.

Back home I flicked through the comic while I ate my sandwich. Unfortunately, some mayo dropped on it. I wasn't too upset about it. I don't think I'll be going back for issue 1.

> One in five houses now stand empty in the city that launched the automobile age, forged America's middle-class and blessed the world with Motown... Detroit has some of the nicest housing stock in the country. Brick, marble, hardwood floors, leaded glass. These houses were built for kings...
> *The Guardian*

Leroy and Steve were doing one last 'house clearance'. Despite the fact that he still didn't have a job, Leroy didn't feel comfortable taking things from houses even if they were abandoned and rotting. Steve had been resistant, arguing that if they didn't do it someone else would and they needed the money, but he was doing more and more photo work for Alison, so he no longer needed the extra income. He'd also done deals with people in the neighbourhood. They had their own mini economy going. By sharing what they grew in their gardens and exchanging their different talents Steve found that he only needed money for the utility bills and the few groceries he couldn't grow himself or get from a neighbour. He was getting by easily on his freelance money and was happy to feed Leroy for as long as it took for him to get back on his feet.

Steve had pinpointed an area he knew had plenty of boarded up houses and they set out early to see what they could find. They got more than they bargained for. As Steve pushed open the door a truly unpleasant smell escaped.

'Gees, what the hell is that?' Asked Leroy.

'I don't know, let's check it out.'

'Why don't we just leave? There's plenty of other houses, let's just go somewhere else.'

'Wait a minute. Oh shit.'

'What?'

'Come here. Look at this.'

Leroy went up to Steve and looked over his shoulder. 'Oh fuck. Let's get out of here.'

'Wait a minute.' Steve pulled out his camera and started taking photos.

'You can't do that!'

'Why not?'

'That's sick. That's not right man. We should go and then call the police. What the hell do you want photos of a dead man for?'

'He's not just any dead man. Look... look at the way he's laid out. This must be a murder. I should call Alison.'

'You should call the cops is what you should do.'

'Leroy, he's been dead for ages, what difference will another half hour make?'

'Well I don't want any part of it. You do what you want. I'll wait in the truck. And make it quick. I don't want to be here. What if someone turns up and thinks we did it.'

'They won't. You can see he didn't just die.'

'Well how are we going to explain what we're doing here? Oh officer we were just stealing some pipes when we found this body and we called you right away. Get real!'

'All right.' Steve had been snapping photos all the time they had been debating what to do. 'Let's go to the truck and I'll call Alison and as soon as she gets here we'll take off OK.'

'How come we have to wait?'

Steve called Alison. She was very excited and said she'd be right over. Leroy wanted to just leave, but Steve wanted to make sure nothing happened until Alison got there. They didn't have long to wait.

'Alison, meet my buddy Leroy.'

'Nice to meet you.'

'Not under the circumstances,' said Leroy.

'Don't be such a grump Leroy. I'll just show Alison the thing and then we'll leave OK.'

Steve took Alison into the house.

'Holy shit!' she said.

'Yeah.'

'Did you call the cops?'

'No, I was waiting until you got here.'

'OK, good. I know a homicide cop. I'll call him.'

'So we can go?'

'I guess. What were you doing here anyway?'

Steve looked sheepish. 'Well... we were looking for scrap to recycle.'

'To steal you mean?'

'If you want to get technical.'

'Not really. I don't care.'

'Good, but the police might.'

'It's OK. I'll call the police, you can go.'

'Let me know if there's any story in it.'

Steve went back to a disgruntled and nervous Leroy.

'Now can we get out of here?'

'Yes.'

'I can't believe you took photos of that man.'

'Your disapproval is noted Leroy.'

'But of a dead guy, that's not right.'

'That's what photojournalists do all the time,' said Steve. 'What about war correspondents and stuff.'

'We're not in a war.'

'We might as well be, the state this city's in.'
'I thought you thought Detroit was great.'
'I did. I do, but there's a lot of crap around too.'
'Tell me about it,' said Leroy. And they drove home in silence.

Washington Times,

The latest tawdry scandal involved the city's youthful and charismatic former mayor, Kemi Hendricks, who approved a multi-million-dollar settlement with police officers who claimed they were fired because of an internal probe into the mayor's personal actions.
September 2007

It felt strange being back in the department after all this time and no contact. A couple of the guys had come to see me while I was in the hospital, but after that it was out of sight out of mind. I didn't take it personally. I wasn't best buddies with any of them. We'd shoot the breeze when it was quiet, we'd go for a beer after closing a big case, but other than that I didn't socialise with them. I got a few handshakes and slaps on the back on the way through to the captain's office. It was nice, but I didn't get emotional or anything.

'Well, well, I wasn't expecting you here Daniels. Take a seat. Are you all finished with the physiotherapy?' said the captain.

'No, not quite.'

'You look good though. Lost weight?'

I wasn't sure if he was being facetious or not. 'No sir.'

'So, are you ready to get back into the saddle?'

'Yes and no.' I pulled out my resignation letter from my pocket and gave it to him. 'I've decided to retire, but there's one last case I want to clear up before I leave.'

'What case? Mick cleared up the June-Bey Jordan thing. That's the last case you had. You don't have any other open cases.'

'Yes, but you'll remember that there was a newspaper found on Jordan's body?'

'So?'

'Well, before I got shot, I was investigating that angle and I found two open cases with the same MO, a neat newspaper left on the body. And, all of them had a name or phrase doodled somewhere on the paper, all of which turned out to be anagrams of Lee Harvey Oswald.'

'What's that got to do with the Jordan murder? We've got someone for the Jordan murder.'

'But we haven't got the right person for it.'

'Now wait a minute, I know you've never liked Mick much, but what evidence do you have that he's got it wrong?'

'The murders have to be linked. The likelihood of there being more than one killer in the city who leaves a neatly folded *Free Press* on the victims has to be zero.'

'OK, but who says Mick got the wrong man? The man he nailed could have done all these three murders.'

Silently I had to admit that was a possibility, but I just didn't believe it. Harvey was our guy. 'But has Mick linked the Jordan murder to any of these other cases?'

'No. He doesn't need to. He was charged with booking someone for Jordan and he did. There's no need to go rooting around in ancient history for other open cases.'

'But…' I tried to explain. I tried to put forward my theory that every murder should be solved if possible. I tried to point out that the killer was still at large, that he would kill again. I failed. The captain was having none of it.

'So run this by me again,' he said, 'you found this guy because there was an anagram on a paper that spelled out Lee Harvey Oswald, then your girlfriend…'

'She's not my g…'

'Whatever. Then your journalist friend finds a blog written by someone called the Lone Gunman, which kind of sounds a bit like he might be a killer.'

'Well it's a bit more…'

The captain held up a hand to stop me. 'Then you executed an illegal search of this man's house and found some comic books, that you think he copied the writing from when he put the anagrams on the newspapers and some books about Oswald and some clippings about people who died, but no gun or any verifiable evidence? And based on that you want me to get a warrant to officially search his property and question him on a murder charge?'

'All the clippings he had are for people who were murdered and a neatly folded *Free Press* was found on the body.'

'He's a paramedic. Maybe these are people he attended and he likes to keep a record of it.'

'That would be weird, wouldn't it?' And incredibly unlikely, I thought.

'Weird, but not illegal,' he said.

'But I have witnesses who heard him badmouthing Shanta Brown at the mayor's party,'

'Alleged party.'

'If you say so sir, but it's all over the press that it actually happened. And I have witnesses saying Harvey caused a scene at Bouzouki and got barred.'

'That doesn't make him Brown's killer. Not to mention that we have someone for the Brown murder, just like we have someone for the Jordan murder. Are you suggesting your colleagues got it wrong twice?'

I was suggesting just that, but I decided to be diplomatic and not mention it. 'But it links him to Shanta. He even said himself that he was at the party, and he as much as confesses to her murder on his blog.'

'In your opinion.'

'Well...'

'Listen Daniels. You've been a fine cop, you've got a good clearance rate, I'd hate to see you retire under a cloud, people speculating that you're losing your touch. Get out while you're on top. Take some more sick time on the city and you've got some vacation owing. You don't even need to come back to work out your notice. Take the pension and go somewhere nice.'

'But I can clear three open cases with this. At least three. The guy had clippings about other deaths too, they're probably people he...'

'It is not going to happen, Danny, not on my watch. We have enough new murders to deal with without going over cases where someone has already gone down for them.'

'But...'

'That was more than advice Daniels. I am not going to a judge with this to get a warrant. I am not going to ask Flanagan if he arrested the wrong man, and I most definitely am not taking this any further up the food chain.'

Sometimes it's best to just be patient and hold your ground and not make a complete dick of yourself. I temporarily capitulated. 'OK, but I don't want a party.'

'What? Oh, I see... Not even a few beers at The Old Shillelagh?'

I didn't know if he was trying to be funny or not, but he ought to know by now that I hate that place. 'No. I'll just slip away gracefully into the night. I've never been much of a team player, especially after Reuben...'

'Sure, sure, well whatever you want Danny.'

What I wanted was to get Michael Harvey for several counts of murder. Son of a bitch, I thought. After twenty-five years of upstanding service the captain couldn't do one lousy thing for me? Well screw him, screw all of them. I'll catch him myself.

I wondered how I was going to tell Alison that there'd be no warrant, no official search, no department involvement in catching Harvey.

I didn't need to tell her, at least not immediately, because she had something way better to tell me.

Freep.com Chapter 8: The Morgue
Silent killer makes its return.
October 2007

'You are not going to believe what I've got for you,' she said.

I loved the way Alison just launched into conversation without a greeting, assuming I knew who she was. 'No, probably not. What have you got?'

'I'm not sure I should say on the phone.'

'Alison, don't go all cryptic on me.' If I'd known then what she was talking about I may have agreed with her.

'I have something you really need to see, right now. Time is of the essence.'

'I'm kind of in the middle of something here.' I was just ragging her, what would I be so busy with that I couldn't drop it.

'Danny!' Her voice went up a couple of octaves.

'OK, OK, I'm just kidding around. Where do you want me?'

'Meet me at the gas station where 39 meets McNichols Road. And bring a handkerchief.'

She'd hung up before I had chance to ask her why the hell I needed to bring a handkerchief. Or give her a hard time for assuming I'd own such a thing. Who has a handkerchief these days? Never a dull moment with Alison. I quickly changed into some more respectable pants and went to the car.

Traffic was light and I was there within fifteen minutes. Alison was loitering with intent in the gas station store pretending to look at street maps or candy, while looking out for my car. I pulled up feeling like a curb crawler and she jumped in the passenger side.

'What's the big secret?'

'I found another one. Another newspaper killing.'

'What? You found another case report or something? You could have just brought the paperwork round. What are we doing here?'

'No,' she whispered, 'a body.'

'You found a body? What the h...'

'Not me exactly. I'll tell you the details later, but we need to get over there and look at it before the cops come. We didn't call it in yet.'

We drove two blocks down to Lindsay Street. It's like a wilderness down there with a few abandoned houses. You can certainly see the tumbleweed rolling in that part of town, which turned out to be a good thing. Alison directed me to stop at one of the boarded-up houses. I had a box of gloves in my door pocket, I pulled some out and gave some to Alison. She led me round the back. Just before we entered, she pulled the scarf around her neck up around her nose. 'You're probably used to this kind of thing,' she said, 'but he's been here a while.'

The back door was hanging off its hinges and we went in. I decided to check the place out before I asked Alison how she managed to come across a decomposing body in what amounted to the middle of nowhere as far as she was concerned. Sun shone through the broken board that covered the windows giving a dusky, dust filled half-light. You didn't need any kind of light to tell there was a body in the room. I lit a cigarette and inhaled. It's the best way I know to mask the smell. Well, cigars are better, but since it wasn't my birthday and it wasn't New Year's, I didn't have one. I followed Alison further into the room and there he was. A middle-aged white junkie who looked older, spread-eagled on his back on the floor, a bullet in his forehead and a *Free Press* folded on his stomach.

I leant over him to see what the headline was. It was another one from the *Free Press* series on fentanyl: "In most industries, rumours of death are bad for business. To heroin dealers, death was marketing gold." Then I picked it up and turned it over, sure enough there was the anagram doodle on the other side. I laid the paper back as I'd found it and scanned the rest of the body. I didn't see any trauma except the gun wound and track marks. He had been an addict for a long time. He was probably stoned when he was killed, didn't know what hit him.

'Did you already take any photos?' I asked Alison.

'Yes and no. I know this guy, Steve, he does freelance photography work for the *Free Press* and he was over here with a friend, well they were here stripping houses, but as you can see this place was cleaned out a long time ago. So they stumble across the body,' I gave her a look. How many idiots had been traipsing around the crime scene, I wondered. 'No, not literally stumbled over it! And Steve called me, thought I might be interested. He was going to call the police straight away, but I talked him out of it. I said I knew a cop personally and I'd take care of it.'

'And where is this Steve character now?'

'I guess he went home. His friend was really nervous. He kept wanting to call the cops right away. But Steve took loads of photos of everything.'

'And where are they now? This is a crime scene; we can't just let whoever take photos and take off with them.'

'I didn't.' She put her hand in her jeans pocket and pulled out one of those camera photo cards. 'I've got them all right here.'

'OK. But we'll need to talk to Steve and his friend.'

'No problem.'

Maybe no problem there, but my problem now was, did I call this in and bring down detectives and crime scene techs and the whole circus, or did I keep quiet about it. If I called it in to my squad, I could show the captain that the newspaper killer was still on the loose and I was right. But even if he agreed, he'd give it to someone on active duty. I was still getting a pay cheque but as far as the captain was concerned, I was already retired. I could just picture them rough-shodding over all of our careful detection to date, disregarding it and laughing, just like the captain had, laughing at the lone gunman and his Oswald obsession and the comics and the lack of tangible evidence. OK, the *Free Press* on all the bodies was evidence, it was proof that one person was responsible, but who cared except me and Alison? No one had missed this junkie. No one had found him. We could pretend no one had found him now. Wasn't it a sign from God that we were meant to find this body? But if I didn't involve the department, how would we ever catch Harvey? I could call in favours all over the place, but they would run out soon enough. There would be a limit to how much I could do on my own. And sooner or later I'd have to involve proper, active police. But was it to be now or later?

'Danny?'

'Yeah?'

'Are you OK?'

'Sure, just thinking how to handle this. OK first we need to completely and carefully check the scene. You stand there by the door and take notes. We don't need any more people than necessary muddying the waters.'

I expected Alison to complain, but she took a few steps back towards the door and stood with pen poised.

'Right, for formality, we'll state the obvious. White male, clearly a drug addict, approximately thirty-five, but age difficult to tell due to lifestyle. Dress and appearance consistent with living rough, either on the streets, or in a drug house. Fatal gunshot wound to the forehead. Looks like a .40 calibre but would need ballistics to confirm. Neatly folded copy of the *Free Press* of June 24, 2007 laid on the victim's stomach. You've already got the headline?'

'Yes.'

'Anagram doodled on the reverse side, consistent with previous MO. Assumed to denote Lee Harvey Oswald. No obvious struggle or robbery.' I knelt next to the body and touched him. Cold. Rigour had been and gone and returned. I felt carefully in his pockets, no wallet or other belongings. 'Why bother to kill this guy? He would have done it himself sooner or later.'

'That's not the point, is it?'

'I guess not. I wonder why he was here anywhere. There's nothing left to steal.'

'Probably looking for a quiet place to shoot up. There's some tools to the left of him.'

I noted the drug paraphernalia.

'Shouldn't we be leaving, or calling the police?'

'I am the police! We might as well take our time while we're here. We're not likely to get another crime scene gifted to us. He's been here a while with no one finding him except your hapless friends. Another half hour or so won't make much difference.'

The more I thought about it, the more I decided to keep quiet about this for now. If it ever came out, I'd be in the shit, but by then I'd be retired, what could they realistically do to me? Reprimand me, put me on desk duty?! The brass might be pissed off but there was nothing they could do and they might even be glad of one less unsolvable murder to deal with. This was no dunker, it had unsolved written all over. No doubt the victim had parents and friends, maybe even a girlfriend who had cared about him once, but he was so far down the addict's path if anyone still cared about him they would probably see his demise as a relief as much as anything else.

'Alison.'

'Hmm.'

'Can I trust you completely?'

'Sure. Where did that come from?'

'We're not going to call this in, I'm going to process the scene, but you absolutely cannot tell anyone ever, not your girlfriend, not Steve, not your grandmother with Alzheimer's, no one.'

'OK, I get it, but why aren't you going to call it in?'

'It's another long story, suffice to say my captain was not too impressed with our case to date and he is not going to authorise a search of Harvey's house.'

'What!'

'We'll talk about it later.' Now was not the time to get into a scene about why the police brass was not taking this seriously. I took off a glove and threw her my car keys. 'In the trunk is a black bag. It's got evidence bags and stuff in. Go get it please. And do you have a camera with you?'

'Yeah, but just my little Fuji.'

'That will do. You're going to document everything we do, then if this ever does come out, we can at least say we processed the scene the best way we could.'

I lit another cigarette and looked around. I was getting used to the smell. It wasn't so bad. It was then I noticed a scrap of blue fabric on the floor near the door. Alison came back with my bag. I crouched down close to it. 'You see this?'

'Yeah.'

'Take a photo of that. A close-up and one that shows where it is in relation to the door.'

Once she'd done that, I took tweezers out and put the fabric in an evidence bag. I'd collected my kit over a number of years, but I hardly used it. Often the bags came in handy, but mostly we'd wait for the crime scene techs and let them do everything to avoid contamination, but I'd have to just hope for the best on this one. I looked up at the door. The most logical scenario was that someone had caught a sleeve on the doorjamb coming in or going out. If we were lucky that person was the killer, unlucky and it was just our poor John Doe, but he was wearing a grey sweatshirt, so I liked my chances. The lock had a slight smear of what looked like blood. I took a cotton bud, put a drop of sterile water on it and wiped the stuff off and put that in a bag. Then I took out my luminal spray and gave the lock a squirt. Just like on TV a few bright blue specks appeared.

'Quick, take a photo of that. It only lasts about thirty seconds.' Alison clicked away. 'I wonder if Michael Harvey has a cut on his arm.'

'So that's definitely blood?' asked Alison.

'Yep.'

'It's just like CSI.'

'Yeah, well don't get your hopes up too much. A lot of times you can't trust the results on trace stuff. The ME's office could be a little more careful if you get my drift, but hopefully... And of course, we'll need the killer's blood and DNA to match to.'

Alison proved to be a good assistant. We worked the scene for at least an hour taking as many samples as we could and pictures of everything we did. If this ever came to a need for evidence, I was confident it was as solid as we could make it. The bullet had gone out the back of the man's skull and into the floor. It was pretty battered so I didn't hold out much hope for matching it to a murder weapon, if we ever got our hands on the murder weapon, but those ballistics guys can do amazing things. I bagged it. We didn't find anything else that was useful. Just before we left I bagged the *Free Press* and put it with all the other evidence in my kit bag.

We left and I pushed the broken door closed. As far as possible I didn't want anyone finding John boy for a very long time, if ever.

'What now?' said Alison, back in the car. 'I could use a drink. That's the first dead body I've seen up close.'

'The first one is always tough. All that scientific stuff kind of works up an appetite though, doesn't it?'

'I guess I could eat something.'

My ideal partner, I thought, but didn't say. 'Let's see if we can find anywhere to eat around here.'

'And drink.'

I didn't answer her.

We drove east on McNichols Road until we spotted Lady Louisa's, specialists in 'comfort food'. We both felt in need of a little comfort, so I pulled into the parking lot.

We ordered rib sandwiches and fries with a beer. Just looking at the menu I decided I was going to have to come back and try some of the other soul food fixins. It was a long time since I'd had yams, collard greens or corn bread. So, if nothing else came out of that junkie's dead body, so to speak, at least I'd found somewhere for soul food, assuming it wasn't awful. I felt a bit bad that our dead man's relatives wouldn't get to hear about his demise, but then even if we'd gone through official channels they might not get to know. He'd had no ID on him, so we had no way of knowing who he was other than running his photo through missing persons to see if there was a match. Years of experience told me there wouldn't be. Plenty of junkies OD'd every year without anyone reporting them missing, and to be honest, without anyone very much missing them. If their people were addicts too, they wouldn't notice and if they weren't they would often have washed their hands of the family member long before they got to that stage of addiction.

The first bite of my sandwich told me I'd be back. We clinked bottles. 'Here's to getting the guy,' said Alison.

'Amen to that.'

'Is this going to help us? I mean will you be able to get those samples processed and stuff? And you never did tell me what happened with your superiors. How come they didn't buy it? We've got loads of evidence, haven't we?'

'We have and we haven't. From a police brass point of view, we don't have enough to throw more resources and time at the thing. Someone was arrested for Shanta Brown's murder and someone was arrested for the June-Bey Jordan murder, so the captain has no reason to re-open them, even if I think they got the wrong perpetrators. And the other murders were on someone else's watch, it doesn't do our squad any good to solve open cases for some other team.'

'So, the police don't care about the truth?'

'That's right. Some do, but most don't care much about the truth. There's too many new crimes to deal with.'

'We've got a new crime and it clearly links to the others,' said Alison.

'I know, but the captain is not going to be interested. He as good as told me to start my retirement now.'

I told her more about my conversation down at police headquarters.

'So, you're basically a free agent on the pay of the police department for awhile?'

'I guess you could put it that way. And, he didn't ask for my badge and weapon back yet, so I need to make the most of that until he does.'

'So where to from here?'

'First up, you need to process all the photos, and the ones from Steve too. Put them all on a CD or something and give me a copy so I can look at them. And you'd better set up a meeting with Steve and his buddy, so I can interview him properly as the first people on the scene.'

'OK. What are you going to do?'

'I'm going to see who I can sweet talk into processing the samples I took and see what we can get from that bit of blood off the door. I sure wish we had some blood or DNA from Harvey to compare.'

Alison wiped barbeque sauce from her chin and put a handful of fries in her mouth. I hoped her lady friend wasn't a fan of fine dining, otherwise Alison would need some training up. 'Speaking of Harvey,' she said with her mouth full, 'he's been emailing me. He wants to know how the article is coming and if I want to talk to him more about the mayor's party.'

'Does he now? And how is the article coming?'

'It's pretty much there, but the editor is waiting for a slow news day. He says we ran the emergency thing not too long ago and he doesn't really need a follow up. To tell you the truth he's pissed off that I didn't consult him before I did the interview and of course I couldn't tell him why.'

'Have him call me, and I'll tell him he needs to run the story, that it's part of an ongoing police investigation and it could help our enquiries.'

'Can you do that?'

'Sure. Sometimes reporters give you grief but usually they'll run stuff, that way they think you owe them and you'll call them first when you get something good.'

I wondered if Harvey's enthusiasm to see himself in print could work to our advantage. 'How would you feel about meeting Harvey again?'

'I don't mind.'

'OK, so we get the story in soon, then you can call him and arrange to meet, say you've got good news for him. The weather is still warm, with a bit of luck he might be in short sleeves and you can see if he's got any scratches on his arms or hands.'

'I like the way you're thinking. Can I buy you another beer Mr detective?'

'No thanks. One's my limit.'

'I'm going to have one.'

'Don't you have to drive home?'

'Yeah, it's just a beer. What is it with you and drinking and driving?'

'It's against the law.'

'I know, but it's more than that.'

I didn't know whether to tell her or not. I didn't like to talk about it, and I don't like to go for the sympathy vote, but we'd been honest with each other and I don't like to lie unnecessarily.

'My wife was killed by a drunk driver, OK.'

'Oh man, Danny, I'm sorry.'

'It was a long time ago.'

'Is that why you became a cop?'

'No, but it may have something to do with why I took the exam to work homicide. Anyways, I'd better get going if we want those samples to go to the lab today.'

> ...what is blight to some is proving an opportunity to remake parts of the city of others living there. [Blight Busters] are pulling down housing that cannot be saved and creating community gardens with fresh vegetables free for anyone to pick.
> *The Guardian*

Leroy MacDonald was now the not particularly proud owner of a glorified shack on Hunt Street. To preserve his friendship with Steve which was getting strained by their discovery of a dead body and their few weeks of living together, Leroy was camping out in the one room that was habitable. He was near a community garden and helped himself to vegetables whenever he wanted. So far he was enjoying the Boy Scout element of his existence and the physical work on the house that left him so tired he fell asleep straight away without thinking about Rhonda or his girls or all that he'd lost.

Steve came by most days and helped him fix up the place. He still gave Steve's address for mail. His house looked so abandoned he was afraid the mail man wouldn't deliver, not that he got much post now he'd paid off the bank and had no house bills to pay, but he'd put in a number of job applications and was desperately hoping he'd soon hear positive news.

Steve turned up while he was brewing coffee on his camping stove.

'How's it going?'

'Not bad. It's getting chilly though. I need to get the heating fixed or I'm going to freeze to death.'

'I know a guy who can look at that.'

'I bet you do,' said Leroy.

'Oh, almost forgot, you got this letter.'

The envelope was plain, no telling from the outside what it might be. Leroy tore it open and read. A slow smile spread over his face.'

'What is it?' Asked Steve.

'I got a job at Blight Busters.'

'That's fantastic. I thought that was all volunteers?'

'Mostly, but there's a few paid positions. I'm going to be project manager. Sounds fancy huh? Glorified building foreman is what it is. The pay ain't great, but hey.'

'Yeah, but you'll get that nice warm glow from knowing you've helped people out.'

'What would you know about it, Mr ambulance chaser?'

'I didn't chase any ambulance, the guy was right there. Anyway, can we drop that? What's done is done.'

Leroy shrugged. 'So, we'd better go out and celebrate.'

'Yeah, we should. Things are finally picking up huh? You sold the house, got this place, now you've got a job.'

'Yeah, lost a career, lost a family, lost a family home, gained a falling down shack and a building job. A good year!'

'At least you got this place cheap.'

'Yeah.'

'And the lady who bought your house is nice, right? She's not going to trash the place or anything?'

'No, she seemed nice, I think she's going to just live there, not try and make money off it or anything. And Rhonda says the girls can spend a week with me at Christmas if the house is fixed up enough.'

'Shit, we'd better get working then!'

'That's for sure. I guess I might meet some people on the job who could maybe give me a hand too, once I tell them about my kids coming.'

'That'll be nice. You'd better get some lights and a tree and everything.'

'I'll start with some fully functioning plumbing and some heat,' said Leroy.

They sat and drank coffee for a while, both thinking how far a year had taken them from the lives they'd known before.

'So, how's your love life,' said Leroy, 'turned anyone gay lately?!'

'Very funny. I'm concentrating on my career. Me and Alison may do a book together, a kind of coffee table photo thing – the fall of Detroit.'

'Really?'

'Yeah, we're talking about it. And I'm finally moving the last of my stuff into the new house. I don't have time for women.'

'Sure!'

'How about you?'

'I've got enough on my plate fixing this place up. My main thing is having the girls visit, then we'll see.'

Leroy stood up. 'Well, I'd better get on it. This house won't fix itself.'

'True. You want me to go out and pick you up some floorboards and pipes and stuff?'

Leroy laughed, 'No, I don't trust you man, you might bring back a dead junkie or something. You could call your heating man though. Oh and you could go and get a Meat Feast and some beers. I've had about as much fresh veg as I can take for a while! We are celebrating aren't we?'

'Yes, we are. Do not let the doomsayers cause us to lose faith in our city.'

'Stop with that Coleman shit. Go on, get out of here white boy.'

Leroy turned on the radio. "Callin' out around the world, are you ready for a brand new beat?" He couldn't help but sing along.

Freep.com Chapter 10: The dead

In Wayne County, fentanyl killed 16 people in January of last year, including a man found with his face in a bowl of food...

October 2007

I was beat. I hadn't had that much excitement for a while, but then I hadn't thought about the dull ache in my shoulder since Alison had first called me hours ago either.

I'd taken the samples over to the lab and asked for a rush on them. It would still take a few days, could even be weeks. They were backed up and understaffed as usual. Fortunately, news hadn't gone round yet about my retirement, so there weren't any questions about that. And technically I was still working for the department.

I sat and looked out at the lights and mentally made a list of what I needed to do tomorrow. I needed to call Louise; she works in personnel at the Fire Department and is married to Reuben's cousin, see if she couldn't get me a peak at Michael Harvey's file. It would be good to look at the rotas too, see what shift he was going to be working. I was starting to think I needed to stake out Harvey. He was too clever. He wasn't going to make a mistake. Well, he had already made a mistake of sorts, catching himself on the door of that house. If I could match his blood to the blood on that door... but even then I needed more. Some lawyer would argue his blood could have got on there at any time it didn't mean he'd killed Mr John Doe. He's a paramedic, he goes to houses like that all the time dealing with overdoses. I could hear the lawyers in my head. So many cases that seemed solid were lost when the lawyers did their word dances and sowed that little seed of doubt. What I need is his fingerprints on the murder weapon and he's never going to be that stupid. What I need is to catch him in the act. Hard but not impossible. All it needs is time and I have time; and the skill to not be seen following someone. That's a skill I have. I may not be up with the latest technology, but I can follow a man.

I closed my eyes, it was black and white, I was Bogart playing Philip Marlowe, following Harvey down a dark alley. I stand under a streetlight, smoke from my cigarette swirling up into the sodium haze. I opened my eyes. I didn't know how this was going to go down, but I knew I was going to catch Harvey if it was the last thing I did. I didn't have anything to lose. My career was over, I have no family, if I go out taking this guy down that'll be OK. I'm not saying that's what I want, but it'd be OK.

Sun was streaming in the next day when I woke – 8.15 a.m. already. I padded through to the kitchen to make coffee and noticed a packet by the front door. It was a brown envelope with a CD inside. The post-it note on it said "here's the holiday snaps, Alison". I made coffee and toasted a bagel. It was on the old side, but it hadn't completely given up and died. I held the refrigerator door open longer than necessary, enjoying the cool air on my legs and despairing at the lack of contents. When this thing was over I was going to start over – clean slate, give up the smoking, eat better, maybe learn how to cook a few more things. It wasn't a great incentive to catch Harvey. No, wrong attitude Danny, it *was* an incentive. Once I'd caught Harvey I could forget about Shanta Brown. I could get on with the rest of my life, read more, get a dog, have the kind of life I'd never had.

I took my coffee into the office and got sidetracked for awhile looking through the crime scene photos. It was a good catalogue, but I didn't see anything new. The phone ringing snapped me out of it. It was Alison's editor at the *Free Press*.

'Hi.'

'Officer Daniels, Alison tells me you have a request concerning the interview she did with some EMS personnel?'

'That's right. I can't go into details, but it would be extremely helpful to an ongoing police investigation if that story could run as soon as possible.'

'I see. And you can't tell me anymore?'

'Not at the moment, no.'

'Can I assume that the *Free Press* will be the first to hear about any breaking story?'

'Absolutely. If the desired outcome is achieved, you'll be the first to know. I've already guaranteed Alison an exclusive.'

'If this ambulance story runs tomorrow, will that be OK?'

'That would be perfect. Thank you for your cooperation.'

I went and refilled my coffee mug. The next piece of the jigsaw puzzle was in place. I hoped Alison would be able to arrange another meeting with Harvey, though it was hard to see why she needed to see him in person, a phone call or email would do it. But we were on a streak of luck that week. Lady Luck was shining down on us and for a while it seemed like we could do no wrong, like we were going to outsmart the son of a bitch.

The phone rang again just as I was contemplating taking a shower.

'Hello.'

'Hi,' said Alison, 'nice work. The EMS story is running tomorrow. And I'm seeing Harvey this afternoon.'

'That was quick.'

'Yeah, I called and gave him some line about if I met him today he could have a look at the article before it went into to print, that we didn't usually do that, but that he'd been so helpful, bla bla. He bought the whole thing. We're meeting at that same crappy diner place at four.'

'Great. Do you want me there?'

She didn't. She said she could handle it. Next, she was going to talk to Steve and line up for me to meet him. Meanwhile, I called Louise and arranged to take her out to lunch. She said if I wanted a favour, the least I could do was buy her lunch, besides she hadn't seen me for so long, getting on for a year and she knew what kind of favours police wanted. I showered and put on a nice shirt and drove downtown.

Louise looked the same. She still had the fluffy blonde hair, the big shapely ass, the twinkly blue eyes. I guess I'm making her sound cute, huh? I suppose she is if you like that kind of thing. I don't particularly, but she's a nice lady. We always got along.

'So how are you stranger?' she said giving me a brushing kiss on each cheek.

'I can't complain. I put in my papers to retire. It's not the same without Reuben.' She nodded.

'But you still need a favour?'

'You know how it is, tying up loose ends.'

'You and Reuben always did like to finish a job off properly. So, what do you need?'

'I'd like to get a peek at the personnel records of a Fire Department employee.' She gave me a look that implied she wasn't keen on the idea. 'You wouldn't be implicated. I could drop by your office on some pretence and the file could be on your desk. Or even better, maybe a copy could be on your desk and it could very discreetly end up in my pocket.'

'You police boys never change, do ya?' I gave her my best smile. 'I suppose something like that could happen. Is that all?'

'If you could possibly get the current EMS rotas that would be great.'

'Not quite so easy, but I'll see what I can do. Now, can we enjoy lunch and talk about other things?'

'Sure.'

Now like I said, Louise is a nice lady. I'd seen her a handful of times at family parties at Reuben's. He had a close family, they had cousins and what not over all the time just for Sunday dinner and cook-outs. Come to think of it, I kind of missed that. But still, forty-five minutes hearing about what her kids were up to and her last vacation, and her next vacation seemed a high price to pay for Harvey's record. But if it showed me what I hoped it would show me it would be worth it.

'You sure get a long lunch hour at the Fire Department.'

'I've been working a lot of overtime, they owe me,' she said.

She polished off the last bite of cheesecake. I always admire a woman who knows what she wants and isn't afraid to take it. She downed the last mouthful of coffee and said, 'well I suppose I'd better be getting back. Nice to see you Danny. You take care.'

'You too Louise.'

She got her cell out of her purse and laid it on the table. 'Come by in about half an hour and bring that, say I forgot it while we were having lunch.'

'You're not embarrassed to be having lunch with a police officer?'

'All the girls have heard about you and Reuben. You're virtually family.'

I half stood as she got up and left. I drank my coffee slowly and paid the bill. Then I walked the long way over to her office.

I'd been there before, a long time ago. Nothing had changed. As I walked up to her desk, I saw a file sitting precariously on the edge. I was about to play one of the oldest tricks in the book.

As I reached over to give Louise her phone, I let my not unsubstantial midriff knock the folder to the floor. I'll spare you the dialogue, you know how the clichés go. In my fumbling pick up Harvey's two-page summary ended up in my jacket pocket.

'So sorry Louise, what a klutz.'

She rolled her eyes at me, and palmed me a post-it as she said, 'nice lunch, don't leave it so long next time.'

I went out into the corridor and looked at the post-it – "second floor, corridor near the locker room, rotas are posted on the wall."

I trundled down to the second floor. Harvey had a week and a half of eight 'til fours left, then he switched to four to midnight. In theory he could do his thing on either schedule. He had the whole night free. But I had this feeling he liked the four to midnight. He'd get off shift, maybe a little hacked off with his lot, his lousy job where nobody appreciated him. Maybe he'd go get a drink, chat to a woman, she wouldn't be interested, he'd relieve the tension by shooting some junkie. What do I know? I don't know what makes the man tick.

But then I started to think about things more logically. He couldn't act so spur of the moment. He needed his gun with him and a copy of the

Free Press, and gloves. Either he carried his kit around with him or he'd have to go home first and tool up. So maybe the early shift did work better? Go home, take a shower, change, eat, pick a location and head out again once it got dark. I wouldn't follow him tonight. He was meeting Alison and getting his name in the paper, that should put him in a good mood. Give it a few days and then I'd set up a tail, see what this guy got up to.

I looked at my watch. Only 2.30 p.m. I decided to go over to the hospital gym and kill time. I didn't have a physio appointment, but I pretty much had a free pass to use the weights whenever I wanted. I went and worked out for a while. Well, I shouldn't give you the wrong impression, I squeezed a few balls, and lifted some of those play dumbbells, you know about one-pound, real heavy stuff. I got a light perspiration going and had an iced tea in the café. While I was sipping my tea, I had a look at Harvey's file. He'd transferred to the Fire Department from the Police Department in 1990. He had all the usual qualifications for a paramedic, as far as I could tell. His mother was listed as his next of kin with his current address in Dearborn. No medical conditions. Not on any medication. Blood group O negative – the universal donor. How ironic, I thought, someone who has the potential to save any life, but goes round killing people. I'd have to look it up, but I remembered something about O negative not being one of the most common types of blood, so that might be helpful. O and A positive I knew were the most popular types so at least we were lucky he didn't have one of those.

I was just leaving when Alison called me. We arranged to meet at the *Free Press*. We didn't want to be seen at Gateway Deli Café together just in case Harvey was still hanging around.

www.bvblackspin.com
Kemi Hendrick's Family to be Deposed About Stripper's Murder
The legendary death of Jessica Rabbit the stripper, which appeared to be a calculated hit, is a tale that has intrigued Detroit residents for years...people have whispered for years about how she was 'coincidentally' found dead shortly after being wrapped in the drama of an embattled and powerful politician.
October 2007

Alison met me at the entrance and took me up to a meeting room. She shut the door.

'So how did it go?' I asked her.

'Fine. He seemed pleased that the article would go ahead, though he doesn't show a huge amount of emotion, so who knows. He made some minor changes to the text and I let him think they would go through. It's such minor stuff it probably will. I guess he wanted to feel in control of it.'

'Yes, I think he's a man who likes to feel in control of things. Any scratches or cuts?' I kind of felt like it was too much to ask for.

'Yes. He had a small cut on the back of his right hand. I asked him if it was a work-related injury, you know, trying to kid around. He said no, he got it pruning his roses. Does he have any roses at his place?'

'I don't remember. But I guess there's nothing we can do with that information. It's going to heal before we can do anything with it. Still if we can ever match the blood on the door to him, it's useful to know he did have a cut.'

'I may be able to help with that.' Alison produced a plastic bag from near her feet and set it on the table. I peeked in the top. It contained a polystyrene cup with a straw stuck through the top. Alison had a huge grin on her face. 'He had this milkshake while we were talking, and I kept looking at it and praying he would leave it. I could see the spit on the end of the straw, you know how milkshake is great for that. Then he gets up to go and just leaves it there, sitting on the table right in front of me. What a gift!'

'That's fantastic. Did you touch it?'

'I had to touch the bottom a little bit to get it in the bag, but I didn't touch the top or anywhere you'd normally hold it if you were drinking.'

'You're such a pro, Alison.' She beamed.

'And what have you been up to?'

'I'll spare you the details, but I know a lady works in the Fire Department and let's just say a copy of some of Harvey's file somehow ended up in my jacket.'

'Nice! Anything useful.'

'His blood group is O negative and he used to work for the police.'

'Really?'

'Yeah.'

'So, can you look up his police record?'

'I guess.'

'Maybe he really wanted to be a cop and couldn't make the grade, so he became a paramedic?'

'I don't know that makes much difference, but I'll take a look.'

'I asked Steve and Leroy to come over here so you can talk to them. They should be here pretty soon. Are you OK to wait in here while I put the finishing touches to the column?' Alison asked.

'Sure.'

I was glad to take a little break, the excitement of lunch with Louise and Alison getting some DNA and fingerprints, was making me tired. But I also wanted to get the milkshake cup to the lab before they closed. I hoped I wouldn't be too long with Steve and Leroy.

We'd come so much closer to Harvey since we'd found the latest body. If we could just get a warrant to search his house, I felt sure we'd find something, some incriminating evidence that would bring Harvey in for questioning and then we could break him. Although I've never been as keen on hard interrogation as some of my colleagues, but a confession always goes down well, especially when you can back it up with evidence. I could apply for a warrant myself, but I wasn't officially working any cases. I was on sick leave and that could be easily checked. It would look dodgy, no judge would buy it. No, I needed someone else to get a warrant for me and I didn't see that happening. What else did we have? Well, now we had some physical evidence at a murder that matched the others. But I knew how things worked. It could be weeks before I got a match on the blood, especially since we didn't have any of Harvey's blood to match with, only his saliva, and here I'm trusting that the straw in the bag next to me has some saliva on it, that means DNA and that means waiting even longer. I didn't want to wait. I didn't want to give Harvey the opportunity to get away with one more murder. I was going to have to start following him and do it soon.

I thought a little more about blood – O negative, the universal donor. Harvey's a paramedic, maybe he is a blood donor. Could I get some of his blood? No, stay real Daniels, that's too complicated. I wanted to check the stats, see how common O negative was. I opened the door and peeked out, hoping to ask Alison to borrow a computer. She was already coming down the hall with two guys, our body finders.

I sat down again. Alison showed them in.

'Gentlemen. Have a seat.' The white guy looked confident, maybe a little cocky, the black guy looked nervous, but not I felt in a criminal way, just like he might get accused of something he hadn't done, or not intentionally. 'I understand I have you to thank for a certain find.'

'I wanted to call it in. I told Steve, but he said it would be cool.'

'It is cool, it's fine. Let's start from the top, what are your names?'

'Leroy MacDonald.'

'Steve Novak.'

'OK, and you were at Lindsay Street for recycling purposes?'

Steve smirked. Leroy looked taken aback, but I wasn't interested in their petty thieving. To be honest, off the record, I thought someone might as well make use of things as let them rot in some abandoned house, but we won't get into that right now. Steve replied, 'yes, that's right. I'd heard there might be some useable stuff in that area. There wasn't.'

'Tell me what happened. Just do it blow by blow, like I don't know anything. What did you see first? What did you smell?'

Steve proceeded to recount their discovery of the body. His account didn't give me any more than I already knew. They'd entered the house discreetly from the back in the hope of finding some pipes or house fittings they could sell. It was almost immediately clear that the house had been stripped already, but there was a strange smell, so they investigated further. Also, Steve is a keen photographer and wanted to get some shots of the general decay.

They didn't move or touch the body. Leroy wanted to call the police straight away, but Steve, for some reason he couldn't really explain, decided to call Alison first, reasoning that the guy had clearly been dead a while, so what difference would another hour make. Alison confirmed Steve's account.

'So, while you waited for Alison, you took more photos?'

'That's right.'

'I waited outside,' said Leroy, 'it didn't seem right taking photos of a dead man like that. I didn't see why we just didn't call the cops.'

'And after Alison arrived then what happened?'

'I showed her a few of the photos, and she said could she have the photo card, so I gave it to her. And I said are we going to call the police now, and she said she knew an officer that she'd been talking to about a story she was working on and she'd call him and we didn't need to worry about it.'

'And then you left?'

'Yeah, we went and had a beer back at my place and then Leroy went home.'

'And you felt OK, about leaving Alison there and not calling the cops like you'd planned?'

They were both silent for a minute looking at each other, then Steve said, 'no, I felt uncomfortable about it, but I think of Alison as a friend and I didn't think she'd do anything wrong. And…'

'And, I kind of didn't want to get involved. I didn't want to get into trouble for stealing stuff, or not calling the police straight away,' added Leroy.

'OK. Thank you. I should say that if you find any more bodies you should call the cops right away. That was a definite error of judgement right there.' Leroy looked into his lap, clearly ashamed, Steve held my gaze but I could tell he felt bad too. 'But in this particular instance, it's very fortunate that you did what you did.'

'It is?' asked Steve.

'Yes. Needless to say, I can't go into any details, but this ties into something else I've been investigating and it was very… well serendipitous, let's say.'

'That makes me feel better, I guess,' said Leroy.

'You shouldn't feel bad, either of you. But I need you to not tell anybody about this. I'm very serious. It could blow a long-running investigation if you mention this to anyone.'

'Like who would we tell?' said Leroy, 'I was knocking off some pipes and I found a dead guy! You think I'm proud of that? I ain't gonna tell anybody.'

'OK, OK.'

'Can I ever get my photos back?' asked Steve.

'I'm afraid that's not going to be possible. Those photos are evidence now. But maybe the *Free Press* can reimburse you…'

'Yeah, we can add a photo card to your next freelance invoice, and some extra hours for your trouble,' said Alison.

They left. Alison showed them out and promised to be right back.

'Serendipitous?' She said, when she returned.

'Well it was, wasn't it?'

'It certainly was,' she said. 'I liked the long running investigation bit too.'

'It is long running. I've been looking for Shanta Brown's killer for years!'

Alison laughed.

I went home and took a long bath and formulated a plan.

Steve and Leroy stood on the sidewalk outside the *Free Press* building talking.

'I think we got off pretty good there, man,' said Steve.

'You did. You're going to get paid for the photos and everything,' said Leroy trying to look sulky.

'Don't worry, I'll split the spoils with you. Or I'll take you out to eat, or something.'

'You're always taking me out to eat anyway.'

'True. But we could go somewhere special.'

'I guess.'

'Oh come on, lighten up. We didn't get into any trouble and we've helped out with a big case. You should feel good about what we did.'

'I don't. It doesn't feel right.'

'Well, it's water under the bridge now, so get over it. I wonder what the case is? Do you think there's a serial killer or something?'

'What killing junkies in Detroit?'

'It could happen!'

'Not much point, that fentanyl shit is dropping them like flies anyway. No need to go round shooting people.'

'Maybe the killer's on some kind of mission.'

'You've been reading too many crime books,' said Leroy.

'It was weird though, the way that guy had a neatly folded *Free Press* on his chest. What's that about?'

'I don't want to talk about it, OK?'

'OK killjoy, but I can't talk about it with anyone else. We're sworn to secrecy, remember?'

'Fine with me.'

'So, you wanna go get a beer or something?'

'Maybe later, I've got some stuff to do.'

'OK, I'll drop you off and go and do some painting at the house.'

'Aw right, later man.' They knocked knuckles.

Freep.com Chapter 10: The dead

It was time, finally, to sound the alarm.

October 2007

I spent a couple of days tidying up loose ends and looking into Harvey's police record. He started as a beat cop in 1989, age nineteen. He'd taken the detective's exam twice and failed, and soon after the second attempt had quit the force. A few months later he had turned up as a basic EMT in the Fire Department and must have worked his way up through the levels to paramedic. His police file, such as it was, said that he had only graduated high school, so he must have done something else between leaving school and joining the police, but I had no way of knowing what that was. Maybe he did a year of college and that made him think he had the smarts to move up quicker. As far as his file was concerned, he was a complete nonentity – no good points, but no bad points either, except failing the detective's exam. I wondered what had made him attempt it so young and with so little experience under his belt. Did he think he was particularly clever and that he could rise through the ranks through book work? Did he have a relative or mentor on the force encouraging him? Maybe suggesting he could pull strings and get him promoted? It would have been a disappointment to him, and after two attempts he clearly gave up. Who could say whether it left a chip on his shoulder? He'd made a pretty good career for himself. He was saving lives and making reasonable money too. Though I still had to wonder why he worked in the metro area when he would have had a much easier and possibly fulfilling time in Dearborn.

On the third day, I borrowed a nondescript car from a friend and began tailing Harvey. It was a boring business. I didn't bother to follow him until he left work. He was still on the eight to four shift. After that I don't know how he amused himself. He went home and he stayed there. On the second day of my tailing him after a couple of hours at home he went to Green Brain Comics for a while, didn't buy anything, and then picked up some food and took it home. Judging by when the lights went off in his house he didn't stay up late. I guess he read comics, watched TV, or wrote his blog, pretty ordinary activities.

The next day got slightly more interesting. It was Friday and he and some co-workers went straight to a bar and drank beer for three straight hours. Then they ate pizza and went to a titty bar. I guess Harvey was maybe feeling off colour, because he left around 11 p.m. and went home and apparently straight to bed. I dozed lightly in my car a little way up the street until 1 a.m., when I decided he wasn't going to go out and kill anyone and I went home. You've always got to make a judgement call in that kind of situation – sure he could have gone out at 2 a.m. and whacked someone, but whatever the cop shows might imply; in reality you usually can't watch someone 24/7 especially when you're the only person watching him. I did think briefly about getting Alison to do a stint, in the daytime, when it wasn't likely that much would happen, but then common sense ruled again. I even thought about getting Steve and his buddy Leroy to watch the guy, but at the end of the day it wouldn't do me any good if something kicked off. And you never knew what would be important. He might do something or go somewhere that seemed innocent, but might make a connection for me.

Anyways, I made another judgement call on Saturday. I knew from the rota that he wasn't working and I decided not to follow him until evening. Of course, that way I ran the risk of him going out earlier in the day and not coming home and rounding the day off with a shooting that I missed, but I needed to do laundry and buy a few groceries and something told me this guy probably acted after dark, though to be honest there were parts of Detroit that were so quiet during the day, you could easily top someone and no one would know. Like that junkie on Lindsay Street, that could have been a daytime kill. But like I say you make your decision, you take your chances.

I slid into Lithgow Street around 5 p.m. and parked between a couple of cars. I could see the entrance to Harvey's house in my side mirror. As I drove past, I noticed his car was in the driveway. So far so good. He wouldn't go far without his car. I didn't have to wait long before I saw him pulling out of the driveway and I followed him into Detroit. I'll spare you the intervening hours, because they were not remotely exciting. Harvey did what normal guys do. He looked in bookstores. He bought stuff. He had coffee. He had dinner. He had a few drinks. He went to a topless bar where he had clearly been before and knew some of the girls and after a while sitting on his own, he went and sat with some guys he seemed to know.

Harvey stayed there a couple of hours. It was an uncomfortable time for me in that kind of environment, nursing a Coke and trying not to make eye contact with any of the girls. The secret to good surveillance is blending in. I didn't feel blended, but looking around there were plenty of single men in their 50s with receding hairlines and expanding waistlines, so I suppose to everyone else I did fit. At least I got to go to the john in relative comfort without losing sight of my subject.

Around midnight Harvey left and drove down to the Riverside Park area. Things were getting tricky now. There wasn't so much traffic to cover me, but I knew Riverside was a dead-end, so I parked on Jefferson and walked quickly over to the waterfront. Harvey was sitting on a bench there looking across to Canada. What the hell was he doing? He just sat there for about twenty minutes. Not smoking, not drinking, just staring out at the water. Still at least it was something. It was the most interesting thing he'd done yet. Then he got up and walked through the park and towards Clark Park and Mexicantown. It was ideal for me that he was walking. Another Godsend. I felt a buzz go through me. Maybe now we were in for some action. I stayed well back and tried to look at the way he held himself, the way he was walking, to see if he was carrying a gun. I couldn't tell. But he didn't have a bag with him and he wasn't visibly carrying anything, so if he had a *Free Press* with him it had to be hidden inside his jacket somewhere and that didn't hold with the pristine condition the papers were usually in. None of the others had looked like they had been carried inside a jacket, even very carefully.

Harvey kept walking, not slow, not fast. He seemed to take streets at random. It didn't feel like he was particularly looking for anything, but my guess was he was looking for a victim. After a while he turned down Clark. It was dark and tree-lined with very few cars parked and not much sign of life. Harvey approached a house that was clearly unlived in, the roof was partly burned and the ground floor windows had board instead of glass, though the surrounding area was not totally abandoned. I held back. If he saw me now, or sensed someone was following him, I felt sure he'd abandon things and head home or at least drive to another part of the city. I'd been lucky so far. Harvey was a very self-absorbed guy. He was confident in that way. He didn't seem that interested in what was going on around him. He didn't look around much. If he was about to go and kill someone, he wasn't nervous about it and he wasn't worried about getting caught.

He slipped into the side of the house. I edged closer. I couldn't go in. For sure he'd know someone was there in an enclosed environment. I ducked down behind a small tree and waited. If I heard a gunshot I would have to make a run for it, or wait and hope Harvey came out the same way he'd gone in and tackle him then. I could hear my own breathing, feel my heart beating. This wasn't the way we usually did things in the police. We didn't follow people and wait for them to act; we arrived after the fact and tried to put together the scraps of jigsaws puzzle left by the body. I felt Marlowe would have been proud of me.

There was a squeak of dry timber and Harvey emerged from the house. There had been no gunshot, so I had to assume the house had been empty. No passed out junkies conveniently waiting for the Michael Harvey touch. Of course, he could have used a silencer, but even then I thought I would have heard the distinctive thunk. Silence is a misnomer with guns. You can mask the noise significantly, but never completely eliminate it. Even given that angle, I didn't think he'd been in the place long enough to have found someone, killed them and laid out his newspaper. And it would have been too easy – another passed out waster submissively waiting for the angel of death to arrive?

I caught a glimpse of Harvey's face. He looked annoyed, but not mad, not angry. He looked at his watch and started to walk back the way he'd come. Now I had to make another judgement call – did I check the house, just in case? Or did I keep following Harvey?

I quickly looked around. No one else was out walking the streets. If I was quick, I could take a look and still catch up with Harvey. I slid out and into the house. The door now hung half open. I took out the Maglite I always keep in my pocket and swung the light quickly over the room. The door opened into a kitchen. Beyond that was a living room. I took a few steps in and strafed the light. Nothing. No one. A sagging sofa and a lot of cobwebs. I went back out into the street and could still make out Harvey, moving more swiftly now, back in the direction of the river.

As silently as I could, I sped up and kept him in sight. He was heading back to his car. I relaxed a little. Something made me think he was done for the night. I was proved right. He got back in his car and drove home. I followed him to the outskirts of Dearborn, then I turned off and headed home. All the murders had been in Detroit. Harvey didn't soil his own back yard. He was going home to bed and so was I.

Huffington Post, Kemi Hendricks, Disgraced Ex-Mayor of Detroit, Living Life of Luxury

If ever a public figure should be down for the count, it is Kemi Hendricks.
Stripped of his job as Detroit's mayor, locked in jail for 99 days and saddled with a felony record, he is legally prohibited from seeking the only occupation he ever wanted – elected leader...
November 2007

To coin a phrase, my pants got a little moist and not in a good way, when I answered the phone and it was the captain. I couldn't think of any reason he'd be calling me other than that he'd somehow found out about the crime scene I'd checked out without calling it in. Maybe one of the lab boys had called to say my samples were ready. It was a bit soon, and I'd made sure to say they needed to call me directly on my cell when they had any results, but those guys aren't that reliable. If it isn't under a microscope, they don't know what to do with it, so they probably just went by routine and called the squad. Damn, I should have thought of that. Now I was going to get it. He wanted to see me in his office in an hour and he didn't want any excuses.

I felt bad driving downtown. I'd screwed up, but what else could I have done? We had to have those samples analysed. You just couldn't trust anybody anymore to do what you asked them to. But it wasn't just that. This was the end of the line. I probably had a couple more weeks of pay, but my life as a police officer was over. Twenty-five years down the pan, and not much to look forward to. Sure, I kidded myself I was going to enjoy all the free time to read and watch movies, but how many books can one man read? It's like the sound of one hand clapping or whistling in the wind, it's pointless.

Sure, I was going to get a dog, I was going to get fit and give up smoking and learn to cook – who was I kidding? Do I look like a new man to you? I'm a guy who likes burgers and pizzas and coney dogs. I like to smoke and I don't much give a shit if I'm a little overweight. I'm never again going to be romantically involved, that ship has sailed. So, if I haven't got the job, what have I got? A big fat nothing. OK, first I have to catch this fucking newspaper killer, but then what? Go PI? I don't think so. Security guard? Puleease, I ain't going back into uniform.

By the time I pulled up in the parking lot of police headquarters I was thoroughly depressed and ready for an ass-whipping. The department seemed strangely quiet, which should have given me a clue, but I was so into my head funk and thinking the captain was going to give me a grilling that I didn't take it on board, so I was totally unprepared when I opened his office and at least ten whistles blew and party poppers popped all around me.

'You didn't seriously think you could get away without a party did you, Daniels?'

I should have known. This is the police. They make a big deal of anyone who's survived twenty-five years on the force. Still, at least I wasn't going to get a drubbing and I'd have to eat my words about the lab techs who hadn't inadvertently grassed me up.

'Yeah, I should have known better. Don't you boys have any murderers to catch?'

'Nah, you've already caught them all.'

'Actually,' said the captain, 'we've currently got the best clearance rate going, so unless someone goes on a rampage tonight, we're all available to thoroughly embarrass you with reminisces and get you mightily drunk.'

That, I knew, was not going to happen. I'd take a beer or two, but I did not like being drunk and I wasn't going to change my habits tonight. Still, it was nice of the boys to think of me.

'OK, everyone out to interview room one,' said the captain.

There was a table set up in the interview room, heaving with every imaginable snack and a bright blue cake in the middle with a shield on it.

'Speech, speech,' they called out.

'Now come on fellas, let the man get a drink inside him first,' said the captain, handing me a bottle of Bud.

I enjoyed the thing for awhile. Shooting the breeze with the fellas and what I didn't drink I made up for in constant raids on the food table, but really, there's only so many police stories you can take. I broke my own rule and had a third beer, not exactly heavy drinking, but it made me maudlin. I missed Reuben. If I'd wanted anyone at that party, it was him. The other guys are all right. Mick was even pleasant and amusing for a change, but Reuben had been my partner for as long as I could remember and all the stories they were telling were about cases I'd cracked with him. I'm not going to admit to crying, but I had to go and hide in the locker room for a while until someone found me and dragged me back to cut the cake. I made some crack about my prostate to cover why I'd been in the john so long and that set them off again on all the old timer jokes.

I cut the cake and said my piece, thanked them all, and raised a plastic cup to fallen comrades and then my luck started to kick in again. Detroit crime waits for no man and the phone started ringing. Pretty soon in turned into a busy night, there was a shooting in Poletown and a suspicious death in McDougall-Hunt, and I managed to slip away.

I wondered if Harvey would pick tonight to strike; the one night in ten that I wasn't watching him. Well, there was no way of telling, but I wouldn't be watching him. I was going home to wallow in my impending retirement for a while, or maybe watch an episode or two of *Homicide:*

Life on the Streets which they'd bought me in case I found I missed the police banter too much. At least as a consolation they'd also bought me the Bogart and Bacall Collection. Now that I was going to enjoy.

Freep.com Chapter 1: The teenager

In the basement anything goes...It's all good. Except tonight, something's bad.
November 2007

I woke with yesterday's fear that the lab boys might inadvertently alert the captain to my activities and as soon as it hit 9 a.m. I called to see if they had any results in yet. It was promising. The blood I'd found on the door was O negative, so it could be Harvey's, although we couldn't say definitively, but at least it was the right blood type. There had been enough saliva on the cup Alison had got from Harvey to extract DNA, but that analysis took much longer and it would be a while still before they would be able to match it, or not, to the blood found at the scene. It was a start. I thanked them and reiterated the need for them to call me on my cell when they got anything new.

Harvey was now on the four to midnight shift and I was planning to tail him after he got off work, so I spent the day pretending like I was already retired. I watched *Key Largo* from the Bogart and Bacall Collection. I even took an afternoon nap. I had a good dinner and a light supper so I wouldn't get hungry while staying up late.

Harvey left the Fire Department right on the dot of midnight already dressed in civvies. He was carrying a black sports bag. He got in his car and drove north-east through Greektown. I was already sitting in my car facing the right way and easily pulled out after him. Greektown was busy enough with its bright neon casino lights and bars. I thought maybe Harvey was headed towards another topless or pole-dancing club. To my relief he kept driving, but slowly as though he was looking for something or couldn't decide whether to stop for a bite to eat.

He dropped down and passed through the warehouse district. There was less traffic and I pulled back to avoid being seen. And then he drove on into the East side. As with much of Detroit, it's a mixture of abandoned houses, wilderness and family homes. It was quiet and dark. I began to sweat a little, I was afraid that Harvey would cotton on to my tail with so little traffic about, but I had to stay close enough to not lose him. I tried driving without my headlights on for a while, but with so many streetlights out, it was hard to see. I had a bad feeling about the whole enterprise. Maybe I should just give up on the case. Maybe Alison and I were mistaken and Harvey wasn't a killer. Maybe I could have one last attempt at showing the captain what we had and trying to get him to search Harvey's house. Or I could try a different officer, or forget how it looked and just go to the judge myself for a warrant. It was crazy following this guy night after night. I wasn't going to catch him doing anything illegal, and if I did, then what? He had a gun, I assumed. I had a gun, but I didn't like using mine. If he was who we thought he was, he'd be very handy with his and not worried about using it. He's a much younger guy than me and he looks pretty fit. If it comes to a chase he'd easily get away.

Just as I was wondering whether to give up this craziness, Harvey pulled up and stopped the car. I pulled in under the shadows of a tree and quickly cut the engine and lights. He got out. He was carrying the sports bag. I got out and walked towards him. I was dressed for a tail, a mixture of blacks and brown and my silent grey sneakers. My gun was holstered under my left armpit, inside my unzipped jacket. Harvey appeared to wander aimlessly among the streets and houses, but I imagined he had some kind of plan. It didn't seem likely that he would just turn up in an area and scout around until he found a suitable victim, but that said, that was what he had done in Mexicantown when he hadn't found anyone and had gone home empty handed. But maybe that had been a different kind of enterprise, he hadn't had a bag with him then and there was something different about him tonight. He seemed to have a purpose. While apparently aimless, his walk was brisk and business-like. I felt that he knew where he was going. Maybe he had scoped something out earlier in the day while on the job? He could have been called to a shooting-gallery, or seen what he knew to be a dealer's house.

I saw Harvey slip down the side of an abandoned house. I moved quicker to get close to where he was. I didn't want to run, but I was walking as fast as I could. I crossed the street and approached the house on the sidewalk next to it. The house had white siding so it was easy to see. Sweat rolled down between my shoulder blades. I put my hand on the butt of my gun. I was outside the house next door when I heard a gunshot and almost immediately a second. Damn, too slow. I hadn't managed to stop Harvey killing again, but with a bit of luck I'd catch him in the act of staging the scene with his signature newspaper.

I pulled out my gun, cocked it and jogged to the side of the house. I crept to the door and peered round it. In the glow of a large flashlight I could see Harvey crouched over a body. Behind him, facing me, a black man was slumped against the wall, blood pouring between the fingers of a hand held over his stomach. He could still be alive. I figured something had gone wrong. There had been two people there when there should have only been one. As far as I knew, Harvey had only ever killed one person at a time before and then set up the scene the way he wanted it.

Harvey was intent on whatever he was doing. He was confident enough to have laid his gun on the floor next to him. I eased around the door and took the few steps towards him. He didn't even notice. It was like taking candy from a baby. I put the gun against the back of his head while kicking his piece away. 'Don't move or I'll blow your brains out,' is what I remember saying, but maybe I'm embellishing that with the beauty of hindsight. I could never have imagined it would be so easy, but he was completely caught up in what he was doing without a thought of being seen, much less caught.

I thought he'd put up a fight. He didn't. You could almost feel him slump and the life go out of him. He wasn't going to run, he was going to face the music and do it proudly.

'Stand up, nice and easy.' He did. I quickly scanned the room for something I could cuff him to. I took the cuffs from my belt and taking one hand and then another I cuffed his hands behind his back. He was wearing paramedic gloves and close up I realised he was wearing a thin hairnet like they wear in food factories. He certainly didn't want any evidence to be left. We'd been lucky that he'd caught his arm on the door of his last murder, if he had. This was not a man given to making mistakes. I pushed him over to a solid looking stove and made him kneel down next to it, then I took my spare cuffs and cuffed his right hand to the stove. He was going to be pretty uncomfortable for a while. He looked at me but kept silent.

I went over to the other victim and felt his neck. There was a thin, shallow pulse. I called 911 and asked for an ambulance, giving my badge number in the hope that they would come quicker. Then I called the squad. I still had the number on speed dial. I got Ramirez.

'Hey Danny, what are you doing calling this time of night?'

'I've got a one eight seven just gone down on East side. I'm not sure what street I'm on. I've got the perpetrator in cuffs and I called an ambulance for the other victim who's currently still alive. Get over here as soon as and bring the tech boys.'

'Ain't you ever going to retire?!'

'Yeah, as soon as I book this son of a bitch, I'm taking a nice long holiday!'

I put my phone in my pocket and went back to the bleeding victim. I felt for a pulse again – nothing, he'd gone.

I walked over to where Harvey had left his bag and used the tip of my gun to ease it open.

'You've got the *Free Press* with you then?' I said to Harvey. He looked surprised, but still didn't say anything. 'Oh yes, I know all about you. You didn't think I'd got you on just this shooting, did you?'

I put my gun back in the holster and went and sat on a crate opposite Harvey, where I could keep an eye on him, not that he was going anywhere. I got my phone out again and called Alison. She'd earned it, she deserved to be there. She eventually answered on the sixth ring.

'Mmm.'

'Sorry, did I wake you?'

'Yeah, Danny. This better be good.'

'Oh it is. Do you want to be the first reporter at the arrest of a serial killer?'

'You're kidding me!'

'No, I am not. I'm looking at Harvey right now.'

'No way! Where are you? I'll be right there.'

I told here where I was more or less. Probably the flashing blues and the whole murder machinery would arrive before she did, so she'd find it easy enough.

So that's how it went down. I sat and waited. The cops arrived first swiftly followed by Alison and finally the ambulance. Maybe Harvey had a point about the state of the city's emergency services. Man, that was sweet, when Harvey's colleagues came in. Were they surprised to find Michael cuffed to a stove, obviously the perp and not the good Samaritan! I'd like to be a fly on the wall down at the Fire Department when they tell that story.

Alison took some photos and got the story from me, but I told her not to run with it until I got back to her. I planned to take Harvey down for every murder he'd done and I didn't want anything released to the press too soon. The *Free Press* were going to have an absolute field day with it once people knew their paper had been placed on every victim.

I followed the wagon down to the station. Harvey was already in an interview room when I got there.

'How the hell did you stumble across this shooting Danny?' asked Ramirez.

'It's a long story.'

'So, what now? Are you going to be the primary on this?'

'No, I'll hand over all I've got to you, but I want first stab at him. You can read him his rights and take over when I'm done. I've only got a couple of questions for tonight.'

'OK. So murder one?'

'No. At least six counts of murder.'

'Six?' Ramirez was incredulous.

'Oh yeah, this is just the tip of the iceberg.'

I pushed open the door and went in. I stood and let Ramirez go through the Miranda. Harvey didn't say a word, just nodded when necessary and signed the form. I sat down opposite him.

'Why did you do it Harvey?'

He remained silent, staring me out defiantly.

'Come on. I know you want to tell me. I know you want everyone to know how clever you are.'

His lip curled up in what passed for a smile. 'Because I could. I've been doing this for years and nobody noticed. No one else gives a damn about clearing up the debris in this city. I even started leaving a calling card and nobody put it together.'

'They did now. Lee Harvey Oswald? Nice touch.'

He looked shocked then, as though he'd believed no one would ever work out the whole story, like no one could be as clever as him.

'Just one more question. Why did you kill Shanta Brown?'

'I don't know who you're talking about.'

'Oh I think you do. You talk about her enough on your blog.'

Harvey shook his head and refused to say more until we got him a lawyer.

'Don't worry. We'll find out in the end.'

I went home then and took a long bath. In the morning I boxed up all my notes, the CD of photos from the John Doe murder we hadn't reported, and the lab reports. I put it in my car along with all the evidence from the older murders I still had – Loomis, Miller and Jordan and drove down to the station.

Ramirez and Jones were still there working last night's murder as though it was a standalone case. The count was up to seven. Last night's other victim had been pronounced dead at the scene. I hadn't included him in my count. I was pretty confident there were even more victims and that eventually Harvey would confess. He was proud of what he'd done, his work to clean up the city of Detroit. He wouldn't be able to stay quiet about it for long.

The captain was there for the day shift. He came out of his office when he saw me.

'You sure know how to make an exit, don't you Daniels?' he said. I figured that was as close as I was going to get to an apology from him for not believing me about Harvey when I'd first gone to him.

'Well, if you'd listened to me when I came to you for a search warrant we could have cleared this up a while ago.' I'd been mad at the lack of support, but it didn't matter now. I'd caught my man. I'd laid Shanta Brown's ghost to rest. I was going out on a high and nothing else mattered.

The captain nodded. 'How many?' he asked.

'At least seven, including, if I'm not mistaken Shanta Brown and June-Bey Jordan.' I smiled. I knew the captain wouldn't want to re-open those already closed cases and admit they'd made a mistake, but that wasn't my problem.

'You'll probably get some kind of commendation for this.'

'Really?' I said. 'I'm surprised I'm not going to be investigated for not following correct police procedure.'

'There'll be no investigation, Daniels. You're retired now, remember? Speaking of which, I'll take your gun and shield now please.'

I handed them over and that was that.

That night I sat in my Lay-Z-Boy and had one last smoke. I threw the rest of the pack away and I haven't touched one since. Alison challenged me to quit when we caught Harvey and I did.

I went back to the station a lot in the following weeks, in a consultative capacity, talking them through the evidence I'd collected. Retirement very slowly crept up on me. I was kept pretty busy. The lab boys came through with the DNA analysis which matched Harvey's DNA to the blood found on the door. And they finally searched Harvey's house and impounded his computer and found all sorts of incriminating stuff me and Alison had missed on our quick search. Turned out Harvey was a trophy hoarder. His loft was full of items taken from his victims, wallets and necklaces, stuff that could have identified them, nothing weird like body parts. Oh and there was a diary written in code hidden under his mattress, describing who he'd killed and when; all very meticulous and orderly. It read almost like a shopping list of undesirables to be taken out, to Harvey's mind anyway. It wasn't a very hard code to crack, but it kept people busy for a while. It was a long time before Harvey finally went to trial and I had to give evidence.

Meanwhile I helped Alison with her story, which ran and ran with all the revelations that kept coming out. It was a gift to a young journalist and she made the most of it. And I tidied up my notes from along the way. I hope you enjoyed the story. It wasn't the retirement project I'd had in mind, but I think it turned out OK.